MO

A Two-Way Tale of Adoption

By Curtis Webster With Trang Elizabeth Webster

ALLOW US TO EXPLAIN . . .

This is a work of fiction, based very loosely on our first year together as father and daughter.

Much of what you are about to read is purely fictitious and has no real-life parallel. For instance, Curtis really wanted to adopt Trang (in fact, adoption was his idea to begin with). Kay (wife and mother) was and continues to be a Rock of Gibraltar when it comes to wise, mature and patient parenting.

We should also note that the legal process of international adoption is far more complex than depicted here. We have taken many liberties for the sake of efficient story-telling

That first year was frustrating for all concerned. But we survived and thrived. Looking back, we can see that there was also a lot of humor.

Today, we are father and daughter and are very proud of each other. We know now that love was growing, even in those really dark and discouraging moments of the early days.

This is not our story factually. But it is very much our story emotionally. We hope you enjoy our two-way tale of adoption.

Curtis and Trang

Kanan-Zephyr Productions. Contact: moonguyennovel@gmail.com

First printing in July, 2014

Books>Fiction

ISBN-10: 0692239502
ISBN-13: 978-0692239506

ACKNOWLEDGEMENTS

No one can achieve a dream or a labor of love alone. We would be remiss if we did not acknowledge a few friends and family members whose love and support have been so vitally important since Day One of our adoption journey.

Our thanks first and foremost to the amazing mommy-warrior Kay, who goes above and beyond the call of duty as wife and mother every day. Special thanks also to Trang's siblings, Andrew Narver, Katie Narver Thompson (and husband Andy), Matt Webster, Ken Webster and Maly Webster.

And an extra-special special thanks to big brother Alex Webster, who designed our cover, created the point-of-view icons you'll be seeing in the text and took our jacket cover photo.

A big thanks to Ms. Linda Jacobsen and all of the teachers and staff of the Las Virgenes Unified School District. Quality public education is alive and very well in the Conejo Valley.

Another big thanks to Master Conrad Ercolono of Agoura Karate and Sue Willett of Sue Willett Music for helping Trang to understand that disabilities don't have to be disabling.

If you ever contemplate international adoption, you could not find a better agency than Dillon International of Tulsa, OK, and its staff, including Jynger Roberts, Cô Trinh and the indefatigable "Thomas" Nguyen Van Trong.

Curtis thanks Forrest Overin and David Quay, two of the best buddies and pals a guy could ever have.

We both thank the remarkable Richard Hatch for all of his encouragement and support, as well as the divine Stacey Stallard for her live reading of Cam's words.

And, finally, a big huge sloppy thanks to the nannies and staff of The Social Support Center of An Giang Province, Vietnam. These men and women work tirelessly and lovingly to care for children who otherwise would have nothing.

Mercy House

How do you know when you're sad? Or miserable?

What does it mean to feel hopeless?

How could you know if you were living in poverty?

For the first ten years of my life, these questions would have meant nothing to me. I would not have known what you were asking and would not have known how to answer.

When I was two months old, my mother without a name brought me to Mercy House, an orphanage in An Giang Province, Vietnam. An American agency, Mercy Worldwide Adoptions, had built Mercy House before I was born.

Even with help from Mercy Worldwide Adoptions, Mercy House was still a very poor orphanage. Mercy House had no electricity. Water came from a well. There were too many children and not enough beds. What beds there were consisted of wooden planks set on cement blocks. Some had mattresses. Some did not.

During the rainy season, the roof leaked and water was everywhere. Mosquitos and other insects had no trouble getting in and making meals out of our blood.

It seemed like there were always a lot of sick children and there was never enough medicine to go around. Sometimes a child with a tummy ache would cry all through the night and none of us got any sleep.

Now that I look back on Mercy House, I realize that every single child there had a physical problem of some kind.

Some children were blind. Some children were deaf. Some children had been born with faces that had parts out of place or were missing some parts altogether. Some children could see and hear just fine, but their brains didn't work very well.

I could see and hear and my face had all the right parts in all the right places, but my left leg was shorter than my right. I guess I had a lot of trouble learning how to walk.

When I did finally walk, it was with the worst limp in the history of limps. It was hard for me to go very far without falling down. I know that I must have hit my head or scraped up my arms pretty badly a few times, but I don't remember that happening.

I've also figured out that we had all been taken to the orphanage because of our problems.

My mother without a name must have thought that she was not going to be able to take care of me because of my leg. Maybe she thought that there must be other things wrong with me that wouldn't show up until I was older. And so she took me to Mercy House.

I didn't think anything of it, though. All I knew was Mercy House. All my friends had problems, most of them seemed a lot worse than a leg that was too short.

I guess I thought that maybe nobody in the world ever lived with their mother. Everybody was born and then their mothers without names took them to an orphanage.

For me, living in an orphanage was normal. It wasn't anything to be sad about. It was just how the world worked.

Of course, there were adults taking care of us at Mercy House. Our nannies loved us. We knew that.

Who needed a mother when there were so many wonderful wife-ladies who loved us and took care of us and made us feel special? When we grew up, our problems would go away and we'd become nannies, too.

Maybe I did have a lot to be sad about, but I didn't know that I was supposed to be sad. As I got older, I became more and more like a nanny. I loved babies and little kids.

The nannies gave me a lot of responsibility for taking care of little kids and sometimes babies, even when I was little myself.

Yes, there were times that I was sad, sometimes very sad, but not because I was living in Mercy House.

One time when I was maybe eight years old, Ai, who was sort of like the head nanny, came and told me that she needed my help. I limped as I followed Ai into the baby room. There was a baby in the crib I didn't recognize.

"This is Hoa. She just arrived. Her mother said that she is two years old and very sick. She needs a lot of water. Can you please watch Hoa and make sure she gets plenty of water?"

At first I smiled. I was happy that Ai would give me a baby of my own to take care of. But then I looked into the crib and I suddenly became very sad.

Hoa did look sick. She looked very sick. She did not look like she was two years old. She was so tiny she could have been only six months old.

Hoa had no hair and there was a big splotch of red skin that started on the top of her head and covered most of the right side of her face.

Ai handed me a baby bottle full of water and walked away. I looked down at Hoa and tried to smile. "Hello, Hoa. My name is Cam. We're going to be friends."

Hoa wasn't crying. Hoa wasn't smiling. Hoa wasn't doing anything at all. If her chest hadn't been moving up and down, I might have thought that she was just a doll.

I picked Hoa up. She was lighter than a feather. I cradled her in my arms and tried to put the nipple of the bottle to her mouth. "Come on, Hoa. This is water. It's good for you."

But Hoa would not take the water. She looked back up at me with her little black eyes. She didn't even blink.

"The water will make you feel better." But Hoa just kept staring up at me. I think I sang her a song, but I don't remember which one.

I sat down on a little wooden stool and rocked Hoa back and forth. Every so often, I'd stop and try to get her to take some water.

All I could do was to dribble a few drops onto Hoa's lips and hope that some would get into her mouth and that she would swallow it.

The sun went down. All of the other children went to bed, but I stayed up and held Hoa.

I kept thinking that Hoa would understand that I was trying to help her and that she would take some water from me. I even started thinking that maybe I could be Hoa's nanny. Hoa would trust me and mind me.

I thought about the day that Hoa would take her first steps. I thought about playing with Hoa on the floor of the orphanage and teaching her how to speak and showing her pretty flowers.

I thought about all of those things. I never left the stool. I never put Hoa back down. I never stopped trying to get her to take water.

I guess I finally fell asleep, but it must have been very close to the sun coming up.

I woke up to Ai taking Hoa out of my arms. Ai was crying. I thought I had made her sad by falling asleep.

"No! I can take care of Hoa. I'm sorry I fell asleep but . . ."

"Hoa has died."

Ai looked like she wanted to say more, but then just turned and walked out of the baby room with Hoa.

I sat very quietly. I don't think I felt anything for a few minutes.

Hoa had died. I had to really think about that. I knew that when someone died they didn't ever come back. I knew that my dreams of being Hoa's nanny were gone.

Why had Hoa died? Ai had told me to make sure that Hoa got lots of water. But Hoa hadn't taken any water from me.

Ai had trusted me to take care of Hoa, but I hadn't done what she told me to do!

It was my fault that Hoa had died!

Suddenly my tummy got very very sore, like someone had stuck a knife in it. I doubled over and fell off the little wooden stool.

Tears came out of my eyes like monsoon drops. I did not know that my body could ever make enough tears for me to cry that much.

When I had finally cried all of the crying I could cry, I slowly got up. I had to lean on the stool to stand.

I hadn't had any supper the night before. I had missed breakfast. Still, I wasn't hungry.

I was just sad . . . very very sad . . .

I had thought that I would spend my life taking care of babies.

But I had killed the first baby they'd given me to take care of by myself.

Hartman House

Adopting Cam was not my idea. Adopting anyone was not my idea. Having any children at all was not my idea.

As much as I was capable of loving anybody at that time in my life, I truly did love Shelley. I was a junior and she was a freshman when we met at Orozco State. The official start of basketball practice was still a month off.

For reasons I cannot articulate now, I had signed up as a Business Administration major and was bored senseless. Fundamentals of Statistics, Administrative Management and Human Resources Management were not classes that fired my blood with academic passion. So, I'd signed up for English Lit 101 as an elective. And that's where I met Shelley.

Shelley seemed to be everything I wasn't, but in what felt like a good way. Shelley lived entirely in the right hemisphere of her brain. Shelley delighted in poetry and drama. Shelley could quote half of Shakespeare's sonnets by heart.

At the same time, she couldn't keep a shopping list longer than about three items in her head for two minutes at a time. I found that charming, actually.

And then there was the doll collection. Barbie dolls, baby dolls, dolls that wet, dolls that cried, China dolls that would crack if you looked at them crooked, plastic dolls that could survive a twenty-story drop. Shelley had like a hundred and twenty or something of them.

Girl-next-door cute, a romantic streak ten miles long, a ditziness that made her intellect seem unthreatening. What can I say? For an egocentric jock with a big need to be worshiped and adored . . . Shelley was made to order.

And nobody would have argued with the "egocentric jock" label. I was doing my best to live the Big Man On Campus life. It was the life that I thought I was entitled to live.

I was a Basketball Star for God's sake! Certain privileges were supposed to come attached to Basketball Star and I was not going to let the fact that I played for a commuter school where 95% of the students could give a rat's furry tail about basketball (or athletics in general) stop me from enjoying those privileges.

Shelley hadn't had time yet to figure out that varsity athletics didn't count for kitty litter at a place like Orozco and so she had gotten a big starry look in her eyes when I'd asked her to go to this little coffee shop frequented by what few of us actually lived on campus.

"Point guard," I'd answered with a tone of prideful arrogance when she'd asked what position I played.

"That's like the quarterback. I get the ball, I size things up and I run the play."

I left out the part about averaging only a minute and a half of playing time per game my sophomore season. I also somehow forgot to mention that Skip Lindstrom, last year's starter, was back for his senior season.

Shelley, though, was under the impression that I was some kind of Anglo Michael Jordan. Maybe I had expressed myself a little carelessly and was partly responsible for her misperception.

Then Skip broke an ankle and I wound up starting after all. I wasn't great. I wasn't terrible. I played for a team that wasn't great and wasn't terrible. But Shelley hung on every dribble, every pass, every free throw and every shot.

Best of all, she swallowed whole my explanation of why I hadn't made the cover of Sports Illustrated just yet.

"My high school coach had no idea what to do with me. The guy was on my case all the time, screaming in my ear. If he'd have just left me alone and let me do my thing, I'd have wound up playing for Arizona or Kansas or someplace. I've been playing catch-up for two years. Wait'll you see me when I've made up for high school.

"If I ever do any coaching, I'm not going to be anything like him. I'm going to treat my guys like adults. A little respect goes a long way."

In the cold hard light of day and with just a tad more maturity, I can see that Coach Tidwell back at St. Olaf was probably the best thing that ever happened to me. The fact that I was playing ball at any college anywhere was major testimony in favor of his ability to get the most out of morons like me.

But that wasn't how I saw it. I mentally stretched my talent to fit my ego. Bad coaching had to be the reason why my name wasn't already a household word.

My talent got me a free education, but that was about as far as it could take me. After I finished out my senior year, I couldn't help but notice that my name wasn't coming up much in NBA draft projections. Actually, my name wasn't coming up at all.

Eventually, I came to the cold hard realization that I had played my last game in organized basketball. I could spin out a long sad tale of all who had failed me and derailed what should have been a glorious professional career. What-might-have-been, though, couldn't change what-was.

Shelley and I got married. Big surprise there. Shelley needed a knight in shining armor. I needed to slay dragons in the name of romance. Perfect, right?

What came next was a pretty standard scenario for all of us NBA never-weres. Teaching credential. Accepting a high school job (the El Lobo Fighting Wolves). Coaching the freshman team. Resenting every minute of every day with a constant muttering about what could have been.

My marriage with Shelley kind of evolved into a mirror of my basketball talent. It wasn't terrible. It wasn't great. It was good enough and not much more.

Shelley put her dream of writing children's books on hold to fully embrace her role as Mrs. Randy Hartman. She got an A for Effort, if nothing else. Self-absorbed as I was, I still put some effort into the marriage. I tried to be careful about toilet seats and diligent about taking out the trash.

Two years in, I moved up to varsity. I had some seniority and something resembling job security. And that's when Shelley started talking seriously about children.

We'd agreed that we would not try to start a family while I was still getting established. In Shelley's mind, that was a temporary necessity. In my mind, it was a long-term reality. Fatherhood just wasn't all that attractive for me.

The excuses were running out and that's when the trouble really began. We spent two years on the verge of splitting up until I finally caved. I guess that divorce just sounded more expensive and inconvenient than having a kid.

A couple of months went by. Nothing.

A couple more months went by. Still nothing.

I knew enough not to say it out loud, but I was kind of relieved that we weren't getting anywhere. Months stretched out into a year.

Shelley tanked into a pretty deep depression. Up to that point, I don't think I'd fully appreciated just how important this was to her. Shelley spent a lot of time crying and a lot of time sleeping and not very much time living.

When we finally got into fertility treatment, Shelley perked back up for a while. But only for a while.

Several more months and many thousands of dollars later, we at last got a diagnosis. Shelley had, at best, a 5% chance of ever conceiving a child. For various reasons I only dimly understood, in vitro didn't look terribly promising either.

Well, you can guess where the conversation had to go after that . . .

I had some serious reservations about adoption, but knew that I would be taking my life into my own hands if I were to object too strongly. Shelley went out and hired an attorney who specialized in facilitating adoptions.

It was right about then that my phone rang.

"Coach Hartman, this is Ty Roberson calling."

Ty Roberson?

You mean like . . . Ty Roberson, the guy whom the press routinely labelled The Greatest Prep Hoops Coach Of All Time? The guy who wrote "Why Aren't You Winning?," mandatory reading for any high school coach who wanted to remain employed?

That Ty Roberson? Calling me? Who is this really?

"I'd appreciate it if you'd keep this under your hat for now, Coach Hartman, but I'll be announcing my retirement after the playoffs. Would you be interested in interviewing for the job at Bishop Mathis?"

Bishop Mathis. A.K.A. Shangri-La. The most storied prep hoops program in the state, if not the country. The pinnacle of coaching success.

Would I be interested in interviewing?

Umh . . . let's see . . .

OH YEAH!!!!!!!!!!!!!!!!!!!!!!!!

Much to my surprise, the first interview led to a second interview which led to a meeting with the Board of Trustees, which led to an offer, which led to an acceptance, which led to buying a new house, moving furniture and getting an office twice the size of our first apartment.

But, it was not yet entirely clear that my name on the door made it "my" office.

Ty Roberson was there to greet me when I showed up with my boxes of mementoes.

"Couldn't be happier to hand you the keys, Coach Hartman."

"Couldn't be happier to get them."

Roberson pointed to a wall full of posters under glass.

"The Wall Of Real Champions, I call it."

Chuck Yeager posing with the X-1. George Patton shouting commands from atop an M4 Sherman tank. Douglas MacArthur wading ashore in his return to the Philippines. Neil Armstrong stepping into lunar dust.

"I've learned more from these heroes about competition than any coach I've ever known. Listen to these men, Coach Hartman, and you will never go wrong. I guarantee it."

So, I guess none of those posters will be coming down anytime soon, humh?

There would be no pretense of me teaching normal academic classes. Any activity that was not related to the success of the basketball program was off my plate. Even so, the job was going to require at least three times the work I'd been putting in at El Lobo. In a slow week . . .

Bishop Mathis thus was a good excuse for me to sort of drift my way out of the adoption process. Whatever Shelley came up with was going to be fine. I didn't really need to worry about it.

My first season coaching at Bishop Mathis began at about the same time as Shelley's attorney finally called with a match.

A single woman six months pregnant had decided to give her baby up for adoption and had chosen the Hartmans. I nodded and signed something. We were upset by Arroyo Blanco in our season opener. Shelley barely noticed.

Shelley started spending a lot of time with the mother. We won seven of our first 10 games. In the grand scheme of basketball history at Bishop Mathis, three losses so early in the season meant the team was already a catastrophic failure.

Keeping my own high school experience in mind, I was determined to stay positive. I didn't yell. I didn't scream. I didn't criticize. "Keep your heads up, guys! We'll get 'em next week!"

On the outside, I was a fountain of optimism. Inside, my guts were churning and my blood pressure was skyrocketing.

My only release was going out into the driveway after work and taking my frustrations out on the basket and backboard the last owner's son had put on the front of the garage.

For about half an hour every night, I would once again be a solid-gold first-round NBA draft prospect.

Dribble. Dribble. Stop. Shoot.

Fifteen-footer on the way . . . Good!

Dribble. Dribble.

Drive the lane . . . SLAM DUNK!

My life got a little better when Bishop Mathis managed to reel off a five-game winning streak that put us back into the Centennial Conference title discussion. We still were nowhere near a Top Ten ranking for the state, but it looked like the Titanic wasn't quite ready to sink yet.

Shelley alternated her time between visiting the mother of her unborn child and investing obscene amounts of money in badly over-equipping the upstairs nursery.

State-of-the-art crib. State-of-the-art changing table. State-of-the-art musical mobile. State-of-the-art disposable diapers. State-of-the-art baby monitor intercom. State-of-the-art car seat. State-of-the-art high chair.

The baby's mother wanted to know as little about the child as possible. She thought it would be easier to give the baby up, so she hadn't tested for gender. That didn't stop Shelley from deciding that her "mother's intuition" guaranteed that we were going to have a daughter.

She went around telling everybody how great things were going to be when "Ashley" joined our family. Ashley Jennifer Hartman. "Jennifer" came from Shelley's maternal grandmother. Since my last name was already part of the deal, Shelley didn't think it necessary for me to have any input there.

Everything was ready. The house was ready. The room was ready. The mommy was ready. The daddy was as ready as he was going to be. Little Ashley Jennifer's due date was imminent. The stage was set. Parenthood was upon us.

And then Black Friday . . .

Needing only to win our final regular-season game against perennial doormat Father Damien in order to earn a tie for the conference championship, my guys were hit with a case of collective basketball amnesia.

In front of a deliriously happy home-gym crowd, Damien handed us our heads and a shocking 66-57 upset loss.

As I sullenly packed up my office that night, I glanced at the Wall Of Real Champions.

Chuck Yeager was smiling contemptuously. George Patton and Douglas MacArthur were glaring. Neil Armstrong just kept his back to me the whole time.

I drove home with my tail between my legs, trying to visualize the resume I was sure I was about to have to circulate. I walked in the front door to find Shelley sobbing hysterically.

Ashley had been born and was perfectly healthy. Only Ashley's mom had decided at the very last second that she was cut out for parenthood after all. And Ashley's name was "Richard" because she had stubbornly refused to be born female.

Shelley spent the weekend in a nearly catatonic state. I wasn't doing much better, what with all of the "Randy Hartman is an idiot" talk coming out of the local sports pages.

Sunday afternoon, Shelley suddenly stopped crying, got up and started her computer.

At almost that exact second, I got a phone call. In spite of our unimpressive regular-season record and our ignominious pratfall at Father Damien, Bishop Mathis had been selected for the sectional playoffs as an at-large participant. We were seeded 15th among sixteen teams, but I didn't care. We would have one last chance to redeem our season and I would have one last chance to keep my job.

I breathed a sigh of relief and walked in to give Shelley the good news. I could hear the printer working as I entered the bedroom.

Before I could open my mouth, Shelley looked up at me with a big wide face-breaking grin.

"If we internationally adopt an older special-needs child, the host country will finalize the adoption almost immediately! Then it's just a matter of getting her entry visa, and then NOBODY can take her away from us!"

Shelley pulled something off the printer and flung it at me. It was a photograph. A photograph of a bronze-skinned girl with very closely cropped black hair and a crooked smile.

"Look at our Ashley! She's from Vietnam! She's beautiful! She's going to be ours and nobody can take her away from us!"

I'm A Nanny

Ai never spoke to me about Hoa again. I didn't ask. I didn't want to talk about Hoa. I knew that I would never forget that horrible night and I didn't need to remind myself.

For the first three or four days after Hoa died, I expected Ai to come get me and throw me out the door and into the street. Why would any orphanage want to keep a stupid girl who had killed a baby? Worse yet, she'd killed the first baby that they'd let her care for by herself.

But Ai didn't seem to be mad at me. None of the other nannies seemed to be mad at me.

Had they forgotten about Cam, the baby-killer? Or were they just waiting for the right moment to kick me out?

I felt so guilty. But nobody was treating me like I was guilty.

Maybe they are going to let me stay after all. I still got to help with toddlers and little kids, but, except for changing potty-pants diapers, no babies.

"I killed a baby," I said to myself. "I'll never get a baby of my own again." That made me very sad, but I didn't complain. It was my own fault.

So, imagine my surprise Ai came to me one day when I was ten years old and said, "There's another new baby and I need your help again."

Part of me was very very happy. Ai had forgotten! I was going to get another chance with a baby. Part of me, though, was kind of mad.

What kind of stupid orphanage would let a baby-killer take care of babies?

"This is Ling," Ai said as I peered down into a crib. "We think Ling is four or five months old."

I gave Ling a long look over. I didn't think Ling was four months old. She looked like she had just been born. She was so tiny. Just like Hoa . . .

"Ling has a bad eye." Then I saw it. Ling's right eye looked like it was almost swollen shut.

"We aren't sure about her other eye. We think it might have some problems, too. Feed Ling some formula now and then again in four hours."

Thanks to Trinh, we had lots of powder formula. Oh, I guess I didn't tell you about Trinh yet.

Trinh was a very pretty girl, almost old enough to be a wife-lady, who worked in someplace called Saigon. Every two weeks, Trinh would come in a big van and give Ai boxes and boxes of formula.

Sometimes, Trinh would bring little presents for us. She'd bring toys and games and new clothes. We shared everything, so the presents were always for all of us.

Sometimes, Trinh would bring strange-looking people to Mercy House and they would take a child with them. We didn't know where the children went. Maybe to a new orphanage. I never paid much attention. I wasn't going to a new orphanage. Mercy House was my home. I was going to live there forever.

I liked Trinh. She was nice. Whenever Trinh came, she would always find time to sit down and have "special talks" with me. Trinh always asked what I wanted to be when I grew up and was as big as she was.

I didn't really think much about growing up. But I hoped that I would always have babies to take care of.

"So, you want to be a nanny, just like Ai?"

"Yes. I'd like to a nanny, just like Ai."

Trinh must have known that Ai was going to give me another chance with a baby of my own, because we had just had a "special talk" about being very careful to boil the water for the formula. Otherwise, formula could make babies very sick.

I remembered everything Trinh had said about formula. I boiled some water, mixed it up with the formula powder and woke Ling up from her nap.

Ling only had one good eye and maybe that eye wasn't so good, but she seemed to know I was standing over her crib. And I think she knew I was supposed to feed her.

Ling was hungry. Really hungry.

What's the holdup? Why won't the stupid girl who killed a baby give me my formula?

Ling started to cry. No. That's not right. Ling started to scream. Feed me, stupid girl who killed a baby!

I reached down into the crib to pick up Ling, but then stopped. If I knew one thing for absolutely sure, it was that I was not going to kill this baby. I had to make sure that the formula was good.

I put the bottle's nipple in my mouth and sucked out some of the formula. It tasted like a water buffalo had made potty in the bottle, but I choked it down.

At first, I thought that maybe I hadn't boiled the water long enough because I felt like I was going to barfy up everything I'd eaten for the last three days.

But then I realized that it was only because formula taste is for babies and my mouth and throat weren't a baby mouth and throat. Once I felt the formula get down into my tummy, I didn't feel like I was going to barfy up any more.

Ling didn't see the need to do any testing, but she saw a big need to do a lot of feeding and to do it fast. I guess maybe she could see well enough to know that I had taken a drink out of her bottle.

Ling had woken up hungry. Now Ling was hungry and mad. Ling was screaming louder than ever.

That's *my* formula, stupid girl who killed a baby!

Feed me, stupid girl who killed a baby!

Be patient, stupid baby who doesn't know anything!

I mean it, stupid girl who killed a baby! Feed me or I'm going to make the smelliest most disgusting potty ever and you're going to have to clean it up!

All right, stupid baby who doesn't know anything! I give up! Here! Drink your stupid formula!

I picked up Ling and stuck the bottle in her mouth.

And, all of a sudden, the stupid girl who killed a baby and the stupid baby who didn't know anything were the best of friends. Ling smiled and then giggled as she drank. I smiled back.

Ling closed her good eye and sucked away contentedly at the bottle. I could feel my smile growing bigger and bigger.

I sat down on the little stool. I started rocking back and forth very gently. When the bottle was empty, I put Ling up on my shoulder. She happily burped for me.

I cradled Ling in my arms. She went right to sleep. Even though she was asleep already, I couldn't help but start singing to her. I sang very softly and quietly.

After about half an hour, I very carefully stood up, trying not to let my Limper Girl leg make me fall. I laid Ling back down into the crib.

Before I could pull my hands away, Ling woke up and started screaming again. I picked her up. She cooed and fell back asleep.

And so, once again, I was up almost all night taking care of a new baby. I missed supper. And then I missed breakfast. But I didn't care. This time was different. Now I was the not-so-stupid girl who did know how to take care of a baby.

Before she left that night, Trinh stopped by Ling's crib and told me what a good job I was doing.

"Ling is lucky to have you for a nanny, Cam!"

Yes!

I was Ling's nanny!

Ling thought I was the only nanny for her.

She would scream out that scream of hers if Ai or any of the wife-lady nannies tried to pick her up. They would call for Cam and the not-so-stupid girl who did know how to take care of a baby would limp in, pick up Ling and then there'd be a happy baby instead of a madder-than-a-scorpion baby.

Everybody started talking about Cam and how good she was with babies. I was carrying Ling around with me most of the time. It was the only way for there to be any peace at all in Mercy House. Nobody wanted Ling screaming and only Cam could keep Ling happy.

I started to wonder if Hoa had just been some bad dream I'd had one time. All of the things that I'd wanted to do with Hoa, I was doing with Ling.

I wanted to teach Ling everything I knew. I knew that the first numbers were "one," "two" and "three." I thought "four" came next, but I wasn't sure. So, I decided to stick to "one-two-three."

"Ling. Let's count. One . . . two . . . three."

Sometimes I would hold up my fingers. Sometimes I would pick up little sticks or pebbles. I didn't know if Ling was understanding about counting, but I thought it was a good idea to keep trying.

One day, I pointed to me and said, "One." Then I pointed to Ling and said, "Two." I kind of tickled her tummy a little and she giggled.

I didn't know what else to point to. A big mosquito landed on the front of Ling's favorite shirt with the bear on the front. Go away, stupid mosquito!

I said "Three!" as I shushed the mosquito off my baby's shirt.

That made Ling giggle really hard. And I giggled really hard.

After that, "One! Two! Three!" was Ling's favorite game. I was always "One!" Ling was always "Two!" And then I'd pretend I was shooing something bad off of Ling for "Three!"

"One!" and "Two!" were Cam and Ling. "Three!" was something that Cam and Ling wanted to go away.

I was very happy. I was a nanny, which was exactly what I'd wanted to be. I had a very special baby to care for. Ling could be a little pain sometimes, but I loved her and I knew that Ling loved me.

As far as I was concerned, life could just stop right where it was and I could spend between now and the end of the world as Ling's nanny.

But that was when I found out that life doesn't just stop and have everything stay the same forever.

It was the day that Trinh came with boxes of formula and then said that she wanted to have an "extra-special special talk" with me.

"Come outside with me, Cam."

I said I wanted to take Ling out with me, but Trinh said that she would be fine inside. We could hear Ling scream as soon as I left the room, but Trinh still didn't let me go back and get her.

For you to understand what happened next, you need to know about school.

Yes, we did go to school. It was only for a couple of hours a day. School was in an old church (I think that's what it was) that was about a five-minute walk from Mercy House. It took me a little longer because I was a Limper Girl.

I know now that we really didn't learn much. Mostly, the teacher talked to us about Ba Ho and how Ba Ho had fought for Vietnam to be free and how the Americans had tried to stop him but Ba Ho hadn't given up and now Vietnam was free.

We also learned that $2+2 = 4$ and rain comes from clouds. There were probably other things, but that's all I can remember.

I didn't really know what "Americans" were or where they came from, but I knew that I wouldn't like to meet one. I knew that Americans had tried to hurt Ba Ho and stop him from making Vietnam free and that was all I needed to know.

I pictured Americans with big ugly horns growing out of their foreheads. Americans were so mean that they probably ate babies.

Yes! Of course! That's why Americans had tried to stop Ba Ho from making Vietnam free! It was so that they could go to Mercy House and eat babies!

So, I almost went potty all over myself when Trinh said: "Cam, I have some wonderful news! You are going to be adopted! You are going to America!"

I couldn't have been more shocked if Trinh had said to me: "Cam, I have some wonderful news! We are going to cut off your arms and sell them to the fishermen so that they can chop them up and use them as bait!"

I didn't know what "adopted" meant. I didn't know where America was. Trinh made it sound like America was a long way from Mercy House.

I guessed that America was so far away, it was probably over on the other side of the river! That meant I would have to ride a ferry boat to get to America.

And why in the world would I want to go to a place where baby-eaters lived? I just knew that they would make me eat babies, too!

Trinh reached into her handbag and pulled out a picture. "This will be your mom and your dad! Isn't she pretty? And doesn't your dad look big and strong and handsome?"

I didn't see anybody pretty in that picture. All I saw were two people with very pale skin. Ugly pale skin.

With skin that pale, these two must be very sick. Why would Trinh make me go live with sick people? Was I supposed to take care of them? I knew that I would refuse to cook babies for these people's supper!

Come to think of it, a lot of the strangers Trinh had brought to Mercy House to take children away had ugly pale skin too! Were all of those kids cooking babies? What was Trinh thinking?

"Isn't it great, Cam? You will get to live in a big house! You'll have lots of clothes and toys and lots of good food!

You'll get to go to school! You'll get to be something special in this world!"

I was already something special in this world! I was a nanny! Ling's nanny!

"And you'll have a room all to yourself!"

I didn't want a room all to myself. I wanted a room that would be big enough for both Ling and me, but that was all I wanted.

"And you'll get a very pretty new name!"

A new name?

"In America, you'll be called 'Ashley'!"

I think it was right then that I started to cry.

I Meet Moonguy

Ty Roberson.

Not an act you want to try to follow.

During Roberson's three decades as head coach, Bishop Mathis basketball went from an afterthought to an institution. Six state championships, eighteen sectional titles and an almost unbroken string of conference championships.

Fifty-six grads who went to the rosters of NCAA Division One schools and innumerable others who played for schools in lower divisions and J.C.s. Nine NBA draftees. Four starters on NBA Championship teams. One NBA Hall of Famer.

"Coach R used to always . . ."

"Coach R always said . . ."

"Coach R would never . . ."

If you listened long enough, you might start hearing stories about Coach R parting the Red Sea, healing leper colonies and leaping tall buildings in a single bound. Everything Coach R ever did on the basketball court turned to pure gold.

Everything I did that first season turned to something else . . .

Actually, objectively speaking, a close loss to Rancho Piedro in the sectional quarterfinals was not such a terrible end result.

If anybody would ever bother to go back through the record books, they would find that B.M. posted a mediocre 14-16 record in Ty Roberson's first year of coaching and would not make the playoffs in any form for his first three years.

Coach R hadn't just waltzed into the gym, waved a magic wand and instantly converted a doormat into a dynasty.

Coach R had needed time. I needed time. But Ty Roberson getting time and Randy Hartman getting time were apparently two different deals altogether.

I got a contract for Year Two, but it was made abundantly clear to me that without substantial improvement there would be no Year Three.

The team had pulled off one impressive upset in the first round of sectionals. Our No. 15 seeding meant we were paired right off with Montgomery Pines. Worse yet, we had to play at their place. It took three overtimes, but we wound up four points to the good, 90-86.

Montgomery Pines bought me back some credibility, but was hardly enough to win over the hard-cores who were determined never to let go of the gauzy memories of Coach R and the glory days.

It didn't help matters at all that good old Coach R attended every single game, sat right in back of our bench and was not discrete about letting displeasure radiate off his weather-beaten face.

We pulled off another upset in the second round, outlasting Agua Fresca in regulation, 56-53. That effort was met with the collective too-little-too-late yawn from the fan base.

How you do handle "what have you done for us lately?" when you have just performed a pair of miracles?

All of which was just a prelude to the firestorm of abuse that hit after Rancho Piedro ended the season for us.

Joe Tyndall, sharp-tongued sports editor for the *South Valley Progress-Bulletin*, headlined his column the day after the Rancho Piedro loss with "RANDY HARTMAN, LANCER HOOPS AND THE ONSET OF THE DARK AGES." The column went on to catalogue all of the reasons why I should not be trusted with sharp objects, let alone the head coaching job for a perennial basketball powerhouse.

When asked about my coaching prowess, good old Coach R had responded: "Coach Hartman is a good man who wants the same thing we all do, more championship banners hanging in the gym. I'm sure he'll do all he can to get Lancer basketball back up to our usual level of greatness."

Translation: "Coach Hartman is an idiot who isn't worthy to wash my sweatpants."

And then I made the mistake of actually reading the garbage people were putting out on social media and bulletin boards.

Every call I'd made, every substitution I'd ordered (or not ordered), every time out I'd called (or not called), every time I'd reached down and scratched my rear end during a game . . . they were all endlessly re-analyzed, second-guessed and ultimately damned as the work of a coach who knew less about basketball than the average third-grader.

But then . . . I came upon this post, this really long post, by somebody with the handle "Moonguy." At first, I thought that I was reading something by the only intelligent fan Bishop Mathis had left.

posted by MOONGUY:
Those of you who are questioning Randy Hartman's game-time tactics are barking up the wrong tree. Hartman's technical understanding of basketball is superb and it is the reason why he was hired.

I smiled. Okay. Here's somebody who gets it. Take that, you ignorant morons! Just keep reading and . . .

The Lancers' fall from grace this past season has nothing to do with strategy and everything to do with chemistry. If only Randy Hartman had a gift to inspire equal to his gift for play-calling. Hartman coached this year not like a man who wanted to win, but a man who wanted to avoid losing. He coached scared. His team played scared. And that is why Bishop Mathis had its worst season in 25 years.

I fumed and mumbled curses all the way home. Moonguy had struck a nerve and I wasn't even sure I knew why.

How could anybody say that my team lacked chemistry? Me, not inspirational? Well, isn't THAT the most idiotic comment of them all? I wrote the book on inspiration! Inspiration is my middle name!

I knew that I was going to need some serious wind-down time dribbling in the driveway. I got home and bounded up the stairs to change.

"Randy? Where have you been? Evelyn will be here in ten minutes!"

When Shelley had first shoved Ashley's picture in my face, she assured me that going the international adoption route was going to be quick and relatively painless.

I don't know if Shelley consciously lied to me or if she'd actually convinced herself that muss and fuss weren't going to be part of the deal.

It seemed like we were constantly going here for this, going there for that, signing some stack of incomprehensible paperwork and (of course) writing checks to somebody or other. There was the whole deal with the State Department on arranging Ashley's entry visa and U.S. citizenship (on the advice of Mercy Worldwide Adoptions, we applied for two visas, just in case a sibling was located within eighteen months).

There were background investigations, parenting classes, CPR classes, classes, I think, in taking classes and . . . last but never least . . . there was Evelyn.

Evelyn was a social worker. Why was Evelyn relevant?

The State Department required that we pass a home study certifying that we were not a couple of sadists, our house was not a death trap and we were not on the verge of poverty. The home study had to be done by a licensed social worker. And so we had the singular privilege of sitting in our living room once a week and listening to Evelyn pontificate on all of the aspects of parenting of which we were clearly ignorant.

"Have you had a chance to work on that little household safety punch-list we put together at our last visit?"

Evelyn's "little household safety punch-list" had detailed repairs whose cost was running somewhere north of $3,000, including a new stairwell railing that probably could have survived a direct hit from a rocket-propelled grenade.

As usual, Shelley was doing all of the talking and that was fine with me. "Yes, we've gotten four bids . . . here . . . let me show you . . . oh . . . what did I do with those bids?"

My mind was wandering, as it had a tendency to do whenever Evelyn came by for one of her "little visits."

I couldn't help but go back and let myself obsess on Joe Tyndall's column, good old Coach R's lukewarm "endorsement" of me, all of the nonsense I'd read on-line and, most of all, Moonguy's comments.

They say you have to have some pretty thick skin to be a coach, but nobody could have skin thick enough to ignore what the public was hurling at me.

From where we were sitting on the couch, I could see the backboard and hoop in the driveway. I had an overwhelming urge to just get up, walk out, grab my ball and start shooting buckets.

I was vaguely aware that Evelyn was lecturing us on "cultural sensitivity."

"Your new daughter will be coming from a very different culture and it will be important for you to show her that you respect her traditions . . ." Blah-dee-blah-dee-blah-blah-blah.

Moonguy.

Why did his post bother me so much? His was the only one that showed the slightest understanding of basketball and the realities of coaching and yet . . .

Shelley was talking, but it was as if she were a hundred miles away. "I've been working with Rosetta Stone . . ."

How could Moonguy say that I didn't know how to inspire my team?

He hadn't seen me in the locker room before games. I always talked to every single player on the team, gave him encouragement and told him to get out on the court and do his best. If that wasn't inspiration, I didn't know what was.

"Well, let's see . . . I know that 'kem' means 'ice cream' in Vietnamese . . ."

I was coaching that team exactly the way I wished I had been coached. I treated my players with respect, like they were adults. They had to love that, right?

"Oh and, it's the cutest thing . . . in Vietnamese . . . a lot of animal names are the sounds they make! Like 'horse' is 'con neigh'! Isn't that precious? A horse says 'neigh' and that's what they use . . ."

Moonguy. I guess Moonguy really knew how to get under my skin . . .

"How about you, Mr. Hartman? Have you learned any Vietnamese?"

I had half a mind to go grab one of those nerd-geeks in Computer Lab and get him to hack Moonguy's account, find out who he really was . . .

"Randy? Evelyn asked you a question."

Moonguy. Yeah, I'd have a thing or two to say . . .

"MR. HARTMAN! Your wife has learned some words in Vietnamese. What have you learned?"

I stared hard at Evelyn. "I . . . umh . . ."

"Really now, Mr. Hartman. I'm going to have to put in some negative comments about your commitment to multi-culturalism."

All right . . . I was just about at my limit for the day . . . Tyndall . . . good old Coach R . . . Evelyn . . . Moonguy . . .

"Honestly, Mr. Hartman. I find it incomprehensible that you would not take the time to learn even a single word of Vietnamese!"

Shelley was poking me hard in the ribs. Evelyn was shaking her head and writing something down on her report pad.

"You say you are committed to international adoption but I really haven't seen . . ."

"Really, Evelyn? And how much Vietnamese do you know?"

"Randy . . ." Shelley hissed in my ear. "Stop this! You're just going to make her . . ."

"I do not know any Vietnamese, Mr. Hartman, but I'm not the one who thinks he's ready to take on the responsibility of raising a Vietnamese daughter! I really have to question whether . . ."

"Basketball!" I almost shouted the word out. Funny how forceful a man's voice becomes when he's lying.

Evelyn fumbled with her pen. "Excuse me?"

"I know the Vietnamese word for basketball. I'm a basketball coach and this is a house where basketball is important. So, I thought I should first learn the Vietnamese word for 'basketball.'"

"And what would that word be, Mr. Hartman?"

I sucked in a deep breath. My mind raced. I had to say something . . .

"Moonguyen!"

I'm A Goalie

A couple of months went by.

Trinh and I had more "special talks," but she didn't say anything more about adoption or about me becoming Ashley Stupidname. Maybe she forgot. Trinh always had so much to do and was so busy. Maybe she forgot and I wouldn't have to be adopted. That would be fine with me.

I just wanted to live at Mercy House and do my job as Ling's nanny.

I didn't want to go live in America Stupidcountry with American Stupidfamily in American Stupidhouse.

What would Ba Ho think? A nice Vietnamese girl going to live in America Stupidcountry that he fought a war against? Changing her name to Ashley Stupidgirl? I think he'd be sad, that's what I thought.

I wasn't going to make Ba Ho sad. I wasn't going to America Stupidcountry. I was staying right here in Vietnam. Where I belonged. Where I was needed.

So, I guess I pushed the whole adoption thing to the back of my head and tried to live my life like Trinh had never said anything about it. Adoption wasn't real. Hoa wasn't real. Ling was real and she was all I needed to worry about.

It was getting harder and harder to go to school every day. I hated to leave Ling.

Ling would scream her mad little monkey scream when I would leave in the morning. I'd be almost all the way down the street to school before I couldn't hear her anymore.

I'd have to stop and wipe away all of my tears before I went into school. If the other kids saw me crying, they'd think I was weak. And I didn't want anybody thinking I was weak.

I started trying to come up with reasons why I couldn't go to school, why I had to stay at Mercy House all day with Ling.

My tummy hurts. I have a cough; here listen . . . (cough)! Ling ate my underwear. A water buffalo made potty in the street and it smells. I can't hear anything; I woke up deaf!

Ai would always listen patiently to my excuses, look me in the eye and tell me that I was going to school.

"What if a monsoon comes up while I'm walking to school and there's a flood and it scoops me up and . . ."

"Then you will wish you had learned to swim. Now put on your clothes, eat your breakfast and go to school . . ."

And so I would go to school. And I would listen to stories about Ba Ho and learn again that $2+2 = 4$ and that rain comes from clouds.

And I would worry the whole time about Ling. Did she ever stop crying? Did Ai feed her enough breakfast? Would Ling forget who I was before I got back from school?

On days when there was no rain, the first thing we would do at school would be our exercises. We'd go out into the yard and do jumping jacks and push-ups and run around the yard six times. Lots of us were from Mercy House and so there some exercises that we couldn't do or we couldn't do very well.

I had trouble with the jumping jacks because my legs weren't the same size and running was pretty hard, too. Instead of running around the yard six times, I'd limp around it two times.

And after exercises we'd play games.

The kids who weren't from Mercy House and didn't have any problems usually went out to this big grassy field to play soccer. The boys had one part of the field for their soccer. The girls had the other part.

The rest of us would play games like "Simon Says" or something else where we didn't run around or kick balls.

At first, I'd liked "Simon Says," except when Simon would say to do something that was hard for me, like more jumping jacks. But by the time I was ten, I was getting bored with "Simon Says."

I didn't want to play Simon Says Stupidbabygame anymore. I kept watching the kids who got to play soccer and wondering what it was like to be able to run without falling on your bottom, kick a ball straight and jump up and down to celebrate.

So, one day when I'd felt really really sad about leaving Ling ("What if there's a great big giant spider in the street?") and I'd felt really really stupid playing "Simon Says" ("Simon says stick your finger up your nose and eat your boogers"), I turned and limped away toward the grassy field.

I didn't understand soccer. I didn't know the rules. I didn't care about the rules. It just looked like it would be a whole lot of fun to run around and kick a ball.

I wanted to do that. I wanted to run around and kick a ball.

The next day, I didn't go to "Simon Says" at all. After I was done limping around the yard two times, I went right to the edge of the grass and watched.

There was this one girl, she must have been two years older than me. Her name was Tham. She wasn't from Mercy House. She seemed like the best soccer player. She could run fast. She could kick straight. She always seemed to know exactly what to do and when to do it.

The more I watched, the more I wished that I was Tham. I wished that I could be just like Tham, but still have my life just like it was and be Ling's nanny.

The day after that, I got done limping around the yard two times, went to the edge of the grass and then I did something that I hadn't known I was going to do. I said the words without thinking.

"Tham! Can I play too?"

A lot of the kids laughed at me. What's this? Orphan Stupidgirl Limper wants to play soccer? Ha ha ha. How funny is that?

I didn't really know anything about Tham, except that she was the best soccer player in the school. I didn't know if she was nice or mean or could sing songs to a baby or change a diaper after the baby had made potty. So, I didn't know what she would say.

Tham didn't laugh. I thought that was probably a pretty good sign.

"Sure," Tham said. "Sure. You can play soccer."

I grinned a great big grin as I limped onto the grass.

Tham pointed to a girl named Mai. "You can be on Mai's team."

Mai groaned and started to argue, but Tham gave Mai a mean look and Mai kept quiet.

"Just remember that your team wants to kick the ball that way. My team is going to try to kick it the other way."

"Okay!" I said. I was so happy to be playing soccer.

The game started. I kept my eye on the ball.

The kids ran up and down, chasing after the ball and trying to kick it in the right direction.

I had a real hard time keeping up. The ball would be going one direction and I'd try to follow it and then a kid on the other team would kick it the other direction and I'd try to run that direction. I was so slow that the ball would usually change direction again before I could get going.

This had been a mistake. There was a reason why they had Orphan Stupidgirl Limper playing Simon Says Stupidbabygame instead of soccer.

Orphan Stupidgirl Limper could never play this game.

She could never in a billion zillion years play soccer.

She was a nanny, not a soccer player.

Orphan Stupidgirl Limper should just stay where she's supposed to stay and not try to do things she can't do.

I was just about to walk off the grass and go back to Simon Says Stupidbabygame when I heard Mai yelling my name. "Cam! Look out!"

I looked up just in time to see Tham running right at me, kicking the ball. I knew I had to get out of her way, but . . .

I had never flown like a bird before. I'd never even wondered what it would be like to fly like a bird, but I was flying like a bird then.

Up, up, up I went.

I wondered if I was going to be able to see the roof of Mercy House.

And then I went down. I went down hard. I landed on my face.

It felt like the ground was pushing my nose back up into my skull.

My mouth was full of mud and grass and little pebbles and maybe a worm. Nothing hurt at first, but then everything hurt all at once and it hurt bad.

The kids were all laughing really really hard.

I felt tears coming to my eyes.

I didn't want tears!

I didn't want Stupidbabytears to make me look weak.

Go away, Stupidbabytears! I don't want you coming out of my eyes and running down my face!

When I was pretty sure that I had scared away all the Stupidbabytears, I pushed up with my arms and got my face out of the mud. I rolled over and sat up.

And then I understood why everybody was laughing so hard. They weren't laughing at me, Orphan Stupidgirl Limper Whoflewlikeabird.

They were laughing at Tham.

Tham was sitting a few feet away from me on her bottom like I was sitting on mine. She looked like she wasn't sure what had happened.

Mai ran over, helped me stand up and started wiping the mud off my face.

"Hooray for Cam!" Mai shouted. "Hooray for Cam who stood up to Tham, the bully girl!"

Was that what I had done? I remembered that I had seen Tham run up at kids like she'd run up at me, but they'd always gotten out of her way.

I think I'd wanted to get out of Tham's way but wasn't fast enough. So, instead of getting out of Tham's way, like she was used to kids doing, I'd stayed in her way.

Tham had made me fly like bird, but I had made Tham fall like a rock.

Tham got to her feet. She was embarrassed.

I could see then that Tham had wanted everybody to think she was big and tough, but I'd just proven that she wasn't.

Big Bad Tham had been knocked to the ground by Orphan Stupidgirl Limper.

Tham walked angrily toward me. "Why did you do that?" Tham yelled.

When Tham got closer, I could see that there were tears in her eyes. Big Bad Tham The Bullygirl was crying!

She was weak!

I hadn't cried! I was strong!

"You ran into Cam, she didn't run into you!" Mai yelled back at Tham.

Tham turned away from me and pushed Mai. Mai stumbled back a little but didn't fall.

"Shut up, Mai! That's not what happened!"

Tham was coming at Mai again. Her hands made fists.

I'd been scared. I'd been embarrassed. I'd been hurt.

But now I was just mad.

The ball was lying right next to me. I picked it up.

"Tham, you big stupid bully girl! Leave my friend Mai alone!"

Tham turned to me. Her hands were still making fists, but it didn't look like she was making them for Mai anymore. She was making them for me.

"What's that? Are you crying, Tham? I didn't know you were so weak!"

Tham raised her stupid fists like she was going to hit me!

The only thing I had to protect myself was the ball. I raised up my arm and threw the ball right at Tham.

Tham's face made a little crunch-crunch noise.

Tham stopped. She put a hand up to her nose. When she saw all of the blood on her fingers, Tham made a really mad girl face and came at me again with her stupid fists up.

Tham punched me on my right cheek.

I had already thrown the ball, so I didn't have anything else to fight with. But that was okay. I didn't need to fight.

Mai and about six other girls tackled Tham and threw her to the grass. They started beating on her back and pulling her hair.

Everybody knew the truth now about Tham.

Nobody was scared of Tham anymore and nobody was going to let Tham beat up Orphan Stupidgirl Limper.

Tham was threatening to do all sorts of bad things to Mai and the other girls, but nobody was scared. Tham started crying even harder and stopped making threats.

A bell rang. Exercise time was over.

One by one, the girls who had tackled Tham got up and started walking toward the school.

Mai took my hand and helped me limp back toward the school. Everybody went back to school.

Except Big Bad Tham The Bullygirl. She just laid on the grass and cried.

Ai asked me what had happened and I said I'd stumbled and fallen down on my face, but I'd been strong and hadn't cried. I guess I looked pretty beat up.

Even Ling looked like she felt bad for me that night. As I was putting Ling into her crib, she reached up with one hand and tried to the touch red spot on my cheek where Tham had hit me.

"Go to sleep, Ling," I ordered, sounding a little meaner than usual.

"It's nothing. I'm strong. You don't need to worry. Remember to be strong, like Nanny Cam!"

The next day, Big Bad Tham The Bullygirl didn't show up for school. I don't think anybody really missed her all that much.

At exercise time, when I was done limping around the yard twice, Mai found me and asked if I'd like to play soccer again. I thought that she was just being nice to me.

I knew in my little heart of hearts that I had no business playing soccer and I'd just get in the way and maybe make her team lose.

"Thank you, Mai. But I don't think I'll ever be very good at soccer . . ."

"But you can be, Cam! You aren't very good at running up and down, but you showed yesterday that you can throw the ball really straight. I think you'd be a good goalie!"

I didn't know what a goalie was, but if it meant I could play soccer with the other kids, I was all for it. Mai helped me down to one end of the grass where there were two big bucket thingees set up a few feet apart.

"This is the goal. All you have to do is stand in front of the goal and make sure that nobody kicks the ball between the bucket thingees. You're the only one who can touch the ball with your hands. You can stop it with your hands and then throw it to one of us. Do you think you can do that?"

"I think I can do that!"

Mai got the two teams together, told everybody that I'd be the goalie for her team and that anybody who tried to knock me down or hurt me would get her bare bottom paddled in front of the boys. That helped all the girls see that it would be a bad idea to hurt me.

And so I became the goalie for Mai's team. I don't know if I was really a good goalie or not. I still couldn't move very fast and many balls got past me. But I did stop a few and then threw them right where I was supposed to throw them. I was a better ball-thrower than ball-stopper.

I thought that life couldn't have been any better.

Once, I had been nothing, just a stupid orphan girl who limped.

Now, I was two things.

I was a nanny.

I was a goalie.

If somebody had come along and said that I could be the Queen of Vietnam if I'd give up being nanny and goalie, I'd have told them to go make potty in their pants and sit on it. I couldn't imagine that I'd ever want to be anything else.

Trinh hadn't said anything more about adoption. It wasn't going to happen. I was going to get to live at Mercy House for the rest of my life taking care of Ling and being a goalie who was good at throwing balls even if she wasn't so good at stopping them.

I didn't have to wait to die to go to Heaven. I was there already.

And then one day Trinh's van pulled up. Trinh said she wanted to go have a "special talk" right away.

"It's all set, Ashley," Trinh smiled.

I felt my tummy twist up when I heard Ai use Ashley Stupidname.

"Your mom and dad are coming next week to take you to America!"

It felt like Mercy House was spinning around me. I was afraid I was going to close my eyes and fall on the grass.

It hadn't been a bad dream! It had been real!

Trinh really had talked to me about adoption and now it was going to happen and there wasn't anything I could do to stop it!

I swallowed hard and fought back Stupidbabytears.

"Yes . . . we have to get ready. We have to get ready. There's so much we have to pack for Ling! Her blanket! She won't sleep without her blanket!

"She still makes potty in her pants, so we'll need diapers! Lots of diapers! Lots and lots of diapers! And her favorite shirt! The little one with the bear on the front . . ."

"Ashley . . ."

"DON'T CALL ME THAT STUPID AMERICAN NAME! MY NAME IS CAM! MY NAME IS CAM AND I'M A NANNY AND A GOALIE!"

"Cam . . . Ling can't go with you to America . . ."

"MY NAME IS CAM! I'M A NANNY AND A GOALIE! "

"Cam! Please! We've talked about this! The Americans are adopting just you! Ling can't go to America with you!"

"I'M A NANNY AND A GOALIE AND I HAVE A BABY NAMED LING! SHE CALLS ME CAM-CAM!"

And then Trinh did something she'd never done before. She slapped me in the face. It wasn't hard, but it was a slap.

"You're going to America, Cam! You're going to America! And Ling can't go with you!"

I was so mad at Trinh. She was making me cry. I looked weak.

I didn't want to look weak.

My Family Grows ... Sort Of ...

High school teams don't recruit. Prep sports is the one last pure expression of amateur athletics left in America. It's all about the competition and not about the result.

A coach's focus is on a player's character, not his talent. We take what players we've got and do our best to prepare them for life as adults. So, high school teams don't recruit.

I have to admit that I made a lot of typos at first when I was typing that paragraph because I was holding my nose. You can pour caramel sauce and whipped cream on manure, then put a cherry on top, but it's still manure.

If you're a coach and want to keep your job, you do everything in your power (and some things technically beyond your power) to win as many games as possible. You look for every edge, every conceivable advantage.

Is that because you are a one-dimensional macho power freak who can't see beyond the final score?

No.

It's because you have a mortgage payment. It's because they don't give food away down at the supermarket. It's because you've got people depending on you to make sure they've got a dry place to sleep when it rains and don't have to walk around naked.

Here's a harsh bit of reality: The same people who make such a big stink out of telling you that "win at all costs" has no place at your school are also the ones who will be the first to scream for your head if you aren't filling the trophy case.

So, OF COURSE high schools recruit. I could tell all kinds of hair-raising tales about coaches manipulating all manner of inter-district transfer shenanigans, but then I'd be throwing stones from the roof of my glass house. I'm no better and no worse than my colleagues.

And private schools have a definite advantage. We aren't constrained by inconveniences like district boundaries. In theory, we've got much stricter academic requirements but it's a pretty dull-headed coach who can't maneuver around that false hurdle.

I can't go after a kid directly. I can't call up his house and say: "Excuse me, but I'm the head coach at Bishop Mathis and I've got a free ride for your potential five-star power forward kid if he'll come play for me."

What I can do is let it be known in a general sense what kind of players I'm looking for . . . nudge nudge, wink wink . . . and then act pleasantly surprised when the potential five-star power forward's dad gives me a call.

Given that we need to keep so much of this under the radar, nobody ever speaks in terms of a "recruiting season," but, make no mistake, a recruiting season there is and you'd better be around when it comes up.

And, if I was going to keep on making that mortgage payment, paying for groceries, sleeping in a dry place and avoiding arrest for indecent exposure, I had to make my first recruiting season at Bishop Mathis count.

The makings of another Lancer dynasty were spread out in eighth-grade classes all over three counties and I was determined to get each and every one of them to commit to my program.

The last thing I wanted to hear right about then was: "We have to drop everything and go to Vietnam for two weeks to finish adopting Ashley."

I'd just gotten a call from Lionel Moncrief, Sr., father of Lionel Moncrief, Jr. The younger Lionel had been turning a head or two playing shooting guard for Malcolm X Intermediate.

Nobody had Lionel down as a five-star recruit, but he wouldn't be a bad start on building that dynasty I had in mind. It had been a promising conversation and Lionel Sr. had made an appointment to come in and see me the following week.

It was after ten o'clock when I walked in the front door, feeling pretty good about my first day of non-recruiting season. Shelley was waiting for me, holding a document that looked suspiciously like a FAX.

"We have to drop everything and go to Vietnam for two weeks to finish adopting Ashley."

"But . . ." I started to protest.

I chuckled a rueful little chuckle to myself three days later as Shelley and I boarded a 777 bound for Hong Kong. Why had I even bothered? Why had I wasted any breath trying to argue?

I had remembered somebody saying something about how the call to go would come with very short notice, but I'd sort of put myself into a state of denial about the reality of it. Sure, we'd be going to Vietnam but we could work something out.

I mean, let's be reasonable, would I really be put to a choice between finalizing the adoption and my professional future?

Yes, naivety can be sort of charming in a man my age, but it can also be extraordinarily costly. And it looked like I was going to pay the price.

I had never flown overseas before. Oh, I'd heard stories, but I don't think any amount of prior research could have truly prepared me for the misery that was eighteen hours in economy class.

I'm sure Einstein could explain it, but those eighteen hours seemed to elongate into about eighteen days.

The in-flight movies available on the little screen on the back of the seat in front of me seemed to have been picked from a Bad Cinema Festival somewhere. The "authentic Asian cuisine" tasted mostly like corn flakes soaked with soy sauce (and sustained for about as long).

Shelley was an anxious little mess who needed more or less constant assurance that the adoption wouldn't be cancelled if the plane were five minutes late.

Our four-hour layover in Hong Kong was just exactly the wrong length. Long enough to get good and stir-crazy; short enough that checking into the transit hotel was impractical.

By the time our little commuter plane touched down in Ho Chi Minh City, I was a wild-eyed sleep-deprived wreck of a human being whose poor confused internal clock was spewing smoke.

I was surprised when the stern-faced immigration officer gave my passport a visa stamp and admitted me to Vietnam. I think I'd have called Security if I'd seen me coming.

After getting our luggage, we walked out of the air conditioned terminal and straight into a wall of the most intense heat and humidity I have ever experienced. Even if I'd have come off the plane feeling perfectly fit and rested, I still would have wilted within about thirty seconds.

A phalanx of Vietnamese men and women, some wearing chauffeur-type uniforms, stood outside the terminal doors holding signs with last names on them.

"There! Hartman!" Shelley shouted.

It took me a couple of seconds to pick her out from the mass of people, but I did spot a pretty and pleasant-looking young woman holding a sign that read: "HARTMAN."

Thankfully, it was only a few minutes later that the pretty and pleasant-looking young woman ushered Shelley and me into an air-conditioned van driven by a stone-faced Vietnamese man.

She introduced herself as "Trinh," although, in one of those inexplicably awkward anomalies of foreign-to-English transliteration, her name was pronounced more like "Gin."

Trinh was Mercy Worldwide Adoptions' person-on-the-ground for all Vietnamese adoptions. Her English was passable and she exuded all of the right enthusiasm and energy.

Trinh explained that we would be getting on the road immediately for the three-hour drive to Long Xuyen, capital of An Giang Province where we would find the orphanage and our new daughter, Cam.

"Ashley," Shelley quickly corrected.

Trinh smiled one of those smiles that suggested we were onto a topic about which she was already frustrated. "That's something that you and your daughter will need to work out."

"There's nothing to work out!" Shelley snapped.

"Her name is Ashley!"

A three-hour drive in Vietnam is quite different from a three-hour drive in America. Road maintenance is spotty, at best, and our van was forced to share two very narrow lanes with motor scooters, water buffaloes, wooden farm carts, large slow buses and wandering pedestrians.

Questions of right-of-way seemed to be determined by the courage (or stupidity) possessed by each individual driver and not by any discernible rule of the road.

When we finally arrived at our hotel in Long Xuyen, I fell into bed fully clothed and slept a sleep that would have made a mummy envious.

Shelley shook me awake the following morning, having done up her hair and makeup to magazine cover specs. I wondered if she'd slept at all.

Trinh and Stone-Face picked us up at 9:02.

At 9:00, Shelley had started winding up on a major fret that something must have gone wrong and we weren't going to be able to get Ashley and her life would be ruined . . .

Trinh smiled that beautiful but obviously patient smile of hers after the van pulled away from the hotel.

"I have been talking a lot with Cam . . . I mean, Ashley, about adoption. She's a very smart girl, but I don't think she understands . . . what's the word . . . I don't think she understands the significance of what's happening. Don't be surprised if she says she does not want to go with you."

"Why would she not want go with us?" Shelley shot back in a tone that suggested Trinh had just deliberately inflicted a grievous insult on her character.

"She's going to have a great house, a great room, lots of nice clothes, plenty of good food, a good school . . ."

"I believe all of that," Trinh interrupted, her smile not quite as wide now.

"I know all of that and you know all of that but . . . Ashley does not know all of that. Mercy House is the only home she's ever known. She does not know you . . ."

"Didn't you give her the pictures?"

Trinh's smile got a little bit smaller. "Yes, we gave her the pictures. The pictures of you, of your nice house, of her nice new school . . ."

"Well then, how can you say that she doesn't know us?"

I hadn't had a drop to drink, but I was having a kind of post-trans-oceanic flight hangover and my tolerance for Shelley's nattering was registering in the low range.

"Shelley, I think that Trinh is trying to tell us something important. We need to . . ."

"I'm not going to listen to somebody tell me that I am a stranger to my own daughter! If Ashley doesn't understand what's happening, the fault lies with . . ."

"WE *ARE* STRANGERS TO HER, SHELLEY! SHE DOESN'T KNOW US!" I could hear my own voice echoing off the interior of the van. Even Stone-Face seemed to cringe a little.

I stopped myself and made a conscious effort to dial it back a little. "And it's not because you're a bad mother or Trinh is a bad . . . whatever Trinh is . . . It's the nature of the deal, okay? Let's just take this thing a step at a time."

Shelley gave me a look that said I'd be sleeping in the dog house for a month after we got home. It was the kind of look that suggested she'd even go and buy a dog.

We rode the twenty more minutes to the orphanage in silence.

We drove up to a long low wooden building reminiscent of a horse stable. The most recent coat of the yellow paint so ubiquitous on Vietnamese buildings had probably gone on sometime before independence from France.

Roosters, chickens and mangy-looking dogs strolled freely about the premises. The place hardly seemed fit for housing swine, let alone children.

The curious faces of various kids started appearing in the paneless windows of Mercy House.

"Which one is Ashley?" Shelley asked anxiously.

"You will meet your daughter soon," Trinh assured, the smile all but evaporated now. "First, we have to meet with some people from the staff."

A Vietnamese woman emerged from the front door. Although she was probably not much older than Trinh, her face carried the worry-lines of someone who did not expect her hard life to get easier anytime soon.

In every organization, there's always that one employee upon whom it all eventually falls. This was clearly that person for the orphanage.

Trinh introduced the woman as "Ai," the head nanny. Trinh explained that Ai's English was, at best, rudimentary.

Ai smiled, shook hands and beckoned us to follow her inside.

Fifty little pairs of child-eyes followed us as we walked through what seemed to be a play-room.

We had been warned that this was an orphanage set aside for children with disabilities, but no amount of verbal warning could have prepared us for the sight of so many kids with obviously deformed limbs or, in too many cases, missing limbs. Cleft palates, misshapen skulls and randomly pigmented skin were also in evidence.

I usually left the anxiety attacks to Shelley, but I had to wonder if we weren't about to find out that we'd been baited-and-switched. Sure, we'd seen pictures of Ashley, but who was to say that they had not been doctored to mask the true depth of her disability.

Ai led us into what I would have described as a staff lounge in the U.S. A kitchen table that could seat about eight was in the middle.

Ai motioned for us to sit at the table. Someone produced a couple of bottles of water for us. I was already learning that the Vietnamese climate made turning down water inadvisable.

Ai smiled a sad but sincere smile and spoke to Trinh in Vietnamese. Trinh translated.

"Ai says that she is very happy that you have come here to give Cam a new home."

I cringed a little, but Shelley managed to suppress the urge to correct Trinh on the name.

"She says that she thinks you are very good people and very generous. She wishes there were more parents in the world who could find it in their hearts to make homes for orphans."

The reality of the orphanage and its unfortunate children was hitting me pretty hard. I could feel my carefully cultivated air of disconnected apathy fading away fast.

Rather than making me feel good about what we were doing, Ai's words suddenly made me feel very unworthy. I now realized what a big huge responsibility Shelley and I were taking on. This woman, whose entire life was devoted to the care of orphans, was entrusting something to us that was very precious to her.

Ai talked to Trinh for what seemed like a good two and a half minutes. Trinh nodded in understanding.

"Ai says that Cam is very lucky to have you. But . . ." Here Trinh seemed to be struggling to find just the right words.

"But Ai wants you to understand that Cam may not appreciate what you're doing. She says that Cam is going to need a lot of love and a lot of patience. She says that Cam is full of love and is going to be a wonderful daughter for you, but she may have a hard time showing that love at first."

I could sense Shelley getting impatient. She wanted Ai to hurry up with the disclaimers so that she could go see her daughter.

I patted Shelley on the knee but I don't think she got the message. Ai's prophetic words were falling on some very deaf mommy-ears.

I nodded and smiled.

"Please tell Ai that we understand . . ." (sometimes little white lies are the kindest things to say) "and that we are honored. We will do the very best we can to be a good family for . . . our daughter."

Trinh translated back to Ai and Ai smiled. She said something to Trinh.

"It's time to meet your daughter."

Shelley was visibly trembling as Ai and Trinh led us back into the play-room. The noisy din died down as we entered.

I don't know if any of those kids understood why we were there or what was about to happen, but they could clearly sense that something big was afoot.

Ai walked into an adjacent room. A moment or two later, she half-led and half-drug a little girl out of it.

The happy smiling child that we had seen in the pictures was not evident. Angry eyes bored in on us from a snarly defiant face. The girl very pointedly limped to the other side of the room and awkwardly sat herself down on a little bench.

Shelley rushed over, almost knocking five kids down along the way. She plopped down on the little bench beside the girl and threw her arms around her neck.

"Oh God, I can't believe this," Shelley sobbed.

"I'm here! You're here! I can hold you at last! My daughter!"

Daughter or not, she seemed unmoved by physical contact.

As I slowly walked toward the bench, the girl's body seemed to stiffen up even more rigidly, if that were possible.

"Hey . . . I'm your dad," I said in what I hoped was coming off as a gentle tone.

"We're going to have some good times together. Shelley . . . umh . . . could you . . ."

Shelley finally pried herself away from the embrace she'd been imposing on Ashley and left just enough room for me to move in close enough that I might be able to offer a little hug.

Trinh said something in Vietnamese. It kind of sounded like it might be: "Ashley, this is your papa! Can you give your papa a hug?"

I smiled as big a smile as I could manage and gingerly held out my arms.

"It's okay," I said. "Look, your mom just got to hug you so I think . . ."

I was just starting to bend down.

The girl shoved herself back into the bench as far as she could go, lifted up her good leg and . . .

Slammed her little foot straight into my crotch.

Kidnapped!

"Are you all ready to go, Ling? Are you ready for a big ride across the river to our new home in America? Are you scared? Are you sad to be leaving? Don't worry. I'll be with you. You don't need to be sad. As long as we're together, nobody has anything to be sad about."

I'd put Ling into that shirt with the bear that she loved so much. I wanted her to feel good about herself.

I was worried that going to America was going to be too much for Ling. I knew that I had to be strong for her. I decided that was why I hated to cry. I'd been saving up all my strong for Ling.

"When are they coming? I don't know. I'll ask Ai."

It really didn't make any difference to me when the stupid people from America came, but I knew that Ling would feel better if she knew, so I went to find Ai.

Ai was sitting by a window in her little office all alone. Ai never sat alone. Ai always had kids or other nannies all around her. She looked sad.

"Don't worry, Ai. I'll make sure that Ling writes you letters. We'll send pictures when we get across the river to America."

Ai turned her head toward me. She didn't say anything. For what felt like a long time, she just looked at me.

"Are you too big to sit on my lap?"

I hadn't sat on Ai's lap . . . or anybody's lap . . . for a very long time. It was a baby thing and I was not a baby anymore. But it seemed important to Ai, so I limped over to her and sat down on her lap.

Ai put her arms around me and squeezed tighter than tight.

"I have a favor to ask you, Cam."

I nodded. I'd do anything for Ai.

And I really liked that she called me Cam and not Ashley Stupidname.

"It may be kind of hard for you."

I nodded again. I couldn't think anything that would be too hard.

"I . . . I'm going to miss you . . . I'm going to miss you a lot. I wonder . . . I wonder if you could help me out . . . and let Ling stay here with me."

My heart almost jumped up out of my chest and out my mouth, but I think my throat caught it just in time.

Leave Ling at Mercy House?

"I'm not supposed to say this . . . but you are . . . you are one of the most special girls we've ever had here. You're very special. Ling is very special, too. I think it would help me not feel so sad about you leaving if Ling were here with me."

I didn't know what to say. When Trinh had first told me that I was going to be adopted, I thought that I would take Ling with me. But then Trinh had said that Ling would have to stay behind at Mercy House while I went to America and slapped me.

After Trinh slapped me, Ai told me the same thing (without slapping me). I couldn't take Ling.

"Why are you being so mean?

"Why won't you let me take Ling to America? I'm Ling's nanny. I'm Ling's nanny and I'm a goalie! I have to take Ling to America. And you can't stop me!"

Ai started crying and then I felt bad that I'd yelled at her. I felt bad, but that didn't stop me from saying that Ling was coming with me.

I thought that I'd won the argument. I thought that Ai had finally seen that Ling had to go to America with me and there was no other way.

Ling and I made plans. Plans about the clothes that we'd take with us. Plans about bringing enough water. Plans about how many diapers we'd need. I didn't know if they had diapers across the river in America and I wanted to be prepared.

But now Ai wasn't telling me I couldn't take Ling . . . she was asking me to leave Ling behind so that she wouldn't be sad.

"I'm sorry that you'll be so sad, Ai. But I'm Ling's nanny! I can't leave her here! It's my job! I'm Ling's nanny and I'm a goalie and I have to take her with me to America."

Ai closed her eyes and nodded.

"I understand, Cam. Believe me. I understand."

"And I need to help Ling get packed . . ."

I slowly got up off Ai's lap and started to limp out of the office.

"Cam . . . what do you think it means to be a nanny?"

I stopped, turned around and leaned up against Ai's desk.

"It means . . . taking care of somebody . . . getting them what they need . . . making sure they eat good food . . . get to bed on time . . ."

"Yes. It means all of those things. You are right. But doesn't it mean something more?"

I was starting to get really confused. That seemed like a lot. What more was a nanny supposed to do? Was there something I'd forgotten?

"Getting them up on time in the morning . . .?"

"Being a nanny means loving a child. Completely. Like I have loved you since you were a tiny little baby. A tiny little sick baby who I was afraid might die. A tiny little sick baby I sat up all night with more than once."

This was the first I'd heard that I'd been sick when I'd come to Mercy House.

"Loving a child means that you put that child ahead of everything, ahead of yourself. It means that if you had to die so that child could live, you would do it."

I knew that what Ai was saying was true, but I didn't know why she was saying it to me.

"Do you love Ling?"

"Yes! You know that I love Ling! Why are you even asking?"

"Have you thought about how hard it will be for Ling to go to America? It's a long long way."

"Ling's been over the river before. Remember when you took her to the doctor's office in Long Xuyen?"

"America is much further away than that, Cam. It will be a very long and a very hard trip, longer and harder than you can even imagine.

"You're a big girl, almost grown up. But Ling is still more like a baby. She isn't growing very fast. What if Ling got very very sick and you didn't know what to do for her?"

"I . . . I didn't know it would be that long to go to America."

"What if Ling died because you took her on such a long journey and she got sick? How would you feel then? And how sad do you think she'd be when she got to America and none of her friends were there? And she couldn't understand what people were saying to her?"

"I'd be there! I'm her nanny! I'm a nanny and a goalie!"

"I've always been here for you, Cam. But has that been enough? Would you be happy if I were the only person you could talk to?"

"No . . . but . . . she'd meet other kids and . . ."

"Cam . . . if you really love Ling like you say you do . . . you'll let her stay at Mercy House. You'll let her stay with me until she's older and maybe it would be easier for her to come to America, too."

Go away, Silly Babytears! I don't need you! I don't need to look weak!

"Are you a good nanny? Are you a good nanny who loves her children and always does what's best for them?"

You win, Silly Babytears! I'm crying! In front of Ai! Are you happy now?

"But . . . you don't know everything about Ling! You don't know . . . you don't know things like . . . how she likes her back rubbed when she's cranky and can't get to sleep! You don't know what songs she likes!

"You don't know which shirt with a bear she loves to wear! How can you be Ling's nanny? You don't know . . ."

"Why don't you tell me all of those things, Cam? Teach me how to be a good nanny to Ling. I'll listen very carefully. I'll even write it all down so you'll know I won't forget."

I was crying pretty hard by then. Silly Babytears were all over my face and dripping down onto my shirt.

"She can come to America when she's older?"

Ai took a very long time to answer.

"Do you know why you get to go to America, Cam? You get to go because you are very very strong.

"Your new mama and papa looked at your picture. They saw a very strong girl. You have to be very strong to leave your home and go to America. I don't know if Ling will be as strong as you."

"I know she will!"

"I hope she is . . . but I don't think we can say for sure until we know she's older. If Ling is ever strong enough, then we'll see about her going to America."

I loved Ling and I was a good nanny. What if Ling got sick and died because I didn't know what to do for her? What if Ling died just like . . . I'd promised I'd never let Ling die. Never never ever ever again was one of my babies going to die!

"Okay . . ." I whispered. "Come on . . . let me tell you all about Ling."

Ai took my hand and I limped back to Ling's little crib. I told Ai everything.

I showed Ai exactly how Ling liked to have her back rubbed. I made her do it so that I could see.

I taught her the special goodnight song that Ling loved to hear.

I told that her that Ling was wearing her favorite shirt, the one with the bear on it.

"I think that's everything," I whispered.

"I'll leave you alone so you can say goodbye to Ling."

I shook my head. "No . . . if I say goodbye I might cry again. And then Ling will think there's something wrong. And I don't want her to think there's something wrong.

"I want her to wake up and have you be her nanny. Like it's supposed to work that way. I don't want her to get scared. She spits up a lot when she's scared."

Ai nodded. "Okay . . ."

Ai took me in her arms again. I could feel a tear drip down off of Ai's face onto my forehead.

"You are a real nanny, Cam. You love the way that only a nanny can love."

I left Ai with Ling and limped back toward my bed.

"Hi, Cam!"

I looked around.

"Mai!"

My friend from the school had come to see me! She'd never come to Mercy House to see me before!

"Is it true? Are you leaving? Are you going to America?"

"I guess so . . . I don't really want to go . . ."

"Is one of your nannies taking you?"

"No . . . I'm going to have a mom and a dad . . . They're coming here today to pick me up."

"A mom and a dad?" Mai made a face.

"Yes. I've seen their pictures. They are pale and look sick, but Ai says that everybody in America is pale and looks sick, so I guess they're all right."

"I've got a mom. But I've never had a dad. Don't you think that's going to be weird? Having a man in the same house?"

I shrugged. I didn't know much about men, except that they were supposed to go find food every day and do what their wife ladies told them to do at home.

"Should it be weird?"

Mai leaned over and spoke to me in a whisper.

"You just be careful. I've heard . . ."

"You've heard what?"

"I've heard that a man will always try to touch a girl's bottom!"

That did sound weird. "Why would a man want to do that?"

It was Mai's turn to shrug. "I don't know . . . they just do!"

"I don't like to touch my own bottom! Why would somebody else want to touch it? Bottoms are dirty. They smell. Yuck! Touching other people's bottoms?"

"I think that's why my mom doesn't have a husband. She knows he'd just want to touch her bottom all day and then she'd never get any work done!"

That made sense. "What . . . what should I do, you think? What should I do if this pale sick American man wants to touch my bottom? He's a lot bigger and stronger. How could I stop him?"

Mai thought on that one for a while.

"You know how boys make potty water different? I've heard it hurts a lot if you kick them in their potty water maker."

I'd changed enough diapers to know about boy potty water makers. I hadn't thought much about them except that they were really ugly, sticking out like that.

"He's still bigger and stronger."

"I guess it hurts so bad that he'll never try to touch your bottom again if you kick him there."

"Wow . . ."

"So . . . I think the best thing . . . if this American tries to touch you at all . . . Just give him a kick right down there."

"But . . . with my leg . . . it's hard for me to kick."

"Always be sitting down when he's around. Then you can squish back in your chair and kick."

That made sense.

Just then, Ai walked into the room.

"Ashley . . . Cam . . . your mom and dad are here."

I gave Mai a hug, said goodbye and slowly followed Ai.

I wasn't in a big hurry to meet these strange people who were going to take me across the river to America so I could get my bottom touched.

Who did they think they were? Why were they doing this to me? Why didn't Ba Ho just kill all the Americans so that they couldn't do all of this to us anymore?

Ai stopped and turned around.

"Big smile now . . ."

She took me by the hand. I didn't move. She moved around in back of me and gave me a little shove.

I stumbled out into the playroom.

There they stood, plainer than day.

Two pale Americans.

Two pale stupid Americans who thought they were my father and my mother. That was a stupid thing for the stupid Americans to think.

I was Vietnamese. They were Americans. Americans can't be fathers and mothers for Vietnamese. Anybody knew that!

Worse yet, Trinh was right beside them! Trinh, with her "special talks" who always acted like she was my friend! Why was she letting the pale stupid Americans think they could be my mother and father?

Didn't she know what was going to happen? Didn't she know that the only reason the pale stupid American man was there was so that he could touch my bottom? Trinh was a traitor to me!

The pale stupid American man was not smiling. He was going to touch my bottom! I could see it in his eyes! I remembered what Mai had told me about making sure I was sitting down when I met him.

I limped over to a little bench under a window, plopped down and made my back good and stiff against the bench.

Here they came, the pale stupid American woman and the pale stupid American man.

The pale stupid American woman was very rude and almost knocked some of my friends down. She sat down beside me.

The pale stupid American woman had Babytears coming out of her eyes. So, she was a weak pale stupid American woman. She put her arms around my neck so hard I thought I was going to choke.

The weak pale stupid American woman made a bunch of sounds with her mouth that didn't make any sense to me. Didn't stupid Americans even know how to talk?

All I heard was gibberish, but the weak pale stupid American woman seemed to think that she was saying real words. She kept making Babytears on her face.

I tried to act like I didn't even know the weak pale stupid American woman was there, but that was hard because she was trying to choke me. I could see the pale stupid American bottom-toucher man was trying to get very close.

"[Weird American gibberish]," the pale stupid American bottom-toucher man said. "[More weird American gibberish]."

The weak pale stupid American woman let go of me. I think she'd let go of me to give the pale stupid American bottom-toucher man room to get at me.

Was this how it worked in America? Did weak pale stupid American wife-ladies actually help their pale stupid American bottom-toucher husbands to touch girls' bottoms?

Traitor Trinh to me said: "Ashley, this is your papa! Can you give your papa a hug?"

The pale stupid American bottom-toucher man finally smiled. I didn't like his smile. It didn't look like a real smile at all! It looked like a smile that a bottom-toucher man would smile to make a girl think he wasn't going to try to touch her bottom.

"[American gibberish]," the pale stupid American bottom-toucher man said. "[More American gibberish]."

The pale stupid American bottom-toucher man started to bend down toward me.

Maybe he was too big for me to stop! And maybe Traitor Trinh and the weak pale stupid American woman were going to help him do it! Maybe that was so, but I wasn't going to let it happen without a fight.

That's it. That's it, pale stupid American bottom-toucher man.

Come closer . . . closer . . . closer . . .

Hong Kong

posted by MOONGUY:
Randy Hartman gets Humanitarian Of The Century Award for taking off to Vietnam with his wife to adopt an orphan girl. But he may wind up as Unemployed Humanitarian Of The Century because of it. After last season's less-than-stellar coaching debut at Bishop Mathis, Hartman can hardly afford to be out of town during recruiting season . . . oops, I meant sit by the phone and wait for completely unsolicited calls from the top prospects in the state season. It appears that the Lancers have already lost out on Lionel Moncrief, Jr., the 6 foot 1 eighth grader out of Malcolm X Intermediate, who will be staying in his home district and Eisenhower High. Sure, Hartman landed Oliver McKee (St. Ignatius) and Eldon Tolliver (Assisi), but they are straight out of the Catholic school feeder system and have probably dreamed about playing for Bishop Mathis since they were wearing bibs at breakfast. Especially since Hartman's biggest weakness seems to be his ability to command respect, it would behoove him to start building those relationships early.

I pretty much rode in silence between Ho Chi Minh City (I think Americans are the only ones who call it that . . . most of the locals still were saying "Saigon") and Hong Kong. The members of the happy new Hartman family were in the middle three seats, me on the aisle to the left, Ashley on the aisle to the right, and Shelley in the middle. I didn't sense that Ashley had any issue with being separated from me. I wasn't all that upset about it either.

We'd tried to take a few days touristing around southern Vietnam. Trinh had ridden back to Ho Chi Minh City with us and so could help translate at first, but then she had to go help with another adoption, which left the three of us alone.

Shelley had been talking non-stop from the moment we'd walked out of the orphanage with an obviously sullen Ashley in tow. Even when Trinh was around, Shelley rarely let the one bilingual member of our group get a word in edgewise.

"Wait until you see your room!" "Wait until you see all of the nice clothes we have for you!" "Wait until you see your new school where you're going to have so much fun!" And on and on and on . . .

I wasn't in a mood to feel particularly sympathetic toward a brand-new daughter whose first interaction with her brand-new father was to kick him in the crotch, but I couldn't help wondering how Ashley was processing her motor-mouth mother. I think I'd get pretty sick of somebody jabbering away non-stop at me for days on end in a language I didn't understand.

Shelley did keep throwing in some of the smattering of Vietnamese she'd been trying to learn.

"Oh, look!" she'd bubble if we'd pass a street vendor selling ice cream. "Would anybody like some kem?"

"What a cute con meow!"

"Ashley, have you ever gotten to ride a con neigh?"

The one area where Shelley's Vietnamese scholarship seemed to be having some impact was in mathematics.

"Mot!" she'd say, holding up her index finger. "One!"

Then she'd hold up her index and middle fingers. "Hai! Two!"

Then the index, middle and ring fingers. "Ba! Three!"

It took a couple of days, but the counting thing finally seemed to engage Ashley. She watched intently as Shelley would run through the one-two-three sequence over and over. She started to mimic the fingers.

Then, hesitantly, Ashley started saying ". . . one . . . two . . . three . . ." as she raised her own fingers. The words were slurred, but close enough. It wasn't much English, but it was a start, I guess.

I'd been following the Hartman-Must-Go campaign via Internet cafes. I felt helpless. I knew what I needed to be doing, but couldn't get to it until we were back home.

I spent most of the flight to Hong Kong working up a good old fashioned deep depression, paying little or no attention to Shelley's persistent efforts to build a bridge to our daughter.

We would be five hours in Hong Kong. Once again, enough time to start feeling really sorry for yourself sitting around an airport, but not enough time to sack out and get any real rest.

The first stop, after restrooms, was lunch. We found a table in a food court.

"What would you like to eat, Ashley?" Shelley asked, making an eating motion with her hands.

Ashley stared back blankly.

"Eat?" Shelley asked again, repeating the hand motions.

"Maybe I should try some Vietnamese?"

I shrugged. If Ashley was hungry for a horse with ice cream on top, we'd be set to go.

Shelley pulled out her Vietnamese dictionary.

"An?" she asked. "Ashley, what would you like to an?"

Ashley was unimpressed. We were getting nowhere and I was getting hungry.

A girl walked by with a bowl of rice on her tray. I pointed to the rice and raised my eyebrows in an expression that suggested I was asking a question.

Ashley looked at the rice and then looked at Shelley and nodded. It was like she wasn't ready to acknowledge the possibility that I might do something right.

A few minutes later, Ashley was shoveling chopsticks full of rice into her mouth and not taking any pains to chew quietly.

I waved my hand to get Ashley's attention and clamped on my lips with thumb and forefinger, indicating (or so I hoped) that

Ashley should keep her mouth closed while eating. I then tried to demonstrate, taking a bite out of the odd Chinese interpretation of a hamburger I had ordered and chewing thoroughly but silently.

Ashley's response was to try to shove in an amount of rice equal to twice the capacity of her mouth, allow the excess to fall all over her side of table and chew the rest in stereo.

"It'll take time," Shelley said. "We have to respect Vietnamese culture. I think that's just how they eat."

"If she's going to live in our culture, then she's going to have to learn that Americans aren't particularly fond of listening to other people chew."

"I know, but . . ."

Ashley contributed a long, slurpy, noisy swig from the bottle of water we'd bought her.

I started to say something, but Shelley interrupted (wisely, for once). "Let's play one-two-three."

Ashley put down the bottle and gave Shelley the closest thing to a smile we'd seen yet from her (so, admittedly, nothing to get too excited about).

"One . . . two . . . three!" Shelley gushed, making the appropriate motions.

"One . . . two . . . three!" Ashley responded.

Shelley pointed to herself. "One!"

She pointed to me. "Two!"

She pointed at Ashley. "Three!"

Ashley's face crumpled up into a frown and she shook her head vigorously.

She pointed to herself. "One!"

She pointed to Shelley. "Two!"

She pointed to me. "Three!"

And then, for the first time in our presence, Ashley started to laugh. And she laughed. And she laughed. And she laughed.

She ran the cycle again. "One! Two! Three!"

She punctuated the Three with an emphatic point of the finger at me. She laughed harder.

"One! Two! Three! . . . One! Two! Three! . . . One! Two! Three!"

Tears were running down her face from raucous laughter. Then she stopped counting altogether, but kept saying "Three! Three! Three!" emphasizing each repetition with a jab of the index finger in my direction.

People were turning to watch.

"Three! Three! Three!"

I smiled weakly.

"Three! Three! Three!"

Clearly, I was the butt of some joke or other known only to Ashley.

"Three! Three! Three!"

"Okay," I said, trying to get some control of the situation. "Three . . . I'm Three. I get it . . . sort of . . . now . . . can we just . . ."

"Three! Three! Three!"

"Ashley!"

"Randy! This is the most positive interaction you've had with Ashley! Don't discourage her!"

"Three! Three! Three!"

Call me immature. Call me competitive. Call me badly jet-lagged and job-stressed. Whatever the reason . . . I was not going to let a little girl get the better of me.

"No!" I growled. I pointed to myself.

"No Three! YOU Three!"

Ashley got a look as if she'd just been punched.

I pointed to myself. "One!"

I pointed to Shelley. "Two!"

I pointed to Ashley. "Three!"

Ashley shook her head and pointed to me. "Three!"

"Three!" I insisted, extending my arm across the table to point directly into her face.

"THREE!" Ashley all but screamed, jumping to her feet and matching my aggressive pointing with a little finger-waving of her own.

"Randy! You're frightening her!"

"THREE!" I barked back with abandon, the tip of my finger now almost touching her nose.

"THREE!" Ashley roared.

This time my finger pushed into her nose. "THREE!"

I had no idea that any human being could move anywhere near that quickly. What was left of the bowl of rice had been shoved in my face before I knew what was happening.

"THREE!" Ashley yelled with an undeniable tone of triumph.

Traitor Trinh told me that it had been wrong to kick my new father in his boy potty water maker. I said that I did not want him touching my bottom.

Traitor Trinh told me that he was not going to touch my bottom and that I needed to get that idea completely out of my head.

That was easy for Traitor Trinh to say that because it wasn't her bottom we were talking about.

I wanted to cry when we drove away from Mercy House, but I wasn't going to let the Americans see me look weak, so I told the Stupid Babytears to stay inside my eyes.

Traitor Trinh was with us and tried to tell me what she thought the weak pale stupid American woman was trying to say whenever gibberish came out of her mouth.

We rode along in a bumpy van for many hours. Ai had been right. America wasn't just over the river. We were going to have to ride longer than I thought!

I missed Ling a lot but decided that, between the long ride to America and having to be with a pale stupid American bottom-toucher man, I was glad she hadn't come along.

We got to a city. It was a really really big city. I hadn't hardly ever left Mercy House and I hadn't seen anything like this really really big city.

America was a big place, I had to admit that. But, as our van moved through the streets of America, I was surprised to see that America seemed to be a lot more like Vietnam than I had thought.

Most of the people had pretty skin like mine, not ugly pale skin. I could hear them talking through the windows of the van and they were all using real words, not gibberish.

I didn't want to talk to Traitor Trinh because she was a traitor but I wanted to know about America, now that we were there.

Traitor Trinh laughed, though, when I said that America seemed to be just like Vietnam.

"You're not in America yet. You are still in Vietnam. This is Saigon, where you and your papa and mama will be staying for a few days. Then you'll go to America. You will get on a big airplane and fly for a long time before you're in America."

Traitor Trinh told me that she couldn't stay with us and had to go help another happy family come together. I didn't say anything, but I thought Traitor Trinh hadn't done a very good job of making a happy family here. Still, I missed her after she left. And then I felt really all alone.

The pale stupid American woman kept making nonsense sounds with her mouth. And she kept making them and making them and making them.

"[American gibberish, American gibberish, American gibberish, American gibberish]!" It never stopped!

The pale stupid American maybe a bottom-toucher man didn't try to make many sounds with his mouth. It seemed like he wasn't happy that the pale stupid American woman was making so many sounds with her mouth.

I wondered if he was even stupider than the pale stupid American woman and couldn't make many sounds of his own.

Every so often, the pale stupid American woman would make sounds like: "[American gibberish, American gibberish], Ashley, [American gibberish], Ashley."

I was trying to ignore her, but I knew that she was calling me by Ashley Stupidname. It was hard not to look mad whenever she did that. So, I think she knew I wasn't happy about Ashley Stupidname. Or maybe she didn't know.

Every so often, the pale stupid American woman would make a sound that was actually a word.

At first, I thought she was saying words by accident. If you keep making sounds with your mouth long enough, you are probably going to say a word once in a while even if that's not what you meant.

But then, one day, we were passing a man selling ice cream. "[American gibberish]," she said. "[American gibberish] ice cream?"

She started making some of the right words about animals.

We'd see a cat. "[American gibberish] cat!"

Once, we saw a picture of a horse. "Ashley, [American gibberish] horse?"

I decided that maybe the pale stupid American woman was starting to learn how to talk. When she would make words, they'd sound strange but I could tell that they were real words.

I was really surprised when the pale stupid American woman started using numbers!

"One!" she said, and held up one finger! But then a gibberish sound.

"Two!" she said and held up two fingers! And then a gibberish sound again.

"Three!" she said and held up three fingers! And then a gibberish sound.

I started figuring out that she was making the same gibberish sounds over and over again. Did Americans really have some words of their own?

It made me kind of sad whenever the pale stupid American woman started doing "One! Two! Three!" because I thought about playing "One! Two! Three!" with Ling.

I didn't want to be sad, so I decided to really learn what the stupid Americans thought the right words were for counting.

The pale stupid American woman would say the American "One!" and I'd try to say it back to her. This made her very very happy.

She'd say the American "Two!" and I'd repeat back.

And then "Three!" and then we'd start all over again.

When we got on the big airplane, I was confused. Riding in the van, I could see the driver and I knew he could see where he was going. What if he got lost and I had to make potty but there wasn't any place for me to make it because we were lost?

The pale stupid American woman sat next to me. The pale stupid American maybe a bottom toucher man was on the other side. I liked it that way.

The pale stupid American maybe a bottom toucher man hadn't tried to touch my bottom, so maybe Traitor Trinh was right. But still, I felt better if he wasn't right next to me.

Traitor Trinh had said that we wouldn't go to America at first. The big airplane had to stop someplace and then we'd have to get on another big airplane and then we'd be in America. That seemed like it was going to take a long time.

I wondered if I would grow up and have a baby before we got to America.

The pale stupid American woman kept doing "One! Two! Three!" with me while the airplane was driving. I was getting tired of it, but it made me not worry about getting lost and not having a place to make potty. So, I let her keep doing it.

The big airplane stopped and everybody started to get off. I was glad that we had stopped. I had wanted to make potty for a long time and I hoped that there would be a place to make potty where we'd stopped.

"I have to make potty." I guess the pale stupid American woman understood me because the first place we went after we got off the big airplane was a place to make potty. It was the nicest cleanest place to make potty I had ever seen.

And then I was hungry. "I am hungry," I said. I guess she understood me again because we went to a place with a lot of tables and a lot of places where people were selling things to eat.

"[American gibberish], Ashley?" the stupid pale American woman said. Then she did something with her hands. I did not know what the hand thing meant.

"[American gibberish]," she said again. She said something to the pale stupid American probably not a bottom toucher man. He said something back in American gibberish.

She reached into her purse and took out a little book. She looked through the book.

"Eab?" she asked. "Ashley, [American gibberish] eab?" She was saying "eab" like it was supposed to mean something to me.

I was getting tired of this. I wanted to eat. Why was the pale stupid American woman talking gibberish instead of getting us some food?

A girl walked by carrying a bowl of rice on a tray. It smelled good. The pale stupid American probably not a bottom toucher man looked at me and pointed to the rice.

Finally! I looked at the pale stupid American woman and nodded. Yes! That's it! Can I please have some rice?

The pale stupid American man who was probably not a bottom toucher went off and came back with some food. He gave me a bowl of rice.

That was really weird. In Vietnam, it would have been the woman who went to get food. But, I was too hungry to care that the pale stupid American woman did not know her job.

I picked up a spoon and started putting rice in my mouth. It tasted so good! I wanted more and more and more.

The pale stupid American okay not a bottom toucher man waved his hand at me. He took hold of his lips with his fingers. I had no idea what he meant by that.

Then he put some of the bread thing he was eating in his mouth. He didn't chew like he was happy with his food. He kept his mouth shut the whole time.

I felt kind of bad because it meant that his food must not taste good. I wanted him to know I thought my rice was good, so I put as much as I could in my mouth and chewed a happy chew.

"[American gibberish]," the pale stupid American woman said to the pale stupid American man. "[American gibberish]."

"[American gibberish]," the pale stupid American man said. He must really have not liked his food because it sounded like he was getting mad.

"[American gibberish]," the pale stupid American woman said.

I was getting thirsty, so I picked up the bottle of water and took a nice long slurp.

The pale stupid American man looked at me like it was my fault his food didn't taste good. That made me kind of mad. Why would he blame me for bad food that he went and got on his own?

The pale stupid America woman said "[American gibberish and then the American sounds for one, two, three]."

"One! Two! Three!" I suddenly thought again of Ling and all the fun we'd had playing that game.

I was a little sad. But then I looked over at the pale stupid American man. I got an idea.

The pale stupid American woman used the American sounds for "One! Two! Three!" using her fingers.

I wanted to make sure that I was making the sounds right, so said back "One! Two! Three!" in American gibberish.

Then the pale stupid American woman did something that was really stupid.

She pointed to herself and said, "One!"

She pointed to the pale stupid American man and said "Two!" and then pointed at me and said "Three!"

What? I am NOT "Three!" I am not "Three!" anywhere. I'm not some stupid mosquito that you can just shush away.

If anybody at that table should be "Three!" it would be the pale stupid American man who blamed me because his bread thing made him think he was eating potty.

I pointed to myself. "One!"

I pointed to the pale stupid American woman. "Two!"

I pointed at the pale stupid American man. "Three!"

Now, THAT made me happy! I had just shushed him away! I started to laugh. I hadn't laughed since before I'd had to leave Mercy House, so I guess I had a lot of laugh stored up.

I went "One! Two! Three!" again pointing at me, the pale stupid American woman and then the pale stupid American man.

I did it over and over again.

"One! Two! Three!"

"One! Two! Three!"

"One! Two! Three!"

I thought that calling the pale stupid American man "Three!" was the funniest thing ever! I stopped counting. I just kept pointing at him and saying "Three! Three! Three!"

"[American gibberish]," the pale stupid American man said. "Three . . . [American gibberish] . . . Three. [American gibberish]."

"Three! Three! Three!"

"[American gibberish]," the pale stupid American man said.

"[American gibberish]!" the pale stupid American woman said.

"[American gibberish] Ashley Stupidname! [American gibberish]!"

"Three! Three! Three!"

I guess they play "One! Two! Three!" in America!

He seemed to get that I was calling him a mosquito who should be shushed away.

"[American gibberish]," he said in a not nice way and pointed to me. "No Three! YOU Three!"

The pale stupid American man pointed to himself. "One!"

He pointed to the pale stupid American woman. "Two!"

He pointed to me. "Three!"

I shook my head. I wasn't going to let him win! "Three!"

"Three!" the pale stupid American man said. He reached over the table and put his finger right in my face!

"THREE!" I yelled.

I jumped up as fast as a Limper Girl could and pointed back at him!

"[American gibberish]!" the pale stupid American woman yelled.

"THREE!" His finger was almost on my nose.

"THREE!" I yelled back and kept pointing at him.

He put his finger on my nose really hard and shouted "THREE!"

He was NOT going to win this game! I had to do something to get him to understand that!

I looked down at the bowl. There was still some rice left . . . but I decided I wasn't really hungry any more.

"THREE!" I yelled as I picked up the bowl . . .

Home Is Where The Hartman Is

*" . . . (click) . . . Hello, Mr. and Mrs. Hartman. This is Evelyn
. . . Just checking in to see how Ashley is adjusting . . . and to
remind you that we need to schedule a post-adopt meeting.
Please call me back when it's convenient . . . oh and, Mr.
Hartman . . . I did some research . . . 'moonguyen' is not the
Vietnamese word for basketball . . . I think it's . . . umh . . . 'bong
ro' . . . I think . . . As a matter of fact, I don't think 'moonguyen'
is a Vietnamese word at all . . . perhaps you confused
Vietnamese with Korean or something . . . have a good day . . ."*

"Oh . . . oh . . . watch this! Watch this!"

Deonte MacBride, 14 years old and already six foot two,
drove past mid-court, took off in flight from the free throw line,
raised the basketball high in the air and slammed it home.

"What'd I tell you? What'd I tell you? That's Dr. J stuff!"

Thomas MacBride, 35 years old and already hanging more
weight on his six foot one frame than it was probably designed to
handle, shook with excitement.

As far as Thomas was concerned, Deonte was ready for the
NBA, and playing prep basketball was a formality imposed on
his son by a set of wrong-headed legalities.

I should be grateful that Deonte was going to deign to hand
me four state championships while he waited around for the big
paychecks to roll in.

And, truth be told, Deonte had a grace and fluidity of motion
unusual for a boy his age and not common for athletes in
general.

He also, small surprise, had a head the size of Madison
Square Garden.

I didn't know Deonte's middle name, but Swagger would have been a good guess.

"Not many of my guys can dunk quite like that," I admitted.

"None of your guys can dunk like that!"

I didn't like Deonte. I didn't like Thomas.

But, I needed Deonte to be a Lancer. And so I was prepared to be as gracious as possible. No request too outrageous . . .

"How about you and Deonte do a little one-on-one?"

"I . . . I don't usually . . ."

I was in pretty darned good shape, but ten pounds separated me from my collegiate playing weight. I was okay horsing around with the guys after practice, but I didn't relish the prospect of getting shown up by a recruit.

"Before I commit my son and all of his talent to your program, I got to know you have something to teach him."

No. Absolutely not. I'm sorry Mr. MacBride, but I am a stickler for discipline and boundaries and I just can't accommodate your request. That's final. The fact that your son could single-handedly turn this team around is irrelevant. I am a man of principle, first and foremost!

"Well . . . sure . . ."

I peeled off my sweatpants. "I'll be happy to work a little with Deonte right now."

Thomas laughed an I-don't-believe-this kind of laugh.

"I think maybe it's a little more like Deonte's happy to work a little with you."

"Hey, Deonte! Your dad wants to see me try to guard you!"

Deonte snorted an audible snort, accompanied by lip-curled sneer. Deonte wanted the world to think that he was ghetto, a hard-edged product of some big city's meanest streets.

In fact, Thomas was a successful trial lawyer whose well-rehearsed street drawl was just part of the act, and his wife, Oleta, ran her own temp agency.

The MacBrides lived in a 3500 square foot lakefront house nestled in a gated community. Few European crown princes had led a more privileged life.

"Take the ball to midcourt. Dribble past me for a layup."

"Layup? Layups is for lame white boys."

"Deonte!" Thomas exhorted. "Go easy on Coach Hartman. He's an old dude!"

I smiled bravely. "Don't hold back, Deonte. Just show me what you got."

Deonte gave me that maddening sneer again and went to mid-court.

"Get a good look at me, Coach, 'cause ain't gonna be nothing but blur."

Deonte's face scrunched up into a 14 year-old's idea of what a determined athlete should look like and he started driving toward me.

I put myself into a defensive stance, but might as well have stood on my head for all the good it did.

Deonte blew past me almost unopposed. Making the layup was an afterthought.

"Deonte! I thought I told you to go easy on Coach Grandpa!"

"I did go easy on him."

Just keep smiling, Hartman, just keep smiling. Don't blow this one . . .

Deonte came at me again. The hip fake was nicely done. By the time I turned around to look, Deonte was already airborne en route to a highlight-reel dunk.

"Okay, Deonte. That's all I needed to . . ."

"Deonte! Show him you can play D."

Deonte flipped me the ball.

"No. Really. We don't need to . . ."

"Come on, Coach. Show us what you got."

Come on, Hartman. It's not about you or your athletic pride. It's about getting the best players you can . . .

I bounced the ball and tried to plot out a strategy. I was still taller than Deonte, so . . .

I dribbled aggressively to Deonte's right. I thought I was just about to get around him when . . .

The sharp jabbing pain in my ribcage made clear exactly what kind of defense Deonte liked to play.

The dirty kind.

I stumbled slightly. After pulling his elbow back from the side of my body, Deonte grabbed the ball, drove the length of the court the other direction and launched himself at about the free-throw line. He made one three-sixty in mid-air and slammed the ball through the hoop.

"He schooled you, Coach! My boy just schooled you!"

I could tell that Deonte's jab was going to leave a bruise.

"Hey, Deonte! Need to understand that the refs aren't going to let you get away with that stuff at this level."

"What stuff you talkin' about? The boy took it away from you clean!"

I bit down on my tongue. "Okay . . . let's try it again."

Deonte brought the ball back down and flipped it to me.

Dribble, dribble, dribble . . . turn . . . fake . . . drive . . .

I hit the court face-first.

"Hey, Coach! Got to remember to tie them laces good and tight!"

"Tripping is a flagrant foul, Deonte. Can even get you tossed from a game if it's that blatant."

"I didn't trip you."

"Yes . . . you did . . ."

"No, I didn't. You just tripped your own self."

Stay calm, Hartman. Stay very very calm . . .

I grabbed the ball.

"Third time's gonna be a charm."

Deonte shrugged.

Dribble, dribble, dribble . . . turn . . . fake . . . turn back again . . .

Stay cool, Hartman. Stay cool . . .

Dribble, dribble, dribble . . . hip fake . . . and . . .

"You got nothing to teach him, Hartman. Nothing at all."

And so, just like that, I'd lost a potential five star recruit for the simple reason that I was a little rusty on my one-on-one game.

I pulled into the driveway, got out of the car and took a moment to look at my nice two-story Tudor style home. "Enjoy it while you've got it," I muttered to myself.

Buying a big house without knowing how things would work out at Bishop Mathis had been stupid.

Adopting an orphan girl from halfway around the world without knowing how things would work out at Bishop Mathis had been stupid.

Thinking that things could ever really work out at Bishop Mathis had maybe been the stupidest idea of all.

I was in over my head and I should have saved all of us a lot of pain and turned the job down.

I glanced at the hoop and backboard hanging off the front of the garage. I knew where I'd be spending the rest of the afternoon.

Baby Talk

The house of the pale stupid Americans was nice. Everything was clean. There were no mosquitoes. There was always food.

It was a nice house, but it was not my home. I didn't care how nice a house it was. It was not my home.

When we finally got to the house after another really long airplane drive (it was really long, but not long enough that I had a baby), the pale stupid American woman made some of her gibberish sounds and then pointed for me to go up some stairs.

Excuse me, pale stupid American woman, but I am a Limper Girl! It's really really really hard for me to go up stairs! Don't make me go up stairs!

But, then, I decided that I didn't want to look weak, like I was a Limper Girl who was afraid of stairs! I was not afraid of stairs! I was a nanny and a goalie, so I could go up stairs even though it was really really hard.

I got to the top of the stairs by holding on to this wooden thing they had going all the way up the side of the stairs. That wooden thing was the first good idea I'd seen stupid Americans ever have.

But, even with the wooden thing, I was very tired when I got to the top of the stairs. I decided that I was not going to go back down the stairs again unless there was a very good reason.

The pale stupid American woman pointed toward a room. I limped into the room and, all of a sudden, there was a big smile all over my Limper Girl face.

This was a room for a baby! It had a crib and a nice table for taking care of a baby after it made potty and pictures of animals and things. It was the nicest baby room I had ever seen.

I could hardly believe it! They were going to go back for Ling! Hooray for the pale stupid Americans! (Did I really just think that?)

I looked up at the pale stupid American woman.

"Ling?"

The pale stupid American woman smiled at me, but didn't look like she understood what I was saying.

I was happy that they were going to get Ling, but you'd think they would have learned her name first. It didn't matter, though. Ling and I would soon be back together again and that's all I cared about.

"Ling!"

Maybe if I said it louder, the pale stupid American woman would remember. She still looked like she didn't know what I was saying. I reached into the crib and picked up a baby doll.

"Ling!"

Just then, the pale stupid American man came into the room. He had some tools with him. He went to the crib and started taking the sides off!

What?

Why are you doing that, pale stupid American man?

Don't you know that Ling will fall off onto the floor and go owie and start crying really loud if you take those sides off? How could you be so stupid?

I was so shocked that I didn't even say anything!

What if this baby doll was Ling? I'd have to hold onto Ling and protect her and not let her get up into that dangerous crib without me!

I held onto the baby doll really really tight. The pale stupid Americans left the room.

I closed my eyes. I was afraid that if I opened them, I'd make Babytears and then I'd be weak.

I thought really really hard and tried to make my brain stop being mad. I was a nanny and a goalie and I had to think about nanny and goalie things, not mad Limper Girl things.

Take care of Ling. That's what I needed to think about.

I opened my eyes.

Take care of Ling. That's your job, nanny and goalie and not Limper Girl.

I looked down at Ling. I thought she was probably pretty tired. I was tired, too, but I couldn't let Ling see that. She had to know that I was going to watch after her.

I crawled up onto the crib that was dangerous because of the pale stupid American man and his stupid American tools. I told Ling to close her eyes. When I knew that she was asleep, I closed my eyes and went to sleep, too.

I don't know how long Ling and I slept, but it felt like a really long time.

I was hungry when I got up and I knew that Ling had to be hungry, too.

I didn't want to go down the stairs. So, I yelled for the pale stupid American woman. If she thought she could be a mother, then let her be a mother! She could get me food, like a real mother would do for me!

I wanted to see if she was going to be lazy and make her husband get the food like she'd done back at that place where I'd had to put that rice bowl in his face.

I heard her yell something back at me in American gibberish. She was downstairs. I am NOT going downstairs, pale stupid American woman! It's too hard for me! I would bring food upstairs and I'm only a nanny! What's the matter with you?

Finally even the pale stupid American woman understood. She brought up a plate with some very weird food I'd never seen before. It looked a lot like the bread thing that I'd seen the pale stupid American man eating.

I was pretty hungry, so I ate it. But it tasted terrible!

It was like I was eating a dead water buffalo between two pieces of bread. I hoped that stupid Americans knew enough to eat rice once in a while.

Those first few days were very hard on me and on Ling. The pale stupid American woman did not understand that it was not easy for me to go down the stairs. I think she tried to be nice, or at least as nice as she could be, at first, but then she started yelling more and more.

I was hearing the same American gibberish sounds over and over again. I guess that stupid Americans do know how to talk a little bit, but have made up their own words, which seems stupid when they could just use all of our good Vietnamese words instead. I didn't know what they meant, but I thought I was starting to recognize sounds like "stubborn" and "brat."

The pale stupid American man was not there a lot. I didn't know where he went. I thought that maybe he went out to the fields where Americans grew bread things that tasted like water buffalo and picked them.

I had not seen the fields, so I did not know for sure. I never saw him carrying any baskets full of bread things that tasted like water buffalo, but there seemed to be a lot of them.

I was confused, but didn't care enough to go looking for the fields, especially since I was a Limper Girl.

From the window in Ling's room, I could see where the pale stupid American man would put his car.

Sometimes, late in the afternoon, he would come back from the bread thing fields and not come into the house. Instead, he would go into another little house (where I wished I could stay so that I didn't have to worry about the stairs) and come out with a soccer ball.

I knew that it had to be an American soccer ball because it was a stupid brown color instead of the pretty white and black soccer balls we used in Vietnam.

It was a good thing that he was using a stupid kind of soccer ball because he played a stupid kind of soccer.

Didn't he know that nobody in soccer could touch the ball with their hands except the goalie? And I was one to know because I was a goalie!

I wished I knew some words in American so that I could tell him he was playing Stupid American Soccer and not Smart Vietnamese Soccer.

The pale stupid American man would bounce and bounce his soccer ball and then he'd throw it up in the air.

Most of the time it went through this orange circle thingee that was on the side of the little house where he kept his soccer ball. Sometimes it didn't. He never seemed happy when it didn't.

I couldn't see what a goalie would do in Stupid American Soccer unless she was supposed to sit up on the orange circle thingee.

I'd been in the new house that was nice but not my home for a little while when I decided that I needed to call the pale stupid American woman and the pale stupid American man something else. They deserved to be called "pale stupid Americans," but those were a lot of words and it made my brain sleepy to use them all the time.

I thought and thought about what to call them. I asked Ling. Ling said that the woman was like a stupid hen, pecking around all the time and making fusses about nothing. Ling said I should call her Peep-Peep.

What about the man? He was so big, Ling said, like a pig. Ling said I should call him Oink-Oink.

Peep-Peep and Oink-Oink It was easier than pale stupid American woman and pale stupid American man.

I thought about Mercy House and all of my friends there a lot. I thought about Ai and all of the other nannies.

I thought about Mai and how it was too bad that we hadn't gotten to know each other better before I had to go to Stupid America.

Thinking about Vietnam made me sad. It made me feel like I was going to be weak and cry Babytears. But I couldn't be weak and cry Babytears in front of Ling.

I knew that Ling was sad, too, because she started sucking her thumb again. Sucking her thumb wasn't good for Ling. But Ling was probably still pretty scared from the long trip over and the strange new house that was nice but not our home. I decided not to say anything.

Maybe I should be sucking my thumb, too, so that Ling doesn't feel bad and think that I think she's a baby or something. I looked down at Ling sucking her thumb and she looked up at me sucking mine. We laughed a little.

I think Ling knew that she was doing a baby thing and that I was doing it too just so that she wouldn't feel like I thought she was a silly little baby.

I think she knew that I would stop sucking my thumb as soon as she didn't need to anymore.

I couldn't leave Ling, not for a tiny little second. I couldn't leave Ling even long enough to go and make potty. So, I just started making potty in my pants. That made Peep-Peep mad. She was mad because she was too lazy to do her mother job.

I'll bet that even my mother without a name in Vietnam took care of my potty pants. I was not a mother but I was taking care of Ling's potty pants, so I didn't see where it was such a big problem for Peep-Peep to take care of mine.

Instead of cleaning me up like a real mother, Peep-Peep would just come into Ling's room and do a lot of yelling when she could smell that I had potty pants.

She would take some new clothes out of a drawer and throw them down on top of me. Then she'd leave the room, but wouldn't stop yelling for a while.

Well, even though it was Peep-Peep's job to clean my potty pants if she thought she could be a real mother, nobody wants to sit around all day in potty pants.

So, I'd get up and carry Ling into one of the special potty rooms where there was water. I'd clean myself up and put on the new clothes.

"See, Ling? I'm a good nanny. I clean your potty pants. But Peep-Peep, who thinks she's a mother, won't clean mine. And she's too stupid to see that she won't ever be a real mother until she cleans potty pants!"

Trouble Ahead . . . Trouble Behind . . .

As far as the whole parenting deal went, I'd been lying pretty low. To the extent Ashley and I had had any contact at all, it was to make a big show out of ignoring each other.

When I got home after the Deonte MacBride catastrophe, I was still in my gym clothes. I didn't even bother going in the house. I went to the garage, grabbed my ball, went back out and starting shooting buckets.

Pretty soon, I wasn't just shooting buckets any more.

I was driving hard to the basket, flying up over the rim as much as my aging limbs would allow and dunking the ball.

Each dunk had a name.

"THAT's for Deonte MacBride!" I growled as I slammed one home.

"THAT'S for Thomas MacBride!"

"THAT's for Moonguy!"

"THAT's for Evelyn!"

"THAT's for my daddy-hating daughter!"

"THAT's for . . ."

"Randy!"

I guess I'll never know who the last one would have been for because Shelley's shrill call messed up my timing.

I slammed the ball off the front of the rim. The hoop groaned like it was about to collapse.

I landed weirdly on my left foot and felt some ligament or another howl in protest.

I came up limping. A minor ankle injury would complement my bruised ribs nicely.

"I need you! Inside!"

Shelley threw down two pairs of potty-soiled little girl pants down on the kitchen table.

"THIS is what I have to put up with all day long while you're out playing basketball!"

After fifteen minutes of listening to Shelley blubber on about how unsupportive I was being and how I needed to get more involved as a father, I found myself gingerly making my way up the stairs to Ashley's room.

The ankle was feeling a little bit worse with every stair step. I made it to the landing and hobbled into the room.

Things still looked pretty much as they had when Shelley had decorated for the first Ashley. All pink and girly. More stuffed animals and dolls than ten girls could have cuddled in their entire lifetimes.

A-S-H-L-E-Y was still spelled out by a series of ceramic wall hangings adorned with pictures of bunnies romping in fields of clover and foxes playing harps made out of cobwebs.

The only difference was that I had taken off the sides of the crib to make a bed . . . sort of.

The crib/bed. That's where Ashley was sitting. And that was pretty much where Ashley had been sitting since we'd gotten home.

One of Shelley's many baby dolls was being clutched very tightly in Ashley's arms. Her right thumb was stuck in her mouth and her head was turned so that she could stare out the window.

"Do something!" Shelley commanded.

"Like what?"

"Say something!"

The absurdity of the thought that me saying something was going to somehow fix Ashley was so enormous that I couldn't even argue with it.

I looked at Ashley.

From the window, I could see the hoop and backboard. Even with my ankle really starting to really hurt, I wanted more than anything to be back out there slam-dunking all my frustrations away.

"All right. I'll say something . . ."

I pulled up a little Humpty Dumpty stool.

"Okay, Ashley. Looks like we've got a situation. You don't want to be here. Truth be told, I don't think I want you to be here either."

"Randy!"

"You've got a nice house. A nice room. Food. Clothes. Toys. Seems like a setup an orphan girl would kill for. But not Ashley."

"Randy! Stop!"

"Now, if I look at this objectively . . . hard to do, I'll admit, but give me credit for trying . . . If I look at this objectively, maybe I can understand why Ashley would rather sit on her rump with her thumb in her mouth crapping her pants than show the slightest bit of appreciation."

"Randy! I said to stop!" Shelley pounded on my back with her fist.

"Strange place. Strange people. Strange everything. So, I get it kind of. But here's the thing. What I don't get. You could meet us halfway on this. Not even halfway. A quarter of the way. An eighth of the way. Some tiny little step our direction. Not happening, though, is it? So, I gotta wonder if you are ever going to be happy here. I'm kind of doubting it."

I could hear Shelley burst out into tears, whisper a statement questioning my parentage and then storm out of the room.

"Your Mom's not happy. I'm not happy. You're not happy. Do you have the slightest interest in trying to fix that?"

Ashley slowly turned her head toward me, as if she'd only just realized that I was standing there.

She stared back at me with an expression that seemed to shout out: "I could not possibly care less about anything that would ever happen in this world than whatever it is you are saying to me right now."

"I'm sorry. This is my fault. No. Seriously. I mean it. I was the one who should have known better and said, 'This going to Vietnam to adopt is a bad idea and it is not going to end well.' Instead, I followed the path of least resistance. And here we are."

Right at that moment, I committed a significant error in trying to stand. Pain shot up my leg, briefly stopped to look in on the bruised ribs, then flew around my shoulder and back down again.

I cursed loudly and rubbed at the ankle.

And that little . . . so-and-so . . . actually smiled.

"Sure, go ahead . . . laugh at my pain. Glad I could brighten your day."

Ashley cocked her head to one side like a curious dog trying to decipher her master's commands. She looked back out the window and then back at me.

"Goalie."

"Goldie? Who's Goldie?"

"Goalie."

"Yeah, okay. Goldie. Whatever."

Ashley pointed insistently toward the window. "Goalie!"

"Goldie. The doll? What does the window have to do with the doll?"

I painfully pulled myself up to my feet and limped toward Ashley.

"Here, I'll be happy to take little Goldie and throw her out the window if that's what you want. The mood I'm in, I'll be happy to tie her to my back bumper and drag her to school tomorrow."

I made a motion to reach for the doll. Ashley scowled and clutched it even more tightly.

"Sing!" she shouted.

"Sing?"

"Sing!"

"Sing to Goldie?"

Ashley pointed out the window. "Goalie!"

"No, Goldie's in here, not out there."

Ashley looked up at me and defiantly shoved her thumb back in her mouth.

"You stay here with Goldie or whoever the doll is and suck your thumb. Stay here and starve to death for all I care!"

Ashley took her thumb back out of her mouth. She pointed to herself.

"One!" She pointed to the doll.

"Two!" She pointed to me.

"Three!"

I was being dismissed. Fine with me.

I turned, steadied myself against the wall and limped toward the door.

"Sing!"

I made it out into the hallway. The ankle throbbed violently. I started down toward the master bedroom.

"Sing!"

Then I heard something that could have been sobbing.

But, I had other things to worry about right then. Like my job. My marriage. My financial situation. An ankle that seemed to be getting in the mood for x-rays.

Ashley could sob. Ashley could sulk. Ashley could suck all of the skin off her thumb.

She wasn't my problem.

One day, I had made potty pants two times already. I don't think I had ever seen Peep-Peep so mad before! Oink-Oink came home from the bread thing that tastes like water buffalo fields and started playing Stupid American Soccer.

Peep-Peep went out and yelled at him. She had yelled at Oink-Oink before, but she had never stopped him from playing

Stupid American Soccer. Oink-Oink came into the house with her. It looked to me like he was a Limper Man. So maybe he was a little bit like me now.

Peep-Peep did a lot more yelling downstairs. Oink-Oink did some yelling, too, but I think that Peep-Peep was way louder. Then I heard Oink-Oink starting to come up the stairs.

Because he was a Limper Man now, Oink-Oink was going up the stairs slow, like me. I knew that Oink-Oink was probably mad at me. I knew that he was probably mad at me because Peep-Peep had told him to be mad at me and a husband is supposed to be mad anytime his wife tells him to be.

That was all right. Oink-Oink didn't scare me anymore. I didn't like him, not one bit, but I knew that Oink-Oink didn't want to touch my bottom. I don't think Oink-Oink wanted to touch me at all.

If Oink-Oink wanted to come in and be mad at me because Peep-Peep told him to be mad, that was all right. Oink-Oink wasn't like Peep-Peep about getting mad. Peep-Peep was mad all the time. It seemed like Oink-Oink would get mad, yell a lot, but then not be mad anymore.

I was glad that Oink-Oink was coming up the stairs. I needed to talk to him. As much as I could talk to a stupid American.

I wanted to tell him that I was a goalie.

Anybody Got Game?

"Peep-Peep . . . Oink-Oink . . . Peep-Peep . . . Oink-Oink . . ."

"We're concerned. Ashley seems to be more childish than when we adopted her."

"Peep-Peep . . . Oink-Oink . . . Peep-Peep . . . Oink-Oink . . ."

"Some regressive behavior post-adoption is normal, Mrs. Hartman . . ."

"Regressive behavior?"

I'd been determined to say as little as possible during the "post-adoption interview." I was hoping Evelyn would be content to ask her checklist of dumb questions and then hop back on her broom stick and leave us alone. But . . .

"Regressive behavior? Evelyn . . . she's sucking her thumb, clutching a baby doll, crapping her pants . . ."

"Peep-Peep . . . Oink-Oink . . . Peep-Peep . . . Oink-Oink . . ."

"And making animal noises . . . constantly . . . I think we're about three off-ramps past 'regressive behavior' here. My career is suffering! My marriage is suffering!"

Shelley slugged me full-force in the shoulder.

"Our marriage is NOT suffering!"

"Ashley can sense your hostility, Mr. Hartman."

"My hostility?"

"Yes. Older adoptees often respond to a hostile environment with immature behavior."

"Hostile? Why would I be hostile? Just because she kicked me square in the crotch upon first meeting, threw a bowl of rice in my face, has demoralized and exhausted my wife to the point where she's barely functional . . ."

"Our marriage is NOT suffering!"

"Of course not. Everything is fine. I enjoy having my wife snarl at me every fifteen seconds and run the Great Wall Of Celibacy down the middle of our bed every night . . ."

"Mr. Hartman! It sounds like you are more concerned about your husbandly privileges than Ashley's emotional well-being."

I threw my hands up in the air. "All right! Okay! I am the bad guy here!"

"Mr. Hartman, this isn't about judging you or . . ."

"It's not? According to you, Evelyn, all of Ashley's problems are because of my hostility . . . oh, and the fact that I am some kind of deviant sex maniac who thinks I should get to have some physical contact with my lawfully wedded wife more than about once every six months!"

"Mr. Hartman, this is very immature."

"If you were home once in a while and all of this wasn't left up to me and I wasn't exhausted all of the time . . ."

I stood up.

"Excuse me if you ladies weren't done yet beating up on me, but I've got some physical frustrations I need to work out!"

Ashley cradled the baby doll and gave me a wicked little Vietnamese grin as I headed out the door toward the driveway.

" . . . Oink-Oink . . ." She stuck her thumb into her mouth, just for emphasis, I guess.

My ankle was at about 50% and I still couldn't walk without some pain. Maybe shooting buckets wasn't what the doctor would have recommended, but I had to do something before I blew myself up into tiny little pieces.

I tested the ankle with a little jump shot.

Ouch! Nope, not ready for that one just yet.

I carefully stepped back a couple of feet. Practicing flat-footed free throws was better than nothing.

I bounced the ball a couple of times and then shot.

Swish. Bounce-Bounce. Swish.

From somewhere off in the vicinity of the porch I could hear Shelley making apologies to Evelyn and Evelyn unconvincingly telling Shelley not to worry about it. Evelyn had not struck me as the kind of girl who easily forgave challenges to her authority.

Bounce-Bounce. Swish.

"I have never been so humiliated!" Shelley's voice called to me from the porch.

"Never!"

I waited for the obligatory door slam.

Nothing.

I wondered how Shelley could possibly have missed that standard dramatic gesture and bounced the ball again.

I shot. Bang! Off the side of the rim!

That sent the ball careening off into the shrubbery by the side of the driveway, where it got stuck in amongst branches and leaves.

I sighed. The ball was pretty tightly wedged in, so it took me a few seconds to pry it back out again. I limped back to the approximate position of the imaginary free-throw line.

Bounce-Bounce.

"Oink-Oink!"

The ball slammed off the front of the rim.

I turned toward the sound of Ashley's shrill little voice. There she stood by the side of the driveway, clutching the doll with thumb poised to go back into her mouth.

The rational part of my brain, the part that wasn't thoroughly fed up with Ashley, remarked that she really could move pretty fast for a girl with a stump for a leg.

"This might be a good time for you to crawl back up into your room and babble nonsense or something. I wouldn't advise messing your pants, though."

Ashley stared back that blank little stare of hers.

"Goalie."

"Yeah, take Goldie with you."

Bounce-Bounce. Swish.

"Goalie!"

"Have it your way! Goldie! Goldie, Goldie, Goldie!"

Bounce-Bounce. Swish.

"NO!!!!!!!!!!!!!!!!!!!"

"Okay then, no Goldie! Bye bye Goldie! Ashley says no to you now!"

Ashley hobbled up to me. She held up the doll.

"Sing!"

"No, I'm not going to sing. And I can't shoot with you standing here!"

Ashley waved the doll at me.

"Sing!"

"Would you please just get out of my way?"

Ashley reached up and shoved the doll into my stomach.

"You want me to hold the doll?"

I dropped the ball and took hold of the doll.

Ashley looked up at me, as if she wanted to make sure I was watching.

"Goalie!"

She tried to kick at the ball, but fell off balance. Instinctively, I grabbed her shoulder to keep her upright. Ashley struggled a little and I let go, but she put out her arm and steadied herself against my waist.

She kicked again, this time making just enough contact with the ball to send it rolling a few feet.

"Goalie . . ."

"It's a basketball. You don't kick it."

I tucked the doll under one armpit, picked the ball up and took a shot at the hoop.

"You throw it. You shoot it."

"Goalie!"

"Here," I rolled the ball to Ashley.

"Don't kick it! You have to . . ."

Ashley tried to kick the ball again, but stumbled slightly. "Goalie!"

"You don't kick the ball! That's soccer!"

Ashley's face lit up like a Roman candle.

"Saw-Ur!"

"What?"

"Saw-Ur! Saw-Ur!"

"Soccer?"

"Saw-Ur!"

Against all odds, Ashley had just said something that made sense!

"You played soccer? In Vietnam?"

I pointed at her.

"You? Soccer?"

"Saw-Ur!"

Ashley backed up off the driveway and onto the grass of the front lawn.

"Goalie!"

"Goldie?"

"Goalie!"

I thought furiously for a second or two.

"Goalie? Have you been trying to say 'Goalie'?"

"Goalie! Goalie! Goalie!"

I gave the ball a gentle little kick in Ashley's direction. She bent down and stopped it.

"Goalie!"

"Yes! Goalie! They let you play goalie in Vietnam? Really?"

"Goalie!"

For the very briefest few seconds, Ashley and I forgot we hated each other.

I raised my arms in what was going to be a questioning gesture.

"But with your leg . . ."

The doll fell from my arm and landed hard on the driveway. Its little head bounced one direction, the rest of its body another.

Ashley let out an absolutely blood-curdling scream.

"SING!!"

I Hate Everything

I hate Stupid America.

I hate Stupid American Soccer.

I hate Stupid American wife-ladies who think they can be mothers for Vietnamese girls.

I hate Stupid American men who drop Vietnamese babies and break their heads off.

I hate Stupid American sun.

I hate Stupid American grass.

I hate Stupid American air.

I hate it! I hate it! I hate it!

When Stupid Oink-Oink dropped Ling and broke her head off, I wanted to run away back to Vietnam.

I wanted to run back to Mercy House and be a nanny. I wanted to run back to my school and be a goalie. I wanted to run back and be friends with Mai. I wanted to run and be anywhere but Stupid America!

But I was a Limper Girl and Limper Girls can't run very far. And I didn't know which way Vietnam was.

And I couldn't ask anybody, because Stupid Americans don't know how to say words and don't know how to understand words.

I would have to say words to Stupid Americans very slowly and would probably get really Babytears-crying frustrated. So, I couldn't run back to Vietnam.

I didn't want to go back into the Stupid American House. I didn't think I could do that without Ling because I'd just be that much more lonely.

There was no place for me to go!

Well, maybe one place: the little house where Oink-Oink kept his Stupid American Soccer Ball.

I turned to Stupid Oink-Oink and screamed at him. I said some bad words to him and called him some bad names.

I don't want to tell you the words I said or the names I called him. They are words and names that only really bad girls use and I don't want you to think that I'm a really bad girl. I only used them this once and I think just using them once doesn't make me a really bad girl. As long as I'm careful not to use them again. So, I won't. If I do, don't tell anybody.

I turned back and limped to the door of the little house. Stupid Oink-Oink was making Stupid American noises, but I didn't have time for that. I opened a door and limped into the little house.

The nicest thing about the little house was that it didn't have any stairs.

I'd tell you some other nice things about the little house, but there weren't any. It was dark and had smells that didn't make me happy. There wasn't any place for a Limper Girl to sit down.

I saw some old blankets in a corner. I limped over and threw myself down on them. I had lots of Babytears now, but I don't think that made me weak. I'd just lost Ling, the most important baby in the whole world, and I think it was okay to cry about that.

Stupid Oink-Oink came into the little house and kept making Stupid American noises. It kind of sounded like maybe he was sorry. Maybe. I couldn't tell.

I couldn't understand what he was trying to say and it was his fault I couldn't understand because he had never tried to learn real words. He was holding Ling's head in one hand and the rest of her little body in the other.

But then Stupid Oink-Oink said something I did understand. "[American gibberish], Ashley Stupidname, [American gibberish]." Well, I'd had about all of Stupid Oink-Oink I could take!

I rolled off the blankets and pulled myself up.

"CAM!

"My name is CAM! NOT ASHLEY STUPIDNAME! CAM!"

Stupid Oink-Oink turned his head a little and looked at me. His face kind of scrunched up the way faces scrunch up when somebody stupid is trying to understand something or when somebody is trying hard to make potty but it won't come out. I didn't think he was trying to make potty, so I guess he was maybe trying to understand me.

"CAM!!!!!!!!!!!"

I pointed to myself.

"CAM!!!!!!!!!!!!!!!!!!!!!!"

Stupid Oink-Oink stood there for what seemed like a long time.

"CAM!!!!!!!!!!!!! CAM!!!!!!!!!!!!!! CAM!!!!!!!!!!!!!!!!!"

I knew I'd done something pretty bad. When I dropped the doll, Ashley had screamed at me.

I don't mean that she yelled at me like she'd yelled before. No, I mean she screamed at me. The torrent of words roaring out of her mouth had a very distinctive sort of tone to them.

It wasn't a little-girl-upset-with-her-dad tone. It was more of a drunken-sailor-who-thinks-you-bumped-into-him-on-purpose-to-insult-his-manhood tone. Whatever the worst the Vietnamese language might have had to offer, I had a feeling that it was being directed toward me just then.

She was upset that I'd dropped the doll. That much wasn't hard to figure. Not at all.

I knew that girls got attached to their dolls, but this was more like a mother whose baby had just been killed. Seriously. Ashley's tone was that vile.

She pointed at me. She pointed at the doll. She pointed at herself. She pointed at the house. She pointed at the basketball hoop. She pointed at things where I wasn't sure what she was pointing at. And then she hobbled in the direction of the garage, staying pretty much with the Vietnamese cuss-word tone.

I looked down at the two parts of the doll lying in the driveway.

It was a doll. It was just a doll. Didn't she know it could be fixed?

Ashley opened the side door to the garage and limped in.

"Randy! What did you do to Ashley?" Shelley yelled from the porch.

I wasn't in a mood to answer. I picked up the doll's head and body and walked into the garage.

Ashley was lying on a pile of rags. She was crying the kind of crying that sounds way more mad than sad.

I tried to lose my Coach Hartman voice and use my Daddy voice (which I hadn't gotten much practice using).

"Look, I'm sorry about the doll. I am really sorry. I didn't mean to drop her. I hope you understand that. I didn't drop her on purpose and I didn't drop her to hurt you. But, she's still in just two pieces. Clean break, right at the neck. We can fix her up. Just like new.

"You won't even know she'd been broken. So, listen, how about if you come back into the house with me and we can sit down together and fix the doll. Okay? How does that sound? Ashley, how does that . . ."

Ashley fell off the rags and grabbed onto the side of the work bench to pull herself up.

"DAMN!!!!!!!!!!!!!!!!!!!!!!"

Well, isn't that great? She finally learns some English and it's a swear word. I raised my hands in a kind of trying not to be threatening motion.

"Whoa! Hey! You know, no need for that . . ."

"DAMN!!!!!!!!!!!!!!!!!!!!!!!!!!!!!"

"I came in her to apologize . . ."

She yelled again, but this time it sounded a little different.

"CAM!!!!!!!!!!!!!!!!!!!!"

She pointed at herself.

"CAM!!!!!!!!!!!!!!!!!!!!!!!!!"

What did "Cam" mean, I wondered. Whatever it meant, she was making it pretty clear that I wasn't welcome right then. And I knew I wasn't going to be welcome until I'd made things right.

I tromped back into the house. Shelley stood in the living room, arms folded.

"Where's Ashley?"

"In the garage."

"Why is she in the garage?"

"Probably because she doesn't want to be in here."

I sat down at the kitchen table and put the two parts of the doll in front of me.

"Make her come back in the house."

"I don't think I'm in much of a position to make her do anything right now. I need some industrial-strength glue."

After finding the glue in a drawer, I sat and very carefully lined up the doll's head with its neck.

Shelley was berating me for all kinds of things. How I'd acted with Evelyn. I'd broken the doll (which Aunt Margaret had given Shelley for her fifth birthday). I was refusing to drag Ashley back into the house.

When the alignment looked as close to perfect as it was going to get, I applied the glue and pressed the head tightly against the neck of the body.

Shelley seemed to have run out of bad things to say about me, for the moment at least.

As I held the doll parts together, I got to thinking about what Ashley had been saying out in the garage. "Cam." Why had I recognized that one word?

And then it hit me.

"Can you get me the adoption papers?" I asked Shelley, who seemed happy for an excuse to not watch me not feel bad about myself and returned a couple of minutes later with the adoption file.

I sat and stared at the English translation of the Vietnamese adoption decree. I was regretting my previous lack of attention to detail.

I looked up at Shelley and almost told her what I'd just figured out. But I knew I wasn't up for another fight right about then. It could wait.

"Can you heat up a couple of those frozen burgers? She's probably pretty hungry out there."

"She hasn't eaten in days. What makes you think she'll eat now?"

I let go of the doll. The glue was holding.

"I've got a hunch."

I guess I'd fallen asleep. A really bright light came on and it woke me up.

Stupid Oink-Oink was standing over me. Didn't Stupid Oink-Oink know I was trying to sleep out here? Didn't Stupid Oink-Oink know that Ling was dead and my life was over?

Stupid Oink-Oink knelt down a little and held something out to me.

"Ling!!!!!!!!!!!!!!!!!!"

There was Ling's head! Back on her body! Just like new! Like she'd never been dropped or killed or anything!

Ling was alive!

Ling was alive and my life was not over!

I reached out to grab Ling, but Stupid Oink-Oink pulled her back.

Then I saw he had something in his other hand. It was a plate. There were two of the bread things that tasted like dead water buffalo on the plate.

I did not want to eat a stupid bread thing that tasted like a dead water buffalo. I wanted Ling!

I shook my head and pointed at Ling. Stupid Oink-Oink shook his head and held the plate closer.

Oh, so that's what Stupid Oink-Oink was up to! I couldn't have Ling back until I ate one of the bread things that tasted like dead water buffalo. I shook my head no. He nodded his head yes.

Come to think of it, my tummy felt really empty. And I really did want to hold Ling and tell her how happy I was that she wasn't dead anymore. So, I grabbed one of the bread things that tasted like dead water buffalo. I took a little bite. It wasn't very good. But it wasn't very bad either.

She inhaled the burger.

I handed her the doll, which she promptly shoved hard into her chest for a very aggressive cuddle.

I had thought that maybe we'd eat burgers together, but from the way she was eyeing the second one, I could see that she was still pretty hungry. I held up the plate. She took the second burger with her free hand and similarly devoured it.

Squatting down was not the most comfortable position. I stood up, found an old folding chair and sat down again.

I looked intently at her.

"You want to be called Cam, don't you?"

She showed a flicker of recognition at the sound of the name that I'd just confirmed from the adoption decree.

"You don't like Ashley, do you?"

"CAM!!!!!!!!!!!!!!!!!!!!!!!!!!!!!!!!!!!!"

"Okay . . . Cam . . ."

I pointed to her. "Cam."

I pointed back at myself. "Dad."

I kept pointing back and forth.

"Cam."

"Dad."

"Cam."

"Dad."

Cam looked up at me. I won't say she grinned. But I won't say she frowned either.

She pointed to herself. "One."

She pointed to the doll. "Two."

She pointed to me. "Three."

I decided to laugh. Cam grinned a little.

I pointed to her again. "Cam."

I pointed back to myself. "Dad."

Cam grinned more broadly and did the "One! Two! Three!" game again.

At least we weren't screaming at each other.

I decided to try a different tack.

I pointed to myself. "Dad."

I pointed to Cam. "Cam."

But before Cam could start one-two-threeing me out of the garage, I pointed to the doll and raised my eyebrows.

Cam gave me a suspicious look, as if I'd just asked for a state secret.

"Ling," she said quietly.

"Ling?"

Cam nodded. "Ling."

"Ling. Well, hello Ling. I'm Dad."

Cam grinned, caught herself and went back to looking suspicious.

"I'm sorry I dropped you, Ling, and broke your head off. That wasn't personal, you understand. Just me being clumsy. But, I hope you're all better now, Ling."

That got a little giggle out of Cam.

I pointed to myself. "Dad."

I pointed to Ling. "Ling."

I pointed to Cam. "Cam."

"One! Two! Three!"

Storm Warning

posted by MOONGUY:

All of the Lancer fans bellyaching about how Randy Hartman fumbled recruiting season are missing the point. This team has plenty of talent. The state championship squad from three years ago didn't have as much raw talent as Hartman can put on the floor next fall. Talent isn't the issue. Coach Hartman's tactical understanding of the game isn't the issue. He knows as much about the science of basketball as any coach on any sideline. The issue is going to be whether Hartman can meld the talent he's got into a viable smooth-working machine. Can he inspire respect? A coach should not be a monster, but neither can he be everybody's best friend.

posted by HARTMAN_HATER:

Why is this [obscenity deleted] idiot still the coach? [Obscenity deleted]. He doesn't know [obscenity deleted] about the game! Idiot! Moron! [Obscenity deleted]. If B.M. doesn't [obscenity deleted] fire this [obscenity deleted] guy, I'm going to [obscenity deleted] his [obscenity deleted]!

posted by LANCERS_HOOPS_BOOSTERS_CLUB:

While we are all understandably passionate about our Lancers, the Lancers Hoops Boosters Club wants to go on record as disapproving of the unfortunate incident late last evening when Coach Hartman was hung in effigy from the flag pole in front of the school. The purpose of a flag pole is to fly our nation's flag and we cannot condone its use for any other purpose.

posted by HARTMAN_HATER:

You want to be rid of this [obscenity deleted] dolt? Sign the petition at my new website [obscene URL deleted].

Last month of school.

If there's such a thing as a breather in my profession, this would be it. Recruiting season was done. Summer basketball camps were still a month and a half away. Maybe I ought to take advantage to spend a little quality at time at home with the family.

The only problem was . . . in order to spend quality time, there has to be some "quality" involved.

Shelley and I were barely on speaking terms. Shelley and Cam ("Ashley," still, to Shelley), on the other hand, were very much on speaking terms, but rarely was it pleasant.

Cam wasn't directing much anger toward me anymore, which was a little bit of something positive but not much.

So, I kept finding excuses to not be at home.

I volunteered for this committee and that committee (telling Shelley that I'd been "asked" in each case). I found it just as easy to work my frustrations out on the floor of the gym as on the driveway.

And that was how I found myself on the Girls' Gymnastics Coach Search Committee.

Yes, that's how low I'd fallen. The boredom of personnel search committee meetings seemed infinitely preferable to the depression of being at home.

I told myself that I could be particularly valuable to the search. The next GGC would be coming in on the heels of the retirement of Candace Mason, another Living Legend of Bishop Mathis Athletics.

Candace (whom no one would ever presume to address as "Candy") had garnered seven state championships in her twenty-year tenure at Bishop Mathis. She'd coached several Olympic gymnasts, including a bronze medalist. I knew what that was like and I might be particularly good at figuring out which candidate was most likely to bear the unbearable pressure. Or so I told myself, knowing rationally that the level of public scrutiny of gymnastics paled in comparison to basketball.

And that was how I met Trish Manders.

We'd narrowed the field to five.

Trish was the fourth we interviewed. Her resume was maybe the weakest of the five finalists. Trish had never made an Olympic team, even as an alternate. She hadn't won any major individual titles.

Trish's competitive career had come to an end when she'd graduated from Benton, a small private college way north of San Francisco that had a much better record of producing folk singers than athletes. Her coaching experience was limited to three years with St. Gertrude, an all-girls school outside of Stockton.

But, Trish had come highly recommended by somebody or other, so I guess we were sort of obligated to give her an interview.

Trish walked into the interview room and I felt something tug somewhere inside my rib cage.

Trish wasn't devastatingly beautiful. She was more really cute. Really cute in the way that a hundred and fifty women I probably saw in a week whose faces I promptly forgot were really cute.

But, there was that something . . . that weird, maddeningly undefinable SOMETHING about her.

We made our introductions around the table. I smiled and made appropriate eye contact as I spoke my name.

Trish's eyes slightly narrowed and stayed locked on mine . . . and stayed locked for that just half a second too long that can't help but make a man wonder . . .

"You're the basketball coach."

I nodded.

Trish smiled.

"My condolences."

A muffled round of guffaws issued from around the table. That seemed to pretty well answer the question of what had been going on in Trish's head when I thought our eyes were getting lost in each other. She had just wanted to confirm that I was, in fact, the buffoon who was trashing Bishop Mathis' long and distinguished basketball tradition.

Trish's face turned a little pinker than it had been as she realized the reaction that her comment had provoked.

"Oh . . . no . . . I didn't mean . . . it's just . . . I know . . . things haven't gone well for you . . . and . . . I should probably shut up, shouldn't I?"

Trish actually recovered nicely and gave a pretty impressive interview. She had one of those gushy bubbly personalities that can run a very fine line between charming and tiresome. Trish managed to keep herself on the right side of that line.

In terms of enthusiasm, Trish blew away her more experienced competition. She was also scoring big points with her understanding of cutting edge gymnastics training techniques. She apologized to me at every opportunity . . . to the point where it became kind of a joke.

The committee all agreed in the after-interview meeting that Trish might deserve some serious consideration.

I was still trying to figure out what, if anything, had passed between Trish and me, so I didn't say much. Besides, it wasn't entirely clear that a rave review from me was going to help her out a lot.

I was headed out to the car.

"Coach Hartman! Wait!"

I turned around and there was gushy bubbly Trish Manders jogging over to me. Something inside me was glad. Something inside me was terrified.

"I just wanted to say again how sorry I am! What I said about condolences! That did not come out right at all! I just want you to know that I really do have the highest respect for you as a coach and want you to know that I'll support you all the way if I get this job and I think you're really great! This has to be a really tough job to take on and . . ."

We stood there talking a lot longer than we probably should have. Well, Trish stood there talking and I stood there listening a lot longer than we probably should have.

I found myself studying her face, her body language, looking for . . . . looking for what?

Was she flirting?

Did I want her to be flirting? Maybe I did. So what if I did?

I'm married! How can that be a "so what"?

I drove home feeling extremely conflicted.

Sure, you can't get away from feeling attracted now and then but I hadn't felt this strongly pulled toward any woman since I'd met Shelley.

A little warning siren was blaring in my head.

Something was wrong.

Something was really really wrong if I could actually have been hoping that Trish Manders was flirting with me. I'd let things at home deteriorate pretty badly.

I slowed and came to a stop for a red light.

A large sign was perched atop a strip center across the intersection.

"Acres Of Adventure! Open Every Day 10:00 to 6:00. 5 miles north on Highway 98."

Oink-Oink had been spending a lot of time out in the fields. I hardly ever saw him. Which was kind of too bad since he'd brought Ling back to life and started calling me by my real name instead of Ashley Stupidname.

Peep-Peep wasn't yelling at me as much as before. Peep-Peep seemed to be very tired. She slept a lot. If I cared, I might have actually felt sorry for her. But I didn't care, so I didn't feel sorry.

Ling was starting to talk and she had lots of questions.

Some of her questions I could answer. "Is it time to eat?" I could answer that question.

"How could Oink-Oink put my head back on and bring me back to life?" I couldn't answer that question.

Kids are like that, you know. Sometimes they ask questions you can't answer. So, you just have to tell them not to ask questions like that and give them a cookie or something.

One day, Ling asked me if I was her mother.

"I'm not your mother. I'm your nanny. I'm a nanny and a goalie." Ling looked like she didn't understand.

"If you're my nanny and you're supposed to take care of me, why do you suck your thumb?"

I told Ling that I was the nanny and it wasn't any of her business if I sucked my thumb. I could suck all of my fingers and all of my toes and it still wouldn't be any of Ling's business!

But that did get to me thinking (don't ever tell Ling that).

I was Ling's nanny and I was going to have to raise her and show her what was right to do. I knew that someday Ling would have to stop sucking her thumb. But she wouldn't ever stop as long as I was sucking mine! For Ling's sake, I had to stop sucking my thumb.

And then the next day, Ling asked me why I still made potty in my pants. I told Ling that I was the nanny and it wasn't any of her business if I made potty in my pants.

I could make potty in my pants, in the bed, on the floor or out the window and it still wouldn't be any of Ling's business!

But then . . . you know what I was thinking. I was Ling's nanny. It was going to be up to me to potty train her.

How could I expect Ling to learn the grown-up way to potty if I was still doing it the baby way? I had to stop! For Ling's sake, I had to stop making potty anywhere other than a real potty place, even if it was a Stupid American Potty Place.

The next day, I took Ling into the potty place.

"Now watch me!" I told Ling. I let her watch me make potty the grown-up way.

I think it was the same day that Oink-Oink came in from the fields real early. He and Peep-Peep spent a lot of time making those stupid American sounds that stupid Americans thought were words.

The day after that, Oink-Oink came into my room. Ling said that she wanted Oink-Oink to hold her. I didn't think that was a good idea, since the last time Oink-Oink had held Ling he'd dropped her, broken her head off and killed her.

Ling said that had been an accident and Oink-Oink had made it all better by putting her head back on. She thought Oink-Oink was nice and that I should give him a chance.

I told Ling I wasn't so sure. Ling asked me what choice I had. I didn't know how to get to Vietnam and maybe it was time I started making the best of things.

I told Ling that I was the nanny and that if I wanted to be mad and miserable all of the time, that wasn't any of Ling's business. I knew that didn't sound exactly right, but it was the truth.

Oink-Oink was making sounds. Ling kept insisting that she wanted Oink-Oink to hold her. That girl can be really annoying! Just to make her be quiet about it, I held Ling up to Oink-Oink. Oink-Oink must have understood because he took Ling from me and held her in his arms like a baby.

He started talking to Ling, which made me nervous because I didn't know what he was telling her and maybe he was telling her that I wasn't really her nanny. But, Ling didn't seem to be upset so I didn't try to grab her back.

Oink-Oink made some motions with his hands.

I figured out that he wanted me to come downstairs. I didn't want to come downstairs because of my leg and because Peep-

Peep would be down there and I didn't want to see her. But then Ling said that she thought it would be okay and that I had to come downstairs someday.

I sighed. I knew that Ling was going to be an annoying baby about the whole thing, so I'd better just go downstairs.

I was a Limper Girl out to the stairs. Oink-Oink stood at the top of the stairs and held his arm out. He wanted me to lean on his arm! He wanted to help me down the stairs!

"See!" Ling said with that little brat voice of hers. "Oink-Oink is trying to be nice! You can be nice back to him! You're my nanny and how can I learn about being nice to people if you don't show me?"

So, just to make Ling be quiet about it, I leaned on Oink-Oink's arm and he helped me down the stairs.

Peep-Peep was sitting at the table. She didn't say anything to me. Which was better than yelling at me.

Oink-Oink showed me that I should sit down at the table. I pointed to Ling. He handed Ling back to me and then went over to the stove.

I couldn't believe what I was seeing!

Oink-Oink was cooking the food! And Peep-Peep was just sitting there at the table, looking tired.

I wondered if all American women were as stupid as Peep-Peep and didn't cook or clean or do anything for their families!

Oink-Oink put a plate in front of me. It had a lot of really strange food on it. I thought I recognized eggs, but the rest of the food was new to me. I looked up at Oink-Oink like I didn't even know what he was trying to get me to eat.

Ling told me to stop being silly and try the food. I said that if Ling thought the food was going to be so good, she should eat some first. I picked up a little strip of meat that Oink-Oink had burned so bad it was kind of stiff.

I put the little strip of burned meat up to Ling's mouth. She nibbled a little bite and told me that it tasted strange but not in a real bad way. So, I ate the little strip of burned meat. Ling was right. It tasted strange but not in a real bad way.

I told Ling that I would eat some of the strange food but only to be polite because I was Ling's nanny and had to teach her how to be polite.

A few minutes later, all of the strange food on my plate was gone. Ling had eaten most of it, which made me feel good because it meant that she was finally learning how to be polite. It seemed to make Oink-Oink happy.

After that, Oink-Oink made motions like we should go outside. I followed Oink-Oink. Peep-Peep followed me. Oink-Oink showed me that he wanted me to get into the car.

Ling asked if Oink-Oink was taking us back to Vietnam. I said I wasn't sure, but maybe we should get into the car and find out.

We rode in the car for a while. Ling asked me what was the first thing I was going to do when we got back to Vietnam. I repeated that I didn't know if we were going back to Vietnam and that Ling shouldn't get her hopes up too much.

We weren't going to Vietnam.

I don't know if I can even tell you anything about the place we went. It was really really strange.

There were some Stupid Americans walking around with their faces all painted up so it looked like they were smiling all of the time or frowning all of the time. I didn't like them, especially when they came right up to me.

There were some horses made out of wood. They didn't go anywhere. They just went round and round and round.

I didn't want to ride a stupid horse, but Ling thought it might be fun. It wasn't fun for me, but Ling laughed and laughed the whole time.

There were little boats and little cars and all kinds of things that looked like they were supposed to go somewhere but just went around in circles and came back to where they'd started.

Ling really liked everything we did that day. I guess she was too young to see how stupid it was to ride in things that didn't go anywhere. For Ling's sake, I acted like I was having fun.

It was way past Ling's naptime, but Oink-Oink didn't seem like he wanted to leave. I think he was having even more fun than Ling.

Ling ate some more strange food. Stupid Americans sure do like their stupid bread things to eat! This one was long and skinny and they put it in a big piece of bread.

I was feeding Ling when one of the Stupid Americans with the smile painted on came up.

"Go away, Stupid American with a smile painted on. You're scaring Ling!"

That's what I said, but it was in Vietnamese so the Stupid American with the smile painted on didn't understand.

He really didn't understand.

Ling Learns A Lesson

The clown was very understanding.

In the clown game, physical assault is apparently viewed as a routine occupational hazard. He assured me that his own nose was not broken and I did not need to reimburse him for the plastic Rudolph nose.

He actually apologized for trying to grab Ling. I told him that I knew it was all in good fun, but that my newly-arrived Vietnamese daughter wasn't as up on the rules of the clown game.

Shelley was absolutely mortified and the proper object of blame was obvious to her. Ashley punching the clown was my fault. We would not have been at Acres Of Adventures if I hadn't come up with the stupid idea of going there.

As a matter of fact, now that she thought about it, this whole thing was my fault because I hadn't tried hard enough to make our own baby with her!

I glanced at Cam in the backseat. She was contentedly cuddling Ling and whispering to her. The girl was clearly oblivious at that moment to everything but Ling.

Shelley moved off of the specific topic of our daughter beating up clowns and moved on to just about everything I'd done wrong since the day we'd met. It was quite a list. Everything from forgotten anniversaries of first dates to violations of toilet seat etiquette. There really wasn't much to say. So, I said nothing.

I said nothing and gradually tuned out Shelley's voice. The more I tuned out Shelley's voice, the more I started picturing Trish Manders' face.

"Families are stupid," I whispered to Ling. "We belong at Mercy House, not with Peep-Peep and Oink-Oink."

I was glad that we were finally leaving the stupid place with the horses that didn't go anywhere. It hadn't been any fun for me and I was afraid that it had tired Ling out too much.

I don't think Ling noticed when the stupid man with the painted face tried to take her from me. I hope not. Ling was so scared and confused already by America.

Peep-Peep must have thought it was a stupid place, too, because she started yelling at Oink-Oink when we were leaving. She was yelling really loud.

I started to feel sorry for Oink-Oink. Yes, he had taken us to a stupid place but Peep-Peep didn't need to yell that loud! I hadn't liked it either, but I wasn't making everybody else's ears hurt about it!

Besides, I was starting to think that maybe Ling was a little bit right and Oink-Oink was the nice one.

Well, not that he was nice. He wasn't. He was Oink-Oink! And he was American, so he really couldn't help not being nice.

But, he wasn't as mean as Peep-Peep, who was also American and couldn't help not being nice either. I guess some Americans tried harder to not be mean than others.

"Why is Peep-Peep yelling at Oink-Oink?"

"You wouldn't understand. You're just a baby and you don't understand these things."

"You don't understand them, either."

"Yes, I do!"

"No, you don't! They're making those stupid American sounds and who knows what they mean? You don't know any more than I do!"

I hated it when Ling tried to argue with her nanny. It wasn't good to argue with a nanny because nannies know all about everything and babies should listen to their nannies all the time and never sass back.

Ling was starting to turn into a Sasser-Back and I didn't like that one bit. I could see that I was going to have to get much stricter with Ling. I didn't want to do that, but Ling didn't leave me any choice!

"Oink-Oink is nice. He put my head back on and brought me back to life. And you know he's really nice. You should be nice to him, too!"

"You're just a stupid baby and you don't know anything! I don't have to be nice to Oink-Oink! I don't have to be nice to Peep-Peep! I don't even have to be nice to you!

"I have to take care of you and feed you and change your pottypants and make sure you don't fall down and hurt yourself because I'm your nanny, but I don't have to be nice to you!"

I don't think I've ever been happier to see my own driveway. Shelley was screaming at me. Cam was screaming at Ling. Cam was also screaming in little higher-pitched voice that I think was supposed to be Ling screaming back at her.

I climbed out of the car and headed for the house. I changed into my sweats and went back outside.

Shelley was nowhere to be seen and, under the circumstances, that was fine with me. Cam was just sitting by the edge of the driveway, still talking to Ling.

Dribble, dribble. Shoot. Miss.

Dribble, dribble. Shoot. Miss.

We're not talking about long jumpers from three-point territory. I was lucky to hit the rim.

Dribble, dribble. Shoot. Miss.

Dribble, dribble. Shoot. Miss.

Dribble, dribble. Shoot. Miss.

Stop dribbling.

Tantrum.

Scream.

Cuss.

Tantrum.

Suddenly aware of being watched.

Cam wasn't arguing with Ling anymore. She was looking up at me with a blank expression. Maybe it was meant to be mocking. Maybe it wasn't. But, in my mood, there was no benefit of the doubt.

"What are you looking at?"

I'll admit that it wasn't the most mature reaction.

"What is your little problem? Don't you get what's happened here? You were living in a stink hole! You had no future! You had nothing! Then we came along and tried to give you a chance! But all you do is mope around, scream at us and make life miserable!

"Should I just call Vietnam up and say, 'Do you have any girls who'd appreciate a good home? That Cam girl you gave us could care less and I hate to waste it on her!

"What's that? Oh, just bring Cam back and you'll give us a nice girl? Great! We'll be there, first plane we can catch!'"

I turned, dribbled, drove to the basket and missed the dunk.

Cam was still staring at me.

"You think this is funny? You try it!"

I rolled the ball to her.

"Go ahead! Pick up the ball and show me how you can shoot a basket! Show me how really good you are that you are qualified to sit there and mock me! Go on!"

Cam said something to Ling. She answered herself back with the Ling voice. Ling didn't sound any happier with her than I was.

Cam gently put the doll down on the grass and wobbled up to her feet. She gave the ball a weak little kick.

"Goalie!"

"NO!" I yelled at Ling. "No, no, no! I am NOT going to be nice to Peep-Peep, Oink-Oink or you, you stupid little baby!"

The car was just stopping at the Stupid American House. Peep-Peep was still yelling at Oink-Oink. Peep-Peep was yelling so loud that I had to yell even louder for Ling to hear me.

"Do you hear me? I am not going to be nice to anybody! I wish I wasn't adopted! I wish I wasn't living in Stupid America! I wish that I wasn't your nanny and didn't have to listen to your stupid little baby talk!"

Peep-Peep got out of the car and slammed her door. Oink-Oink got out of the car and slammed his door.

Ling started to cry.

"Ling! Don't do that! Don't cry! It isn't nice to cry!"

"Well, it isn't nice to say that you wish you weren't my nanny!"

I started to say that I could say whatever I want and it wasn't any of Ling's business, but I stopped myself.

Did I really say that I wished I wasn't Ling's nanny? Oh no! That wasn't right! I loved being Ling's nanny! Why would I say such a stupid thing! Ling was a stupid baby, but even she would know not to say that!

"I'm sorry. I didn't mean to say that I wished I wasn't your nanny. I didn't mean that. I'm just mad at Peep-Peep and Oink-Oink and . . ."

"If getting mad at Peep-Peep and Oink-Oink makes you say things to me that aren't nice and hurt my feelings and make me cry, then you shouldn't get mad at Peep-Peep and Oink-Oink!"

"I have to be mad at them! Look at what they've done to me! They took me away from my home! They took me away from babies! I was a goalie and a nanny and now I'm not anything . . . except your nanny!"

"You don't have to like them. You just have to stop being mad at them."

I didn't want to stop being mad at Peep-Peep and Oink-Oink. But I didn't want to make Ling cry anymore either.

Oink-Oink was bouncing the Stupid American Soccer Ball and throwing it up at the circle thingee.

"You could teach Oink-Oink how to play soccer right!"

"I don't know how to make Stupid American Sounds! How could I teach him anything?"

"Maybe you could just show him."

I sighed. I didn't want to do any of this stuff, but it seemed important to Ling.

Oink-Oink seemed to be getting really mad at the Stupid American Soccer Ball. He was sweating and grunting like a good Oink-Oink.

"Go on! Get up and show him how to play the game right."

"He's a Stupid American. He'll never learn anything."

Ling was quiet. She was pouting.

"Oh . . . all right . . ."

I looked up at Oink-Oink.

Oink-Oink looked down at me.

And he started to yell!

"Goalie!"

That one word snapped me back to reality. I was screaming hateful things at a ten year-old girl who had no idea what I was saying. Maturity gradually started to re-assert itself.

"Goalie . . . right . . . soccer . . . okay . . ."

The whole point of Acres Of Adventure was to try to connect with Cam. That hadn't worked. Spectacularly. And now here she was, telling me how to connect.

I took in a deep breath and swallowed hard.

I nodded. "Goalie . . ."

Cam put Ling down on the grass and unsteadily came to her feet.

"Goalie," Cam repeated.

"Goalie." I rolled the ball to her. She reached down and stopped the ball before it could roll between her feet.

"Goalie!" Cam smiled.

"Goalie," I shrugged with a smile.

I motioned for Cam to roll the ball back to me. Balancing on her longer leg, she gave the ball a weak little kick with the shorter.

The ball rolled maybe three feet. I started to move forward to get the ball, but Cam stumbled up and gave the ball another little kick.

I hate it when stupid little babies are right and I'm wrong. I hate it. I hate it ! I HATE IT!!!!!!!!!!!!

But Stupid Little Ling was right. Stupid Oink-Oink played Stupid American Soccer but he did know about Smart Vietnamese Soccer.

Oink-Oink kicked the ball and didn't use his hands. He didn't try to throw it through the circle thingee. It didn't make any sense. Why would he play Stupid American Soccer when he knew all along about Smart Vietnamese Soccer?

It's not good when stupid little babies are right and their nannies are wrong. It makes stupid little babies think that they're smarter than they are and don't need to listen to their nannies. I had to do a smart nanny thing to keep Ling from thinking that.

"All right, Ling, now I want you to listen to me. I knew all along that Oink-Oink could play Smart Vietnamese Soccer. I just wanted to see if you'd be mean to me about being right. It's not nice to be mean to somebody when you've been right and they've been wrong. See how much I do for you?"

Ling didn't say anything. I think she knew that I'd just shown that I was smarter and more grown-up than she was. So, my idea worked.

Oink-Oink and I played Smart Vietnamese Soccer until the sun started going to sleep. I won the game because I kicked the ball more times than he did.

Then we went inside the Stupid American House. Oink-Oink made more of the water buffalo things. I guess Peep-Peep wasn't hungry because I didn't see her.

When we were done eating the water buffalo things, Oink-Oink turned on the TV. We had had a TV at Mercy House, but it never worked very well. Even though this was a Stupid American TV, it worked.

Oink-Oink pushed some buttons on a gun thing he pointed at the TV and a bunch of Stupid American TV Things went by real fast. But then, he stopped pushing the buttons.

"GOAL!!!!!!!!!!!!!!!!!!!!!!!" the Stupid American TV yelled.

I could feel my face making a great big smile. Men in short pants were running around trying to kick a ball.

Stupid American TV had Smart Vietnamese Soccer!

Don't Stand So Close

I stared hard at the little piece of blank paper. No matter what I wrote, I was going to feel like a fraud.

"Indicate your first choice and put your ballot in the middle of the table."

It was a perfectly sensible way to handle selection of the next Girls' Gymnastics Coach. And Principal Claire Frank, as Chair of the Search Committee, was explaining it quite lucidly.

It wasn't the process that was troubling me. It was my role in the process.

You look at all of the resumes. Whose was most impressive?

Not Trish Manders. Truth be told, that was probably Amy Vandercroft.

You look at the interviews. Whose was the strongest?

Not Trish Manders, although she did a pretty good job of it. Amy Vandercroft.

Who was the smartest, safest choice?

Not Trish Manders. Amy Vandercroft.

"If we do not get a unanimous consensus, we will discuss the candidates, narrow the field down to two choices, and take another ballot."

The best result for Bishop Mathis and the best result for me personally would be that Trish Manders would get a form letter.

Thank you very much for your interest in Bishop Mathis athletics. While your qualifications were very impressive, we have decided not to offer you the position of Girls' Gymnastics Coach. Please be assured that this was a very difficult decision. We wish you the best of luck on your continued success in the future!

The seventeen year-old Randy Hartman within, the innocent romantic guy who wanted to be in love all the time and was absolutely dying to get another shot at it, was screaming out at me: "TRISH MANDERS!"

The mature adult Randall Hartman, the one who knew that the seventeen year-old was suggesting something outrageously reckless, was screaming at me: "AMY VANDERCROFT!"

My pen hovered over the ballot. My hand trembled slightly.

"Come on, Randy! You KNOW you want an excuse to hang around with Trish!"

That was Seventeen-Year Old Randy.

"Randall! How could you even THINK about voting for Trish Manders just because you've developed a massively hopeless crush on the woman?"

That was Adult Randall.

"Dude! You are like SO not any fun anymore!"

"And you are an irresponsible little . . ."

"Coach Hartman! Your ballot please?"

I looked up at Principal Frank. The entire committee was staring at me. Oh God, please tell me I didn't just actually verbalize what Seventeen Year-Old Randy and Adult Randall were saying to each other?

Please, please, please . . .

"Are you all right? You look as if you are sweating?"

Oh. Okay. I didn't actually say it. I just look it.

"Yes . . . yes, I'm fine, Principal Frank. Fine. You know, it is a little warm in here. Anybody else think it's warm in here? Well, then, I guess it's just me . . . you know . . . thinking it's warm in here . . ."

"Your ballot, please, Coach Hartman . . ."

"Oh . . . yes . . . my ballot . . . Just trying to come up with the best choice, you know . . ."

"TRISH MANDERS!!!!!!!!" Seventeen Year-Old Randy bellowed.

"AMY VANDERCROFT!" Adult Randall demanded.

I took in a deep breath . . . wrote down my choice . . . folded the ballot . . . and put it in the middle of the table on top of the other four ballots . . .

"Thank you, Coach Hartman."

Principal Frank picked up the ballots.

"Amy Vandercroft . . . Amy Vandercroft . . . Amy Vandercroft . . . Amy Vandercroft . . . and . . . the handwriting on this one is . . . Amy Vandercroft . . ."

"I am never speaking to you again!" Seventeen Year-Old Randy barked.

"I am SO proud of you!" Adult Randall beamed.

"All right," Principal Frank smiled. "We seem to be in agreement. No need for further discussion. I will call Amy and let her know that she's our new Girls' Gymnastics Coach."

I wiped away the sweat from my forehead. I had the feeling that I'd just dodged a bullet. Trish Manders would be nothing but trouble for me and it was just as well that I was probably never going to see her again.

"And I think that each of the other candidates needs to hear from one of us directly. I hate form letters. Each of them took the time to apply and interview. Could each one of you please contact one of the candidates we did not choose? Let's see . . . Coach Hartman, could you please call Trish Manders?"

I'd found something about America that wasn't stupid.

TV!

When Oink-Oink showed me Smart Vietnamese Soccer on the TV, Ling and I watched for hours and hours and hours. I didn't sleep that night. Neither did Ling.

Ling kept pestering me with questions about Smart Vietnamese Soccer.

"Why do they stop like that? Why don't they just keep playing?"

"They stop because they have to make potty, stupid baby! It's in the rules of Smart Vietnamese Soccer!"

"They have to all make potty at once? How do they do that?"

"They practice it. They play for a while and then they stop and say: 'Time for us all to make potty together!'"

"Why don't they just pick the ball up and throw it?"

"Because it's in the rules. You have to kick the ball. You can't throw it."

"Why not?"

"It's in the rules."

"Oink-Oink throws the ball."

"That's Stupid American Soccer, not Smart Vietnamese Soccer!"

Sometimes that girl just has too many questions!

I was happy watching Smart Vietnamese Soccer and didn't even think that there might be other things on Kind Of Smart American TV.

I'd seen Oink-Oink push some buttons on the little gun thing he pointed at the TV to make it work. So, one time when the players were all off making potty together and I was bored, I pushed buttons on the little gun thing.

The picture changed. No more Smart Vietnamese Soccer. A man and a woman were smack-smacking their lips together. Ooh, yuck! I pushed the button again.

A big ugly monster was breathing fire and burning a city down. I wasn't scared, but I was afraid that the big ugly monster would scare Ling, so I pushed the button again.

Some Stupid Americans were sitting at a desk and yelling at each other with Stupid American Sounds. Boring. I pushed the button again.

Stupid American Woman! Didn't she know everybody could see her if she was on TV? She should at least wrap a towel around herself!

I pushed the button again. I thought I'd found Smart Vietnamese Soccer again, but then I saw that the men in shorts were touching the ball.

"You told me that the rules said that they couldn't touch the ball!"

That girl!

"No, you stupid baby! That's only for Smart Vietnamese Soccer! I think this is Stupid American Soccer!"

And then one of the Stupid American Soccer players threw the Stupid American Soccer Ball up in the air. It went through an orange circle thingee like Oink-Oink had outside.

Another player got the Stupid American Soccer Ball and threw it. Another one caught it. He threw at another orange circle thingee. It went in.

Now Stupid American Soccer seemed stupider than ever! There was no goalie! That's why the ball kept going into the orange circle thingee!

Maybe it was good that I was in America, after all. They needed somebody to teach them how to play soccer!

"Thank you so much for meeting with me, Coach Hartman."

I smiled weakly as I stirred my steaming hot cup of cappuccino.

I was trying to avoid making eye contact with Trish Manders without looking like I was trying to avoid making eye contact.

"Sure. Happy to do it. I just have to warn you again . . ."

"That you can't discuss specifics of the decision-making process. I understand. It's confidential. I'm just wondering if you think there's anything I could have done differently. You know, when I interviewed or something."

Trish was asking if there was some way I could tell her about the process without technically violating confidentiality. I really shouldn't have said anything . . .

"The only thing you could have done differently, Miss Manders . . ."

"Trish . . ."

" . . . would to have been born ten years earlier so you'd have at least five more years of coaching experience at the prep level."

Trish bit her lower lip. "Okay . . . but . . ."

"But, if that's true, why was I hired as the boys' basketball coach when, on paper, I don't really have any more experience than you?"

Trish blushed. "No. That's not what I was going to . . . well, okay . . . maybe I was."

"I've asked myself that question. Over and over and over again. The best I can come up with is that I am the sacrificial lamb of Bishop Mathis Lancer basketball."

"Humh?"

"Ty Roberson was a living legend . . . is a living legend. Whoever followed Roberson was going to be, by definition, inferior. Not good enough. Can't possibly fill the shoes.

"You don't hire the coach of the future to follow the giant of the past. You hire a guy who will come in, suffer through the inevitable slump, take the blame and hit the road after two seasons. That's when you hire the next Ty Roberson."

"But Coach Mason . . ."

"Different deal. Whether it's fair or unfair or neutral, boys' basketball gets a whole lot more attention than girls' gymnastics. Amy Vandercroft can afford a couple of rebuilding seasons. I can't. That simple."

"So, you think you'll be fired?"

"Nobody ever gets fired. Pressure will be put on me. I will resign to 'pursue other opportunities.' The school will deny that I was pressured to resign. I'll deny that I was pressured to resign. We'll all be lying through our teeth, but that'll be okay because nobody will believe a word we say anyway."

"That sounds pretty cynical."

"No, it sounds pretty realistic."

"What if you turned the team around? What if you went undefeated next year and won the state championship?"

"As hard as it was, I let go of Santa Claus years ago."

"Is it really that bad for you?"

"No. It's worse."

"Want to tell me about it?"

"Not really. No."

Trish stared at me in stony silence for several seconds before asking: "Are you still offended about what happened in my interview? Is that why you're being rude to me?"

My heart froze up for about half a second and then started pumping again. Yes. There is a reason why I'm being rude to you.

I'm being rude to you because I think I'm attracted to you and I don't want to be attracted to you and I'm scared to death of what might happen if we were to really hit it off.

I'm being rude to you because it really is the best thing for both of us and if you understood the situation, you'd thank me for it.

"I'm sorry," I half-spoke and half-mumbled.

"I . . . please . . . accept my apologies. I didn't mean to be rude. Honestly. It's just that . . ."

It's just that . . . what? Come on, Hartman, you overplayed your hand. You overplayed your hand and she's calling you on it and she has every right to do that.

It isn't Trish Manders' fault that your marriage is dangling at the edge of a cliff. Don't take it out on her just because she made the mistake of showing up and being cuter than a little bug right when you happened to be most vulnerable.

"Well, you said it yourself at the interview. I'm under a lot of pressure."

"Under a lot of pressure" is a phrase that always sounds lame, but it was the best I could fumble around and come up with.

"I guess I'm trying to lighten the load of my anxieties a little by dumping some of them on you. I'm sorry for that. If you need to hate me, go ahead. But you'll have to stand in line."

Trish's long cold look held for about another two seconds and then softened. She leaned forward, grasped her cup and took a long soothing sip of whatever exotic mix of caffeine she'd ordered.

"Apology accepted."

"No, really . . . my sarcasm was uncalled for . . ."

"I said I wanted your honest feedback. You've given me your honest feedback. You've told me that I'd have been in over my head at Bishop Mathis."

"No. I didn't mean that exactly . . ."

"You've told me that what can look like a dream job from the outside can be a nightmare from the inside. You've told me that maybe I should be thankful for being where I am and just get comfortable with it."

"No, I'm not telling you anything of the kind. I'm just saying how it looks from my little corner of the room. Like I said before, with girls' gymnastics, I'm sure it's different. Nowhere near the visibility. Nowhere near the 24/7 sense of people who have no idea what they're talking about looking over your shoulder and dissecting every move you make."

Trish got a thoughtful look on her face.

"I'll ask again . . . if you're going to be nice about it this time. Is it really that bad for you?" Her tone hovered somewhere between sympathetic and clinical.

"Yeah . . . it is. Back when I was playing prep ball, it was nothing like it is today. The Internet means that any moron with a computer can spout all he wants to."

"I can see where that might get a man down. Even a good man like you."

"Even a good man like you?" Geez, Miss Manders, could you be a little more ambiguous?

Any other confoundingly complimentary phrases that push the frontiers of politeness and encroach on flirtation? And, while you're at it, could you make your facial expression just a little bit harder to read?

"That's kind of you."

"Not kind. Just honest. Like you were with me. Why do you let it get to you when ignorant people say things that aren't true? Can't you just tune all of that out?"

"Humh . . . yeah, you know, the idiots aren't the real problem. They're annoying and make you want to go strangle somebody, but that's not what really gets to me."

Without thinking, I leaned in a little bit closer and dropped my voice.

"It's when people who do know what they're talking about say things . . . and those things are true. There's this one guy who posts all of the time. He's always right. He tries to be fair and always words his criticisms in a very civil way . . . but somehow that just makes it worse . . . if you know what I mean."

Trish smiled. "Moonguy?"

"What? You've actually been reading . . . Okay. Yeah, Moonguy. He knows everything's that wrong with this program. He knows everything's that wrong with me. Every time he posts I'm thinking 'So, would it kill you to be wrong just once?'"

Trish giggled. Unfortunately, it was a very human and very charming little giggle.

"That was funny. I don't know why. Just the way you said it. I really felt your frustration."

"Not hard to do right now . . ."

"So, if Moonguy knows what's wrong with you as a coach, why not just listen to him and fix it?"

"You mean why not just turn into Ty Roberson, get the team's respect and go be brilliant?"

"You think the team doesn't respect you?"

"I think they respect me . . . or is the lack of disrespect not the same thing as getting respect? Whatever it is, they don't respect me the way they respected Coach R.

"Ty Roberson's teams would follow him straight through the gates of Hell. They'd do anything for that man, anything. He knew how to inspire guys not just to play their best, but to play better than their best. I don't know how to do that."

"Neither do I . . . so maybe that's why it's best I won't be coaching at Mathis."

"That's really it, isn't it? Respect. I don't have their respect, at least not the right kind of respect."

"Your wife must be very understanding and supportive."

Thanks, Trish Manders.

Thanks for the beautiful opening to pour out my heart and my soul to an attractive young single woman about everything that is wrong with my marriage. Thanks for the chance to express how neglected I feel.

Thanks for the perfect segue to talking about the needs a man has and how, even if he's loyal and means to honor his marriage vows, he can't help but be tempted when those needs aren't being met . . .

"Yeah. Shelley's great. You know, the perfect coach's wife. Right there at the front door with a martini all ready when I come home. If I told you what she's wearing, that would be way too much information, but, trust me, it usually looks pretty good. Supportive. Understanding. Affectionate. That's Shelley."

Trish Manders, do not flirt with me because I have this like totally cool and great marriage and I am not looking for a girl on the side and you could never ever in a million years measure up to the absolute goddess I married.

Trish hesitated for just about a tenth of a second. "Good. This isn't a job you can do alone."

"No, it isn't."

Trish was quiet for a few seconds and then got a where-are-my-manners sort of look on her face.

"I heard you'd adopted? How's that going?"

"Oh . . . you know . . . it's two steps forward and one step back off the cliff."

"SLAM DUNK!!!!!!!!!!!!!!!!!!!!!!!!!!!!!!!!"

"What was THAT?"

"Umh . . . my phone . . . ringtone thing . . ."

A text was coming through. Something told me that I needed to read it.

"FRANK" showed on the screen.

"CALL ME ASAP!"

"I've got to make a call. I think we were probably done?"

"Oh . . . sure. Yes. Oh! Look at the time!"

"And . . . I am sorry about the rudeness and the sarcasm. You just happened to wander across my firing range when I was practicing with live ammo."

"Umh, no worries, Coach Hartman. I understand completely. And, you know what? You've made me realize that this job just wasn't for me anyway. Way more stress than I want to have to process."

Trish got to her feet and stuck out her hand. "Friends?"

I did my best not to let my face flush too deep a shade of red. I shook her hand.

"Friends."

I took a sip of way too cooled off cappuccino as I watched what-could-have-been-but-I'll-never-know-now walk out the Starbucks door, pony tail bouncing as she went.

I allowed myself another couple of seconds for a little sigh before calling Principal Frank.

She picked up on the first ring.

"Coach Hartman, we have a problem."

My gut dropped about three hundred feet below sea level. So, the axe really was going to fall and it was going to fall a lot sooner than I'd thought.

"A problem?"

"Amy Vandercroft just called. It seems that the Australian Olympic Committee decided she's destined to be the savior of their gymnastics team."

"What? I thought she'd accepted."

"Don't get me started. Just get to school and get here like fifteen minutes ago. I'm calling an emergency meeting of the search committee."

Hello

"The ballots read as follows: Trish Manders . . . Trish Manders . . . Trish Manders . . . Trish Manders . . . and . . . I can't read the writing . . . Allison Deaver . . . all right . . . so . . . who wants to speak up for Allison?"

I didn't sleep in the Stupid American Bedroom anymore. It was all the way up the stairs and Limper Girls don't like stairs very much. It didn't have Kind Of Smart American TV. Ling thought the paint on the walls reminded her of Mercy House and made her sad.

I spent almost all day every day and most of the nights sitting in front of the Kind Of Smart American TV.

I could see Smart Vietnamese Soccer. I could see Stupid American Soccer. I could see people singing and dancing. I could see people smack-smacking their lips together, but I never watched that for very long. I could see dogs that talked and turtles that fought with swords.

And at first I didn't even notice, but I could hear things on Kind Of Smart American TV. I could hear Americans making Stupid American Sounds with their mouths.

"Why don't Americans use words, like we do?" Ling asked again for about the eighty-eight hundred million billionth time.

I didn't know why Americans didn't use words. But Ling had been doing so much back-sassing that I couldn't let her know that I didn't know.

"Americans used to use words. But then they all got sick. They got sick with bad coughs. They all coughed so hard that they broke the word-makers in their throats. So they couldn't make words anymore and had to just make noises like monkeys."

"I thought it was just that they were too stupid."

"Well, yes, Americans are pretty stupid and when they could make words they couldn't make as many words as Vietnamese make. They could say things like, 'Hello' and 'Goodbye' and 'Hungry' and 'I have to make potty now,' but not much else. It's really kind of sad. Because Americans are stupid they had to work so hard to make even just a few little words and now they can't make any words at all."

"On the Kind Of Smart American TV, it looks like they think those sounds are words."

"I guess so. They keep making sounds to each other, like Peep-Peep makes to Oink-Oink all the time."

"Oink-Oink doesn't make many sounds now. Do you think he forgot how to make even Stupid American Sounds?"

"No. Oink-Oink is a Stupid American but he isn't more stupid than other Stupid Americans. I think he just doesn't want to hurt Peep-Peep's feelings. She seems so happy making Stupid American Sounds."

"Peep-Peep never looks happy to me."

"I'm starting to think that Stupid Americans must have some other way of looking happy instead of smiling."

"Why don't they just smile?"

"I don't know, stupid baby. It's Stupid America, that's why."

We were quiet for a few minutes. Some men were shooting lots of guns at each other.

"I don't want to watch this," Ling said. "It's going to give me bad dreams."

"It's not going to give you bad dreams, Ling. Close your eyes if you don't want to watch."

"Stupid American Sounds would be pretty easy to learn."

"Why would I want to learn Stupid American Sounds?"

"You're afraid that if you try, you won't be able to learn them and that will make you as stupid as a Stupid American Girl."

"I am not afraid! I just don't care!"

"I thought you had to be smart to be a nanny."

"I AM smart, stupid baby!"

"But if you can't even learn Stupid American Sounds, then I guess you're not very smart after all!"

"You are going to bed without any water buffalo things to eat and your pants full of potty and no good-night kiss from me!"

"No. Not very smart . . ."

I put Ling down on her face so that she couldn't talk anymore. It would be a long time before Ling called her Nanny stupid again!

I pushed the little gun thing. Sometimes the Kind Of Smart American TV would get kind of stupid because there wouldn't be any color, like the pictures they took of us at Mercy House. This was one of those times.

Even though the Kind Of Smart American TV forgot to put color on, it was still pretty interesting. An American woman was cooking on a stove! Just like she's supposed to! Not all American women were stupid like Peep-Peep and didn't know how to cook for their families! This was something I wanted to see. I wished Peep-Peep were downstairs so that maybe she could learn something.

An American boy walked in and the American woman turned around and smiled at him. She made a sound.

I think it was something like . . .

"Hello."

"I don't think Trish Manders is really ready to coach at this level. That's all."

The room was silent. Principal Frank gave me a stink-eye stare that was asking if I had any idea how big a hole I was digging for myself. She had a problem. The problem had a solution. I was the idiot standing in the way.

"Some might have said the same of you when you were hired," Principal Frank replied with an arctic tone.

Now there was a piece of live bait I needed to let keep dangling.

"But, more than that . . . I don't think Trish wants the job."

"Excuse me? A coach who would NOT want to work at Bishop Mathis?"

She said it in such a way as to imply any such phenomenon would be in defiance of the basic laws of the Universe.

"Trish thinks that this would be a pressure-cooker environment. She's thinks that if she comes to coach at Bishop Mathis she'll have an ulcer inside of a month. She thinks that this dream job would become a nightmare."

"And why does she think that, Coach Hartman?"

I hesitated, cleared my throat looking hopefully for any signs of sudden laryngitis.

"Because I told her so."

"Heh-low."

"That doesn't sound right."

"Shut up, stupid baby! You try making the sound and see if you can do any better. See! So, shut up and let me learn the sound. Heh-low."

I thought I'd heard a lot of people making that sound in the place where the Kind Of Smart American TV forgot to put color. They made that sound whenever some new person showed up.

It was kind of funny. Once I figured out that "heh-low" was a real word I all of a sudden was hearing it all the time. I wondered how many times I'd heard "heh-low" and thought it was just American gibberish.

"Heh-low. Heh-low. Heh-low."

"I still think you're saying it wrong."

"You know, Ling . . . I think that 'heh-low' may be like 'hello.' The Americans seem to say it a lot when they are meeting people. Somebody walks in a room and everybody says 'heh-low'!"

"Why don't they just say 'hello' instead of 'heh-low'?"

"I told you, stupid baby, the Americans don't have word-makers in their throats. They can't say 'hello' so they make this weird 'heh-low' sound."

For a simple sound made by Stupid Americans, "heh-low" was kind of hard to say. I decided to just keep practicing.

"Heh-low. Heh-low. Heh-low. Heh-low. Heh-low. . . ."

"Hello?"

Just the sound of Trish's voice made me grimace a little, knocked me a little off stride. It made me want desperately to go back to the conversation we'd had over coffee and give her the honest answers.

What I said about my wife being supportive? I lied. I totally lied to you, Trish Manders. Do you know why I lied to you?

I lied to you because you are the Woman Of My Dreams. I lied to you because I thought that I was stronger than destiny. I lied to you because I'm afraid that an honest answer would be a lit match landing on two-story stack of kerosene-soaked hay.

But you can't ignore your dreams. You can't fight destiny. I am lighting the match, Trish Manders. Let the chips fall where they may.

"Trish? Hi, it's Randy Hartman . . . from Bishop Mathis. Hey, listen, the conversation we had this morning , you know the one where we decided that you had no business being the girls' gymnastics coach . . . well . . . umh . . . a funny thing just happened and I kind of hope that maybe we can re-open that discussion and look at some other factors . . ."

"I accept."

"Because you see . . . here's the thing . . . sometimes in order for us to grow professionally, it's necessary that we . . ."

"I accept. Whatever you're paying, I accept."

". . . go through some experiences that aren't entirely pleasant and . . . excuse me?"

"I heard an hour ago about Amy Vandercroft going over to the Aussies. I didn't know where I was in the finishing order the first time around but I had my fingers and toes crossed that I was next up on the list."

"Yeah. I guess you were. The committee met and . . . the job is yours if you want it."

"I already said I accept."

"Yes, you did . . . so . . . umh . . . you see, we're in kind of a rush and . . ."

"I'm packing up my office as we speak."

"All right, Dude. Par-tee time!" Seventeen Year-Old Randy bellowed.

Adult Randall just stood there in my mind, arms folded and a very disappointed look on his face.

"Heh-low. Heh-low. Heh-low. Heh-low. Heh-low."

I was getting good at making that stupid sound.

"Heh-low. Heh-low. Heh-low. Heh-low. Heh-low."

The front door opened. Oink-Oink walked in. He looked like he was thinking about something real hard.

"Heh-low."

Oink-Oink didn't even seem to see me as he walked past the Kind Of Smart American TV and went up the stairs.

"Heh-low. Heh-low. Heh-low. Heh-low. Heh-low."

He came back down the stairs wearing his Stupid American Soccer clothes and went back outside.

That was great!

I could teach him about goalies and how Stupid American Soccer could be more like Smart Vietnamese Soccer.

I picked up Ling and limped outside.

But I didn't stop practicing the sound.

"Heh-low. Heh-low. Heh-low. Heh-low. Heh-low."

Trish had accepted the job.

After all that.

After all of the "I don't think this stress is for me."

After me doing my best to make sure that the temptation that was Trish would be out of my life . . . Trish had accepted the job. Just like that.

Worse yet, when I'd called Principal Frank to report that I'd managed to avoid talking Trish out of taking the job before she'd heard the offer, she opined that Trish could take the office next to mine in the athletic building.

"She'll need a friendly face to show her around," Principal Frank had explained.

Which led me to an awful thought. Somehow, some way, Principal Frank had found out that I was madly in crush with Trish Manders!

This was her way of torturing me for having dared to suggest that Bishop Mathis wasn't necessarily the coolest place in the whole wide Universe to work! Putting Trish right next door to me and making me look at her and talk to her and never once get to . . .

How could she have known? What had I said? What had I done? They say that women have a way of sensing these things, but Principal Frank didn't strike me as the kind of woman who'd be real good at that.

No. Of course not. Absurd. It was all a coincidence. A painful coincidence. Nobody had made Randy Hartman the punch line to this joke but Randy Hartman.

I was in a daze by the time I got home. When I walked in the door, I was vaguely aware that Cam was watching TV (where else would you find her?) but otherwise wasn't noticing much about my physical environment.

I changed clothes (quietly, so as not to disturb Shelley's daily 18-hour nap) and headed out to the driveway.

Dribble. Dribble. Dribble. Shoot. Bucket!

Dribble. Dribble. Dribble. Shoot. Bucket!

"Hello!"

Dribble. Dribble. Dribble. Shoot. Bucket!

"Hello!"

Or, well, it sounded like "hello." It was more of a "heh-low." I turned to see Cam standing in the grass, holding Ling and looking very pleased with herself.

"Hello!" Cam insisted.

"Hello," I answered.

That brought a gigantic grin to Cam's face.

"Hello! Hello! Hello! Hello! Hello!"

"Yes . . . Hello . . ."

"Hello! Hello! Hello! Hello! Hello!"

"Okay . . . Hello . . ."

"Hello! Hello! Hello! Hello! Hello!"

I turned back to the basket.

"Hello! Hello! Hello! Hello! Hello!"

Dribble. Dribble. Dribble. Shoot. Basket!

"Goalie! Goalie! Hello! Goalie!"

"Yes. You're a goalie. Hello, goalie! Can I get back to my game now?"

"Hello! Goalie! Hello! Goalie!"

Dribble. Dribble. Dribble. Shoot. Basket!

I grabbed the ball out of midair and turned to go back and position myself for another jump shot. Instead, I almost tripped over Cam, who'd managed to put herself right in the middle of the driveway.

"Goalie! Hello! Goalie!"

"Yes! Fine! You're a goalie."

"Goalie! Hello! Goalie!"

"This is basketball! No goalies in basketball. Now, if you would please get out of my way . . ."

"Hello! Goalie! Hello!"

"Have it your way . . ."

I dribbled toward Cam and then easily around and laid the ball up and in.

"See? No goalie."

"Goalie."

I took the ball back up the driveway and started to drive again. This time, though, as I was trying to go by Cam . . .

I wanted to teach Oink-Oink something important and he wasn't paying any attention. He wouldn't even let me show him where the Goalie should stand. He just kept bouncing the ball and throwing it up until the little orange circle thingee.

"Goalie," I said with my meanest now-you-listen-to-me-Oink-Oink voice.

He ignored me.

He started running at the orange circle thingee bouncing the ball.

So, when he got up next to me, I made a mad-girl fist . . .

For the second time since we'd met, Cam had nailed me right where it hurts a man the most. I dropped the ball and then dropped to my knees. I let the pain slowly migrate up through my stomach and then dissipate.

"Hello!"

I came to my feet. Cam was holding the ball.

"Goalie!"

"If you ever do that to me again . . ."

"Hello! Goalie!"

"This . . . is . . . basketball. There . . . is . . . no . . . Goalie."

Yes, Hartman, that's the ticket! Speak slowly and she'll understand every word.

I reached to take the ball. Cam clutched it tightly.

"No, please . . . just give me the ball . . ."

I grabbed the ball.

Cam raised her right hand and then her right forefinger.

"One . . ." Cam pointed to herself with her left hand. She then dropped the forefinger and made a fist. She pointed to me with her left hand and shrugged.

"No . . . That's not how it works . . . You did not just score a point . . . I'm sorry, but punching a man in the groin and then taking the ball doesn't get you a point."

Cam repeated the sequence of forefinger up, point to Cam, forefinger down, point to Dad. As far as Cam was concerned, she was leading, 1-0.

"Okay. Try this."

I backed off a little and dribbled. Cam steadied herself on her good leg and held up her hands to block. I dribbled toward her, but then stopped, jumped, shot and hit the bucket.

I smiled sarcastically. I held up two fingers on my right hand and pointed to myself.

Cam frowned. She shook her head. She held up her right hand. Only one finger.

I held up the forefinger of my left hand and pointed it toward Cam, while still keeping my right hand with two fingers up.

"2-1."

Cam frowned a sneering frustrated frown. She held up both hands, with only the single forefingers raised. She pretty clearly was under the impression we were tied at one.

I could feel my blood pressure starting to climb. All I'd wanted was to blow off a little steam. Instead, I was arguing the rules of basketball with a ten year-old, a ten year-old who was making a habit out of nailing me in the crotch with some pretty vicious blows.

"All right, that's it! Enough of this nonsense! You go inside and stare at the TV, which is what you do best. I'll stay out here and play basketball, which is what I do best."

Cam dropped her left hand and pointed to herself.

"One . . ."

Cam pointed at me.

"One . . ."

"I have had just about all I can take for one day. I do not need to stand here and . . ."

Right at that moment, it hit me like the backside of a shovel to the forehead.

We were communicating!

I took in a deep breath, swallowed some big dumb male pride and nodded.

I pointed to Cam.

"One . . ."

I pointed back to myself.

"One . . ."

Cam grinned a great big grin and went back into her defensive stance.

"No hitting this time!"

I retreated back up the driveway a little and started dribbling.

"Ready or not . . ."

"Goalie!"

Moonguyen

"Tonight on Prep Focus, we continue our look at how local powerhouses have fared this past school year. Who were the Winners? Who were the Losers? Who's On The Way Up? Who's On The Way Down? Who Doesn't Have Clue One?

"You want a Winner? How about Arroyo Rojo football? Athletically speaking, A.R. was so far off the radar you'd have thought it was a Montessori. But, last fall, the Toreador gridiron squad stunned the experts by going 8-3 in the regular season, upsetting Kennedy in the first round of the playoffs and giving eventual sectional champ Truman a big scare in round two before surrendering two late scores in what can only be described as a valiant 38-23 loss.

"You want a Loser? Look no further than Bishop Mathis basketball! Some questioned whether the inexperienced Randy Hartman could step into the Paul Bunyan shoes left by Ty Roberson. Yes, some questioned Hartman's readiness. And now many, if not all, are questioning the wisdom of hiring Hartman. The Lancers played with a disturbingly listless lack of inspiration under Hartman's dubious leadership.

"Cleon Wilkerson, senior power forward on his way to the Weber State hoops program had this to say [cut to Wilkerson on camera]: 'I don't know. Coach Roberson, you know, you just wanted to play for, you know. You wanted, you know, to please him, you know, win for him. Coach Hartman, you know, he's all right, but he's not, you know, like Coach Roberson. He's an okay guy, you know, but he doesn't make me think, you know, that winning is, you know, important, you know.'

"The Lancers' woes have led to an avalanche of on-line fan commentary that makes me wonder if there's enough bandwidth on the World Wide Web to handle all of the anti-Hartman posts. One Lancer fan, known only as 'Moonguy,' has practically become a cult hero among Hartman haters . . .

"Moonguy!"

I pointed the remote and flipped to a children's channel that was showing a cartoon about what appeared to be a maggot and his best friend, a mute amoeba.

"Moonguy!"

I sighed.

After the "hello" breakthrough a week before, Cam's English vocabulary was expanding exponentially. She had mastered "goodbye," "couch," "door," "ball," "potty," and now, unfortunately, "Moonguy." Why she had to pick that word out of everything the moron hosting Prep Focus had said . . .

"Moonguy! Ball! Ball! Ball! Moonguy!"

My phone barked out "SLAAAAAM DUNK!"

I looked at the screen.

TRISH MANDERS

"SLAAAAAM DUNK!" the phone bellowed again.

"Hello, Trish?" I answered, aiming for a tone of voice that was appropriately cordial without sounding overly familiar.

"Randy. I am SO sorry!"

"About . . .?"

"Didn't you see it? That awful thing on Prep Focus just now? I couldn't believe that Cleon actually went on camera and criticized your coaching! I thought he was one of the nice guys on the team!"

"He is . . . once you get past all of the 'you knows.'"

"Oh . . . well . . . if you need to talk . . ."

"Naw, I'm fine," I lied. "Just goes with the territory."

"Well . . . okay . . . Just don't hesitate to call . . ."

"I won't," I lied again. "Goodbye."

"Bye."

"Moonguy! Moonguy! Moonguy! Ball! Ball! Potty! Moonguy!"

I really needed to shoot some buckets and, five minutes later, that's exactly what I was doing.

Dribble. Dribble. Dribble. Drive. Lay it up and in.

"Moonguy! Moonguy! Moonguy! Moonguy!"

The persistent little voice was getting louder as Cam hobbled her way across the lawn to engage in what was becoming a ritual for her: cussing me out about basketball. I guess it was good to know that she was fitting into the local culture in at least one area.

Dribble. Dribble. Dribble. Drive. Lay it up and in.

"Moonguy! Moonguy! Moonguy!"

"How about we learn a different word today? Dad, or whoever I am, is already just a little bit tired of that one."

"Moonguy! Moonguy! Moonguy!"

"Isn't this the part where you tell me about goalies in basketball?"

"Goalie!"

Cam limped over and took up her usual station in front of the basket. So, I had managed to distract her away from repeating the handle of my most incisive critic, but had opened the door to another frustrating session of non-basketball.

"Goalie"

"All right, all right . . ." I rolled the ball gently toward Cam. She reached down and stopped it. "Goalie!"

Clutching the ball, Cam raised her arms in triumph.

"Okay, nice stop, Goalie. Now, if you could . . ."

Cam turned and threw the ball up toward the basket. The ball landed on the rim, wobbled for a second . . .

"Oink-Oink needs a new name."

"I'm making potty, Ling. We can talk about this later."

That girl . . .

"Why can't we talk about it now? You aren't doing anything except make potty and that's not very hard, is it?"

That girl . . .

"How can I be thinking about Oink-Oink and do a good job making my potty?"

"Thinking about Oink-Oink will make you forget how to make potty?"

"All right, all right! What do you want to say about Oink-Oink?"

"He needs a new name! Oink-Oink is a mean name. We called him Oink-Oink back when we thought he was mean. And he isn't. He isn't and you know it. And I've been saying he isn't mean for a long time and you haven't been listening! So, he needs a new name!"

"Listen, you stupid baby . . ."

"And don't try to make it look like you know more than I do, Cam! Don't refuse to change Oink-Oink's name just so you can show me you think I'm stupid!"

"That is NOT what I'm doing! I would NEVER do that!"

"Yes, you would. You do it all the time."

"And don't call me 'Cam.' Call me 'Nanny Cam.'"

"You want me to think that you're grown up and a really good nanny that I should listen to? Think about this. Grown-ups change their minds.

"Grown-ups think one way about something and then they find out something they never knew before and they change their minds. It's only stubborn kids who don't change their minds!"

"You would know all about stubborn kids, I guess."

"I know enough to know that you are acting more like a stubborn little girl than a grown-up nanny lady! How can I learn anything if you don't start trying to be more like a grown-up!"

"Turn around! I am getting off the potty now!"

"We're both girls!"

"I don't care! It's not dignified for a baby to see her nanny with her pants down! It was okay when I was trying to potty-train you, but that's over! Turn around!"

"I'll turn around if you'll change Oink-Oink's name!"

"All right! I'll change Oink-Oink's name! Turn around!"

"Tell me his new name!"

"I didn't say I'd change it right now! I have to think about it!"

"Okay . . . But you promise that you'll change his name?"

"I promise . . ."

That girl!

After I was done making potty and listening to Ling tell me all about how to be a grown up, I went downstairs to watch Kind Of Smart American TV.

Oink-Oink . . . I mean Whatever His Name Is . . . was already watching. It was something about Stupid American Soccer and maybe some other Stupid American Games I didn't know anything about.

I didn't want to watch, but there wasn't anything else to do, so I sat down on the couch.

"[American gibberish], [American gibberish], [American gibberish]," some Stupid American kept saying on TV.

I didn't have anything else to do, so I decided to think about a new name for Whatever His Name Is. What name could I give him that wouldn't be kind of mean like Oink-Oink?

He was big. What else is big? Horses are big. I could call him "Neigh-Neigh."

Water buffaloes are big. I could call him . . . I don't know. Water buffaloes don't make any noise.

Ling said that he was nice. I wasn't sure about that, but maybe, just to make that impossible girl happy, I could give him a name like a very nice animal. What animals are nice? Cats are nice. I could call him "Meow-Meow."

Just then, the Stupid American On TV made a sound that was kind of funny. He said: "Moonguy." I didn't know what "Moonguy" meant, but maybe it would be a good name for Whatever His Name Is.

"Moonguy!" I said. Whatever His Name Is didn't seem to like that very much. So, I decided not to give him that name.

But it was still a fun word to say, so I kept saying it. "Moonguy! Moonguy! Moonguy!"

Whatever His Name Is's telephone yelled at him that somebody was calling. He answered and talked American gibberish for a while.

I thought I heard a girl's voice on the other end, but couldn't be sure. Maybe he had a girlfriend! That would serve stupid Peep-Peep right, wouldn't it? Then she'd be sorry she never cooked dinner or cleaned house or washed clothes or any of the other things good Vietnamese wives do.

I wanted to go upstairs and tell her that her husband had a girlfriend and she should get herself up out of bed and do something about it, like make him dinner and then smack-smack his lips and tell him he's her lovey-dovey! But I didn't think Peep-Peep would do that.

Whatever His Name Is turned off the TV and went outside. I knew that he was going to go play Stupid American Soccer. I knew that I had to keep trying to show him how to do it right.

I told Ling to stay on the couch. I didn't want her out there asking me about new names when I was trying to teach Whatever His Name Is Smart Vietnamese Soccer.

I was a Limper Girl all the way out to the Stupid American Soccer Field (which didn't even have any grass on it).

I really liked my new word.

"Moonguy! Moonguy! Moonguy!"

Whatever His Name Is was doing it wrong, just like he'd been doing it wrong all along. He bounced the ball with his hands and then threw it up at the orange circle thingee. I limped out and stood in front of him.

"Goalie!"

He rolled me the ball.

"Goalie!"

I think he wanted me to roll the ball back. I wanted to do something to show him how silly Stupid American Soccer was.

What would be really silly? How about if the Goalie threw the ball at the orange circle thingee? That would be really stupid and silly. Then maybe he'd start to understand what I was trying to tell him.

So, I turned around and threw the ball up at the orange circle thingee. It bounced onto the orange part . . .

And then fell through the white rope thingees hanging down from the orange circle thingee.

I stood there, like a complete moron, staring at the hoop. Had Cam just done what I thought I'd seen her do? Had she just actually made a basket?

On her first try?

Cam caught the ball, turned and grinned at me before rolling the ball back my direction.

"Moonguy!"

I picked up the ball. Had to have been a coincidence. Pure dumb luck. Right?

I rolled the ball back to Cam. She stopped it.

"Goalie!"

She was about to roll the ball back to me when I motioned for her to stop.

I pointed to the basket and to the ball.

Cam kind of shrugged, turned around and threw the ball toward the basket.

Swish.

"Moonguy!"

I sprinted up and grabbed the ball out of the air. I motioned for Cam to take a couple of steps back, further away from the basket. I gave her the ball and motioned for her to take another shot.

Swish.

I took her back a couple more steps and gave her the ball.

Swish.

I was about to walk back a couple more steps, when she grabbed my leg, pointed to the ball and then pointed to me.

I nodded and took an easy jumper.

Swish.

"Moonguy!"

I retrieved the ball and then walked Cam back a couple more steps.

She took the shot. The ball hit the rim and then ricocheted back.

I took the rebound and then shot from the same spot.

Swish.

Without thinking, I said: "Moonguy!"

Okay, now THAT was losing my head, wasn't it?

Cam shook her head, turned her back to the basket and motioned for me to shoot.

I did exactly that . . . and missed . . .

"Moonguy!" Cam shouted.

I picked the ball up and bounced it absently for a few seconds.

Something was familiar . . . very familiar . . .

Evelyn's face popped into my head. Oh yuck gross. Why would I be thinking about HER right at that moment? Why not something more pleasant like root canals?

And then . . . I remembered . . .

"No! Not Moonguy!"

Cam looked at me expectantly.

"Moonguyen!"

My Apologies

posted by MOONGUY:

With summer hoops camp only two weeks away, it looks like Randy Hartman might finally have something to crow about. Shane Henderson, the freakishly tall eighth grader who up until last week called Tacoma, Washington, home, has enrolled for the fall semester at Bishop Mathis. Henderson, rated as the top prospect in the entire state of Washington, abruptly became available when his mother, Ruth, decided to head south after her divorce from Shane's father became final at the end of May. Little is known about Shane, except that his size and athletic prowess qualify him as one of the biggest catches of this or any other season. If Coach Hartman can mentor Shane and develop his talent, he'll find himself coaching a once-in-a-Halley's-Comet superstar.

I zipped the car into the driveway and skidded to a stop. Something loud and raucous and testosterone-laden was blaring from my radio. Whatever the song may have lacked in artistic content, it had the virtue of matching my mood.

For the first time since the start of last year's basketball season, I was feeling good about being Randy Hartman.

Shane Henderson was a gift from heaven, an obscenely huge pot of gold sitting at the end of an unexpected rainbow.

There wasn't a prep hoops coach in the nation who hadn't heard of Shane Henderson, hadn't drooled over his massive and still-growing frame and hadn't fantasized about the kind of utter dominance that the kid would impose on any and all opponents.

And I hadn't had to lift a finger to land Shane Henderson, except to pick up the phone when it had started buzzing urgently in my office at precisely 1:58 that afternoon (yes, I noted the time).

"Coach Hartman? This is Ruth Henderson. My son is Shane Henderson. We are moving to your area and I wish to enroll Shane at your school. Will you see to it that all of the paperwork is taken care of?"

And, just like that, Bishop Mathis High School seemed to be back in the business of winning basketball championships.

I flew out of the car and all but floated over the lawn. Life was good. Life was very very good.

All it took was opening the front door for all the air to bust right out of the balloon.

On the couch sat Shelley, dressed as if heading for a job interview. That should have been another big dose of good news . . . if it weren't for the two large and clearly very packed suitcases.

Shelley hit me with an accusation-laden stare.

"Come to counseling with me, Randy. It's that or I leave!"

"Why don't you just call him 'Papa'?"

That girl . . .

There she was, as usual, trying to tell me, her nanny, how to do things.

"Because he is NOT my Papa! He's just a stupid American man who thinks he can be my Papa!"

"If he isn't your Papa, who is?"

"My Papa is whoever my mother without a name was married to when she had me."

"Who was that? What was his name? Was he nice? Or did he have two great big ugly teeth that hung out of his mouth even when it was closed?"

"What kind of question is THAT?"

"The kind of question that shows you don't know who your Papa was!"

"Well, it doesn't make any difference WHO my Papa was! It's the mother who has the baby, not the Papa! The Papa doesn't have anything to do with it!"

"Then why do women wait to have babies until they get married?"

"Because, stupid baby, they need a husband to go out and work in the fields and bring home food for the baby. They get married and then they say, 'Okay, I'm married and there's a man here to go out and work in the fields and bring home food. I think I'll have a baby now.'"

I was getting really irritated with Ling.

I didn't want to be explaining things like having babies to a stupid baby. I wanted to be out playing American Soccer with Whatever His Name Is.

We'd been playing American Soccer for about a week and I guess I didn't think it was so Stupid anymore.

I was able to throw the American Soccer Ball through the round orange thingee and that seemed to make Whatever His Name Is very happy.

Except I didn't think that what we were playing was real American Soccer.

We didn't run like the American Soccer players on American TV. Which was good, I guess, because I was a Limper Girl and there wasn't any Goalie in American Soccer.

And this was right when I should have been out playing American Soccer with Whatever His Name Was, but it had been a real upsy-downsy kind of day.

Peep-Peep had finally gotten out of her bed. That was upsy-downsy right there.

But then Peep-Peep talked American gibberish into her telephone for a long time and went into her room for making potty and stayed in there for a long time, too long to just be making potty.

I didn't see any of this, but I heard it when I was sitting downstairs.

Then, Peep-Peep came downstairs. She was dragging two big bag things. And she was dressed very nicely (for a Stupid American Woman). I hadn't seen Peep-Peep dressed like that since she and Whatever His Name Is kidnapped me.

She sat down like she was waiting for Whatever His Name Is. I thought for sure she was going to tell him that he was her lovey-dovey and they were going to smack their lips like lovey-doveys do.

I didn't want to see any yucky lip smacking, so I Limper Girled upstairs to put Ling down for her nap. Ling didn't want to take a nap, but I didn't care.

And then I heard Whatever His Name Is come in the front door. But I didn't hear any yucky lip smacking.

A few minutes later, Whatever His Name Is came into my bedroom and moved his hands to show me that he wanted me to come with him.

And so now, instead of playing American Soccer, I was sitting in the back of the car, arguing with Ling (and nannies should never have to argue with their babies).

"You should call him Papa."

"And you should be quiet!"

"Call him Papa."

"YOU call him Papa. Now be quiet!"

I wasn't a happy Limper Girl at all.

Ms. Chaves. My judge, jury and executioner. Or so I imagined.

Ms. Chaves advertised herself as a "family dynamics counselor" and the waiting room bore that out. Toddler toys were scattered all about the floor. One entire wall of shelving was taken up by a doll collection that must have made Shelley emerald with envy.

Ms. Chaves opened her office door and beckoned us to enter. I took one look and concluded that this wasn't going to go very well for me.

With the withering stare she gave me, I got a feeling that our counselor already had her mind made up about who was the bad guy here.

"So, Mr. and Mrs. Hartman, what seems to be the problem?"

No "hello, how are you?" No "would you like some coffee?" Straight to the point.

"The problem is that Randy is just not very supportive."

About twenty minutes later, Shelley had said more than I had heard from her in the previous four months combined.

"For the sake of my own identity as a person, I have to know that Randy is going to change."

Ms. Chaves held up her hand in a "stop talking" motion, wrote furiously on a yellow pad and then turned to me.

"Mr. Hartman, how do you feel about what Mrs. Hartman just said?"

"Well . . . umh . . ."

Peep-Peep and Whatever His Name Is went into a little room with a woman whose face looked very unhappy.

I sat down on a couch and looked around. I didn't know what this place was. I didn't know who the unhappy woman was. I didn't know what we were doing there.

"I'm bored," Ling said. "There's nothing to do."

"Be patient," I said, not wanting Ling to know that I was bored too. "This is a place where stupid babies come to learn how to be patient."

"Is that why there are all of those babies over there?"

I looked where Ling was pointing. I saw a whole bunch of dolls. Ling was a stupid baby so she thought they were all real babies and not dolls.

"Yes. That's what all of those babies are doing. They're learning how to be patient. Look how nice and quiet they all are. You should be nice and quiet, too."

"They're not all being nice and quiet."

"Yes, they are!"

"Can't you hear her?"

"Hear who?"

"The baby on the bottom shelf, right in the middle. The brown one. I think she's Vietnamese, like us."

"The baby in the middle is being nice and quiet, like all of the rest. If she's Vietnamese, then she's probably being nice and quiet better than the stupid American babies."

"I'm Vietnamese and I'm not nice and quiet."

"I know and you're embarrassing Ba Ho."

"I think she's crying."

"No, she isn't! She's . . ."

I stopped. I listened very hard. Stupid baby Ling was right. The Vietnamese baby was crying.

I got up and limped over to the shelf with all of the nice and quiet babies. I picked up the Vietnamese baby and held her in my arms.

I kissed the Vietnamese baby's forehead.

"What's wrong? Why are you crying?"

The Vietnamese baby looked up at me. She stopped crying. Which was because I was such a good nanny . . . right?

I limped back over to the couch.

"Don't you be jealous, Ling. I'm just holding this baby until she stops crying and goes back to sleep and then I'm going to put her back with all of the stupid American babies."

I looked down at the Vietnamese baby.

"You're a very nice baby. What is your name?"

The Vietnamese baby stared back at me.

"Why did you kill me, Cam?"

" . . . so . . . I don't know . . . I want to be a good husband and I want to be a good father. And I'm sorry for not being supportive enough of Shelley and not understanding everything's she's going through.

"I don't know. Maybe this whole adoption thing was a mistake. I just . . . don't know . . ."

Ms. Chaves hadn't let up with her cold hard if-it-weren't-for-men-there-wouldn't-be-any-problems stare the whole time I'd fumbled my way through answering her question.

"Do you have anything else to say, Mr. Hartman?"

"No . . . just . . . I'll try harder . . . I guess . . ."

Ms. Chaves' pen was a blur as she made a bunch more notes. Shelley and I were both very quiet as we waited.

"I don't believe you, Mr. Hartman."

"I . . . what do you mean . . . you don't believe me?"

"The whole mea culpa speech you just gave us. It's all your fault. That's really how you feel?"

"Now, look, Ms. Chaves . . ." I did my best to scowl up into a look of indignation.

"I came here in good faith. A lot of husbands wouldn't have even . . ."

"Mrs. Hartman virtually abandons you emotionally as a response to her fertility issues. She shoves adoption down your throat as a quick fix to her own self-image deficit and expects you to jump in with both feet."

Shelley's lower jaw began to slowly drop.

"After the American adoption falls through, she commits emotional blackmail by sinking back into a depression and then demands you acquiesce to the Vietnamese adoption."

"What . . .?" Shelley spluttered.

"When your new daughter turns out be a flesh and blood human being with a mind of her own and not a little brown Barbie who instantly delights in playing dress up, Mrs. Hartman sinks back under the bed covers, leaving you to try to raise a girl you really didn't want in the first place while trying to keep your career from falling apart.

"She then drags you into counseling, whines like a spoiled princess about your 'lack of support' and sits back waiting for the feminist counselor she's lobbed at you like a grenade to put you in your place, force you to absorb all of the responsibility for the extreme dysfunctionality from which your family suffers and demand that you move heaven and earth in order to clean up the mess she's made of all three of your lives.

"So, Mr. Hartman, when you say that you are consumed by an overwhelming sense of guilt about the last several months, I have a hard time finding credibility in your statement."

Ms. Chaves was beginning to grow on me.

She turned to an astonished Shelley.

"Yes. I know. I'm a woman. I was supposed to eat up your self-absorbed bellyaching with a knife and fork and verbally slap your husband around until he waved a white flag.

"I will say that, while Mr. Hartman seems sincere in many ways, he is obviously lacking some basic parenting skills. He doesn't get off scot-free by any means, but I'm really very clear where the bulk of the responsibility lies. Mrs. Hartman, a little girl cannot raise a child. Only an adult can do that. You want this to work, Mrs. Hartman?

"Grow up. Fast."

Shelley gaped at Ms. Chaves.

She looked at me.

She looked back at Ms. Chaves.

She looked at me.

She looked back at Ms. Chaves.

She looked back at me.

"Randall Hartman! Are you going to let this woman speak to me that way?"

Whatever I was going to say is now lost to history.

Because, at that very second, Cam began screaming out in the waiting room.

"I'm sorry! I'm sorry! I'm sorry! Hoa, I am sorry!"

I burst out into the waiting room, followed closely by Ms. Chaves.

Cam lay on the rug, clutching a doll and sobbing incoherently. At first, I thought that the doll was Ling, but then I saw Ling face down on the rug, looking as if she'd been flung away. And I couldn't help but notice this new doll's brown skin.

I looked helplessly at Ms. Chaves, who herself seemed pretty unnerved.

"Cam? I . . . umh . . ."

Cam kept repeating something in Vietnamese over and over and over again.

I reached down and gently touched Cam's shoulder.

Cam rolled away, spat out something at me in a pretty vile tone and then continued cradling the doll while she cried.

"What do I do?"

"Be her father!"

"No . . . I mean . . ."

"I know what you mean, Mr. Hartman. And I am telling you. Be her father!"

I sat down on the couch. Shelley appeared in the doorway from Ms. Chaves' office.

"And what about her mother?" I asked in what was probably a pretty unkind tone.

Ms. Chaves turned and looked at Shelley and then looked back at me.

"When she's ready . . ."

"What? And you think *I* am ready?"

Ms. Chaves unconsciously licked her lower lip in a little half second of seeming indecision.

"You're going to have to be, Mr. Hartman."

I looked back down at Cam and then closed my eyes.

Who was that rolling around on the floor, crying her eyes out? Was that really my daughter?

That woman in the doorway. Was that really my wife? Was I really her husband?

Was I really this girl's father? Were we really a family? Was I about to wake up? Was it still five years ago in the real world and had this nightmare taught me something?

I opened my eyes.

The girl was still crying.

The wife was still a statue.

And I was still sitting on that couch, wondering what had happened to my life and fearing that it was all beyond fixing.

"I can't tell you what to do, Mr. Hartman. But maybe I can give you a hint. She can keep the doll."

I nodded as if I understood.

"Well, that's something . . . I guess . . ."

"Can you and Cam come back to see me on Friday? 3:30?"

"I . . ."

Cam's crying began to soften.

"If you have any interest at all in getting your life back, Mr. Hartman, the answer is yes."

"All right then . . . yes."

"Then I will see you and Cam on Friday."

Cam's crying stopped altogether.

"Friday . . ."

Ms. Chaves closed the door to her office. I looked up at Shelley.

"Friday. Cam and me. 3:30."

As if Shelley hadn't been standing there the whole time.

"And she can keep the doll."

Shelley just kept staring.

"Don't look at me. You picked her."

Shelley stopped staring and walked over to Cam.

"Ashley . . ."

Cam screamed something up at Shelley. It sounded like it was probably obscene.

"I wouldn't call her that, if I were you."

"Ashley, I'm your mother and . . ."

Cam screamed something else that didn't sound any friendlier.

"Cam. She wants to be called Cam. That's her name, Shelley. What if I suddenly starting call you 'Marcia'? How would you like that?"

"Ashley! Listen to me!"

Cam screamed yet a third really nasty-sounding scream at Shelley. She struggled to her feet, still holding the doll tightly. She stumbled to the waiting room door and struggled to get the knob turned.

"Cam! What about Ling?"

I reached down and picked Ling up off the floor.

"You can't just leave Ling here because you have a new doll!"

Cam pointed to Ling and then pointed to me.

"You want me to take Ling?"

Cam started trying to open the door again.

"Ashley! I am your mother! You listen to me this instant!"

Cam ignored Shelley. I stood up and walked to the door.

I looked at Shelley.

"Earn it. Earn it and then tell her to listen to you this instant."

What You Wish For

I couldn't tell right off which Henderson I disliked more intensely. Confusing insolence with manhood is a common malady among 13 year-old boys, so I was willing to cut Shane a little slack when he sauntered into my office wearing a backward Mariners cap and cool-guy shades with a smirk to match.

But then there was Ruth. A less gallant man might have described Ruth as "horsey." I think that the more polite word is "statuesque."

With the over-stylized pile of platinum on top of her head, flimsy white blouse and black skirt tailored in a why-did-you-even-bother-wearing-it length, Ruth seemed to be having a hard time letting go of seventeen. I'm sure it had been a glorious past full of prom dresses, letter-jacket boyfriends and varsity cheerleading.

Glorious.

But in the past.

Ruth wasn't terribly subtle about sizing me up as we shook hands and I offered mother and son comfortable chairs.

Ruth's cheesy wow-I'm-good-at-flirting smile told me that she was measuring to see if I could wrap comfortably around her little finger. She took a seat, expertly crossed her legs and raised her eyebrows slightly as if to say "Your move."

"First off, Mrs. Henderson, I just want to say how excited we are to have Shane enrolling at Bishop Mathis."

"As well you should be."

Okay . . .

"Our summer basketball camp opens next week. It's not mandatory that Shane attend, but I highly recommend it. We waive part of the fee for boys in the program . . ."

"Is that your wife?" Ruth asked, pointing to the picture of Shelley that was strategically positioned on the credenza in back of my desk.

"Yes, it is."

"She's cute." Something in Ruth's tone suggested that she intended less of a compliment than the word "cute" might imply in the abstract.

"I agree. Otherwise we wouldn't be married."

Ruth threw back her head in moderately exaggerated laughter. "I can't argue with your logic, Coach Hartman."

Why she didn't just come out with "There's no accounting for taste"? Shelley wasn't right at the top of my Favorite People In The World List right then, but that didn't excuse Ruth's cattiness.

"I'd like to take Shane out to the gym to assess . . ."

"Do you have any children, Coach Hartman?"

Hoa was starting to take a little bit of water. And she was looking a little bit better.

Ai had been right. Hoa needed water. There were lots of bottles in the Stupid Bedroom at the Stupid House and I'd filled one up.

I didn't want to watch Smart American TV or play Moonguyen with Whatever His Name Is. I just wanted to take care of Hoa.

The stupid doll that I'd called "Ling" was sitting way up high on a shelf that I couldn't reach. Whatever His Name Is had put the stupid doll up there after I'd thrown her out the door three times. And that was only because I didn't know how to open the window.

"You're just a stupid doll," I glared. "I don't want you anymore. Your skin is pale and sick like an American's. You're not Vietnamese at all. I just said that so you wouldn't feel bad about looking sick.

"I can't play any more stupid games with you because I have to take care of Hoa. Hoa needs water and she needs love. So, you can just sit up there and look sick all the time!"

After we'd gone to the place where I'd found Hoa, Peep-Peep had gotten quiet again. Whatever His Name Is kept trying to talk to Peep-Peep, but Peep-Peep didn't want to talk to him.

A couple of days later, Whatever His Name Is came into the Stupid Bedroom early in the morning. He motioned that he wanted me to come with him.

"Is this really necessary?"

I nodded. "If you want the discount on the summer camp, he has to be on my roster. To be on my roster, he has to try out."

Ruth sighed as if no one had ever tried her patience quite so thoroughly.

Shane sauntered out onto the gym floor with a sense of fashionable disaffection.

His physique was indeed impressive even if his manners were underwhelming. The biggest uniform we had still looked about two sizes two small. Instead of stretching tortuously over Shane's enormous frame, his arm and leg muscles already gave a sense of definition more worthy of an 18 year-old.

I'd expected awkward gawkiness, but Shane's body seemed to have sacrificed little in the way of coordination in exchange for size.

I tried to picture Shane playing eighth-grade ball and kept coming up with a man among boys, a redwood among mulberry bushes.

Shane absently put his hands on hips and gave me a what-do-you-want-me-to-do-now look. I tossed him a ball.

I didn't have to see him work in the paint. I already knew that he would dominate even the biggest centers under the basket.

"Let's see you dribble." Ball-handling is the one weakness that seems to be universal among big men. That's why you coach your centers to fire off passes to point guards after a defensive rebound.

But there stood Shane, dribbling adeptly and moving gracefully. It almost made me think that I might be able to trust him to bring the ball up court on occasion.

"All right . . . now . . . take it up to the top of the key and give me a jumper."

Shane went one better than that. He retreated back beyond the three-point line and fired at the basket. Nothing but net.

He was big . . . no, he was huge. He was strong. He could move like a ballerina and shoot like a sniper. No weaknesses.

Shane's was a face that would soon be sneering off the cover of Sports Illustrated. A vision of a spectacular future in which four state prep championships would just be little preludes to the NCAA Final Four, the NBA Finals, trophy cases full of awards, celebrity endorsements, Hall of Fame inductions.

In short, Shane Henderson was . . .

Perfect.

Right?

At first, I got excited because I thought Hoa and I were going back to Vietnam. I recognized the place where airplanes drive. Why else would Whatever His Name Is take us there? But then Peep-Peep got out of the car, Whatever His Name Is got her big bag things for her and we drove away.

I wondered where Peep-Peep was going. Maybe there was a special school for Stupid American Women who didn't know how to cook or sew. Whatever His Name Is should have sent her to that school a long time ago. I'll bet he'd have been a lot happier.

We didn't go back to the Stupid American House. We went someplace I'd never seen before, with lots of buildings.

I had to limp a long way following Whatever His Name Is, but we finally got to a really really big building. He took me down to a room where a Stupid American Woman was sitting, except she wasn't so stupid for an American woman.

She pointed to herself and used an American gibberish sound I had a hard time understanding. But she said it over and over again until I heard "Trish."

I decided not to call her Peep-Peep or Oink-Oink or Moo-Moo or anything mean like that. I'd just call her "Trish."

Trish was nice. Trish was a lot nicer than Peep-Peep, but I guess that wouldn't be too hard. She showed me some pictures of a pretty girl doing exercises and then pointed to herself.

I looked really close at one of the pictures. Yes, it was Trish!

I didn't have any American friends. I hadn't wanted any Stupid American friends. But Trish was nice. I wanted her for a friend.

"So, does my son make the team, Coach Hartman?"

I suppressed a grin. "Yeah . . . I guess so . . . Just wish he wasn't so short."

Ruth laughed artificially. "Well, I'll try to feed him more. Maybe he'll be tall enough someday."

I laughed back just as artificially. We could have been reading off a script. Repartee for the sake of repartee as we tried to fill the ten minutes or so that would pass before Shane came back from his post-non-workout shower.

Ruth bit down a little on her upper lip, as if she were trying to decide whether to speak her mind.

"How long has your wife been gone?" she asked abruptly.

Well, now we were a little off-script. And I wasn't entirely sure about my line.

"Uh . . . who says she's gone anywhere?"

"Your tone of voice when I asked about her picture. Your body language. The whole presentation, I guess. Women aren't really mind-readers, but, when it comes to this kind of thing, we may as well be."

I shrugged. "Well, Mrs. Henderson . . ."

"Actually, I'm taking back my maiden name. Colton."

"Miss . . . or whatever . . . Colton. At the risk of offending the mother of the greatest prospect I've ever seen . . . I don't discuss things like this with people I've just met."

"Oh, don't worry. No need to discuss. It's plain as sunrise. And call me Ruth."

Trish spent a long time looking at my leg. The short one.

I didn't like people looking at my short leg. I didn't like being a Limper Girl and I wished sometimes that I could just forget that's who I was.

But I didn't mind Trish looking at my leg. She was very nice and very gentle.

I felt like Trish understood what I was saying even though she did not know any real words.

Maybe Trish wasn't American. She sure wasn't Stupid!

I think Hoa was liking Trish too because she didn't cry the whole time!

Which got me to thinking . . .

Okay, so asking Trish to watch Cam while I met with Shane and Ruth may not seem like the smartest move, but what else could I do?

Shelley deciding she needed "time to think" and going to her sister Doreen's place in Oregon to do it was, in many ways, a blessing. Less tension. Less frustration. Less to remind me that my life was a chaotic mess.

But Shelley's departure left me with one major problem.

Cam.

I couldn't just leave her at home. I didn't have Clue One where to search for reliable day care. Time off was not an option.

So, that meant Cam was coming to hoops camp with me.

Every day.

For the foreseeable future.

I did everything I could to pump myself up after Ruth and Shane left.

Shane wasn't going to be a problem. No attitude issues. He hadn't been "sullen" or "egocentric." He'd been nervous. We were going to get along fine.

Right?

Ruth wasn't a manipulative control freak who'd sensed my loneliness like a shark senses blood and was going to play me like a cheap violin.

She'd been nervous, too. Anxious to protect Shane. Maybe feeling a little awkward herself in changed marital circumstances.

Right?

I'd willed myself into a good mood. I deserved it.

Right?

I could hear the laughter and giggling from all the way down the hall as I approached Trish's office.

I was an adult. I was a mature adult man completely in control of his emotions. I wasn't interested in Trish. Naw. The crush was just a response to the marital tension. Nothing serious. It was all so clear now . . .

I smiled as I walked into Trish's office.

Trish and Cam were sitting on the floor, Cam's leg resting in Trish's lap.

"It looks like things went well. Thanks for watching her, Trish."

"No. Thank *you*! Your daughter is wonderful! Oh, and I was thinking . . . about her leg . . ."

Cam looked up at me and pointed at Trish.

It came out as plain as day. No ambiguity at all.

"Trish your girlfriend!"

Meeting Of The Minds

"She your girlfriend!"

Cam pointed to the undeniably attractive blonde standing on the street corner we were passing.

"Smack! Smack! Smack!"

The smack-smack-smack part was a new addition Cam had slipped into her explosively expanding English repertoire just in time for our return trip to Ms. Chaves' office. I assumed it had something to do with kissing.

"No. Not girlfriend."

If I were the blonde, I wouldn't have felt too awfully special. In the space of five minutes on the road, Cam had designated roughly fifteen women, two of whom were using walkers, as my "girlfriend."

"She your girlfriend!"

Trish and I had managed to laugh off Cam's ineffectual match-making.

"I don't know where she got THAT!" I had spluttered out with an extremely embarrassed chuckle.

"Well," Trish had similarly spluttered, "at least she's giving me credit for good taste!"

Which was, truth be told, not what I wanted to hear.

How about: "I have a boyfriend already, Cam."

Or maybe: "Your dad is a very nice man, but he is not my type."

I'd even take: "Oh yuck gross! What makes you think I'd be interested in a goon like him!"

Anything but yet another ambiguous non-signal of Trish's possible interest in me.

I'd wanted to get good and self-righteously angry at Cam for embarrassing Trish and me, but she'd gotten this impish grin that I hadn't yet seen, almost like she thought she was sharing a joke rather than making me the butt.

"She your girlfriend!"

Cam pointed.

"Smack! Smack! Smack!"

I glanced out the window at the sidewalk for a confused second or two. There was no one in the vicinity. Only a stray cat.

Cam broke into convulsive laughter.

"Con meow! She your girlfriend! Smack! Smack! Smack! Meow! Smack! Smack! Smack!"

I wasn't going to dignify that one with a denial, but I was also having a hard time keeping a straight face.

"Meow! Smack! Smack! Smack! Meow! Smack! Smack! Smack!"

No point in fighting it. I laughed.

Cam turned and looked at me. She was quiet for ten consecutive seconds, so I figured she was thinking about something.

"You Randy!"

Peep-Peep was gone. She was really really gone! Hooray!

"We don't have to worry about Peep-Peep any more, Hoa. Now we can have fun!"

I was glad Peep-Peep was gone, but now I saw a new problem.

Whatever His Name Is needed a new wife. A new wife would have a lot of work to do because Peep-Peep hadn't been cooking or cleaning or lovey-doveying. We had to get the new wife in fast.

But I was a Smart Vietnamese Girl and I knew that Whatever His Name Is couldn't just go pick out a new wife.

He had to find a girlfriend first. That's just how it works. He had to find a girlfriend and bring her flowers and take her to dinner and hold her hand and tell her that she was his lovey-dovey.

I know! It seems like a stupid waste of time. Why couldn't he just smack-smack-smack-a girl and say: "You are my wife now. Come home and cook and clean and lovey-dovey with me"?

I don't make the rules. We'd have to do the whole girlfriend thing first.

Of course, I'd wanted Trish to be the girlfriend for Whatever His Name Is. Trish was the first Un-Stupid American I'd met. I liked her. She liked me. She was pretty. A perfect girlfriend! A perfect wife! A perfect American mother!

But Whatever His Name Is hadn't brought Trish flowers or taken her to dinner or held her hand or told her that she was his lovey-dovey.

Don't blame me, Whatever Your Name Is, when some other man brings Trish flowers and takes her to dinner and holds her hand and tells her that she's his lovey-dovey! I told you that Trish was your girlfriend, but you did not listen to me!

Since Whatever His Name Is was so stupid about girlfriend stuff, I knew I'd have to help him find one!

With Peep-Peep gone, Hoa and I got to sit up in the front seat of the car. Which was good because that made it easier for me to find a girlfriend for Whatever His Name Is.

There were so many maybe-girlfriends out there! All he had to do was stop the car, get out and smack-smack-smack one of them!

But no matter how many times, I'd pick a girlfriend for him, Whatever His Name Is never stopped! Not once! You'd think he could at least go talk to a maybe-girlfriend!

I saw a cat. I told Whatever His Name Is that he was going to wind up having to smack-smack-smack a cat if he didn't get to work.

I think he got my point because he started to laugh.

But he still didn't stop for a girlfriend.

So, I decided to take a rest from girlfriend-hunting.

Hoa was asleep in my arms. I loved her so much! I knew that Ling hadn't been real but I missed having Ling to talk to (even though she could be a stupid back-sassing baby sometimes) and Hoa was too little to talk yet.

I looked over at Whatever His Name Is.

I didn't hate him anymore. I really didn't. Ling had kept saying he was nice and I hadn't wanted to believe her, but I could see now that Ling really was pretty smart for a stupid baby that wasn't even real.

I had promised Ling to give Whatever His Name Is a new name. A promise is a promise, even if you make it to a baby who's not even real.

What name to call him?

I'd heard Peep-Peep use lots of words that could have been names for Whatever His Name Is but I don't think they were all nice names.

There was something Trish had said. Trish was an Un-Stupid American so she probably knew what she was talking about.

I didn't have to make up a new name.

He had a name already. Maybe I should start using it.

"You Randy!"

Ms. Chaves summoned us into her office at precisely 3:30.

I was a little startled to see that a fourth person was joining the session.

"This is Katherine Nguyen. Katherine is a Psychology major and is bi-lingual in English and Vietnamese. I asked her to assist today in communicating with Cam."

Cam pointed to Katherine. I knew what was coming next and was powerless to stop it.

"She your girlfriend! Smack! Smack! Smack!"

Ms. Chaves gave me a sternly questioning look.

"Smack! Smack! Smack!

I shrugged. "I have no idea."

Cam pointed to Ms. Chaves.

"She your girlfriend!"

Daggers shot straight out of Ms. Chaves' eyes.

Cam stopped mid-smack-smack-smack and sat down, clutching her new doll tightly.

"Now that we have whatever that was out of the way, I think it would be best if Cam and Katherine chatted a little bit and got to know each other."

I was confused.

But it was a good confused.

I think.

Katherine looked Vietnamese. But she said she was American.

She could talk in Vietnamese. Which made her the second Un-Stupid American I'd met.

Katherine told me that her parents had come to America from Vietnam and that she had been born in America.

"Why did your mama and papa want to come to a place where everybody is stupid?"

Katherine told me that I shouldn't say things like that. America was a wonderful place to live. Things had been very bad in Vietnam and her mama and papa were happy to have come some place where they could get a new start.

Well, that was fine for Katherine's mama and papa, but I hadn't wanted a new start and I told her so.

I told Katherine about how happy I'd been at Mercy House and all of my friends and how I got to be a nanny and a goalie.

I told Katherine everything.

Except I didn't tell her about Hoa dying because I took bad care of her. I only told her about Ling and how I'd been a good nanny and had let her stay at Mercy House even though my heart hurt to leave her.

I wanted Katherine to like me. And I didn't think she would if she knew the truth about Hoa.

Katherine translated most of what Cam told her with a very straight face.

And Cam had been talking non-stop.

She loved the orphanage. She loved the babies and the toddlers. She loved her nannies, especially Ai. She had loved Trinh, but didn't anymore because Trinh was a traitor.

She had not wanted to be adopted. She'd told Ai and anybody who would listen that she did not want to be adopted. They made her get adopted anyway.

Because they made her get adopted, she had to leave behind a baby named Ling. (Light bulb pops on in my brain.)

She loved Ling and was very worried about what would happen to Ling. Cam was the only one who understood Ling and knew what she needed.

She had wanted to take Ling to America but didn't want Ai to be sad and miss her too much so she'd let Ai keep Ling.

She hadn't liked Shelley or me very much. She thought that we were pale and looked sick.

And then Cam talked for a while and Katherine didn't translate. Katherine put her hand over her mouth like she was shocked.

"What is it?"

Katherine looked at Ms. Chaves with eyes that pleaded "don't make me tell him."

"You are here to translate, Katherine, not censor."

Katherine cleared her throat and had the look of a woman who was composing herself so that she could do a very distasteful job.

"Cam says that . . . please do not get mad, Mr. Hartman. Cam says that she was afraid . . . that you were going to molest her."

Ms. Chaves raised an eyebrow.

"Molest her? What? You mean like . . . *molest* her? Why did she think that? What did I do to make her think that?"

Katherine asked Cam in Vietnamese.

"She says that she had a friend at school who told her that men always tried to touch girls' bottoms. That was the only reason Americans came to Vietnam, so that men could touch girls' bottoms. And their wives help them touch girls' bottoms. So, she was scared of both you and Mrs. Hartman."

Cam chattered in Vietnamese. Katherine's look of distaste mutated into horror and then . . .

Katherine laughed. Katherine laughed one of those oh-my-god-I-shouldn't-be-laughing-but-I-can't-help-it laughs.

"And then she says that she . . ."

Katherine hesitated.

Cam laughed, apparently knowing exactly what story Katherine was having to tell.

Katherine hesitated another couple of seconds.

"She kicked you . . . right in the boy potty water maker."

Ms. Chaves raised her other eyebrow.

I had done something bad, hadn't I?

I should not have kicked Randy in his potty water maker.

I hadn't forgotten that I'd kicked him. But it was like I had forgotten. I guess part of me knew it was a bad thing to do and I was hoping that I hadn't really done it.

But telling Katherine about it, I got a kind of an I've-been-bad feeling and told her in a I've-been-bad kind of voice.

I was embarrassed. I wanted to tell Randy that I was sorry, but I didn't want to think about it anymore. I wanted to talk about something else.

"I'm glad Peep-Peep is gone!"

I decided that whatever Ms. Chaves had told Katherine she would be paid, I was going to have to double it.

"I . . . I don't know how to . . ."

"Just tell us what the girl said," Ms. Chaves commanded.

"Cam says that she did not know what to call you and Mrs. Hartman. She made up names."

Katherine hesitated.

"She says that she called Mrs. Hartman . . . Peep-Peep."

"Peep-Peep?"

"Peep-Peep. Because Mrs. Hartman reminds her of a chicken, peep-peeping all the time . . ."

Ms. Chaves seemed to be having some difficulty maintaining her professionally stony exterior.

"Peep-Peep?"

About five seconds passed before I absolutely detonated with laughter.

Maybe it wasn't anywhere near as funny as it sounded at the time, but I think I needed to laugh and laugh hard.

Cam started laughing again. We briefly made eye contact, as if some secret understanding passed between us.

I was still laughing pretty hard when Cam started talking again.

Poor Katherine had the look of a woman who wanted desperately to find a large hole and crawl in.

"And she made up a name for you, Mr. Hartman."

"She did . . . did she? What . . . I'm sorry . . . composing myself now . . ."

"Oink-Oink . . ."

Ms. Chaves fumbled with her pen as it dropped to the floor. From how snugly she was clutching her stomach, she appeared to be in some degree of pain.

Ghosts

"MOONGUYEN!"

I raised my arms in mock triumph.

"3-1."

Cam twisted up her face in a look of exaggerated disgust.

"No Moonguyen! No 3-1! 2-1!"

"What do you mean 'No Moonguyen!'? I made the shot!"

Cam firmly shook her head. Grabbing my hand, she hobbled her way to the space behind the trash cans. She pointed to the space. She pointed to the basket.

"Moonguyen."

"What? No! You changed the rules! How come I have to shoot from here for a Moonguyen and you get to stand right under the basket?"

Cam giggled, but did not back down. She pointed to the space. She pointed to the basket.

"Moonguyen!"

"Cam initially was very angry with both of you."

In my mind: "And I need to pay you $110 an hour to figure that out?"

Instead: "She seemed to be angry, yes."

"Coming from the Vietnamese culture, she has what we would regard as some strange ideas about gender roles. In her mind, a wife should keep house and raise children."

I wanted to say: "I may be starting to come around to the Vietnamese way of thinking."

Instead, I said: "American culture would be kind of a shock then."

"Yes, it has been quite a shock. I think we can safely say that Shelley came as a disappointment to her."

"There's been plenty of disappointment to go around."

"The professional literature suggests that there is a pretty standard pattern for a non-infant adoption. The child has two very intense emotional needs.

"First, sheneeds to mourn the loss of the previous caregiver. Second, she needs to attach with a current caregiver.

"That presents a bit of a dilemma for the child. In mourning, the child needs to blame someone. But, in attaching, the child needs to trust someone. It is not at all unusual for a child to split those needs between the adoptive parents.

"One parent takes the brunt of the rage; the other is vested with the child's love and trust. There is no definitive research yet, but I think it's safe to say that the more normal course is for the child to hate the father and love the mother."

"That seems pretty sexist."

Dry, ironic humor.

It's a gift.

Before I could shoot, Cam changed her mind.

In order to score a Moonguyen, it wasn't going to be enough for me to stand behind the trash cans. I was going to have to stand IN a trash can.

And shoot with my back to the basket.

With my eyes closed.

I flung the ball backwards over my head.

"Moonguyen!"

Since what happened next sounded suspiciously like a basketball bouncing off a garage door, it seemed that my optimism was premature.

"You appear to have made certain assumptions about me and my attitudes toward men, Mr. Hartman. Those assumptions are no more constructive than if I had decided, based solely on your profession, that you were a lumbering Neanderthal whose social views were more in line with medieval thinking."

"All right. I'm sorry. I just sometimes use humor to . . .defuse tense situations."

Ms. Chaves eyed me for several pregnant seconds.

"I understand. If, at any point, you elect to display any actual humor I will excuse your conduct accordingly."

She held the ice sculpture expression for two or three seconds before allowing just a flicker of a smile to skirt briefly across her mouth.

"Truthfully, though, Mr. Hartman, I guess I have to admit to making that very assumption. I trust we can each get past our prejudices?"

I smiled. For real.

"I will if you will."

"MOONGUYEN!"

"Oh come on! You didn't even draw iron!"

"5-2!"

"How was THAT a Moonguyen?"

"Cam had to make a decision. She needed a caregiver. Shelley defaulted on her motherly obligations. So Cam chose you."

"Humh . . . things did seem to get better real fast between us."

"That sort of whipsawing is not uncommon. One day, you're the personification of evil. The next . . . you're daddy."

"No! I am sorry! I am NOT going to hop on one foot and try to shoot!"

"I think there's something else."

"What?"

"I'm sensing a trauma. Something beyond abandonment. Something beyond peer group hazing. Something happened to your daughter, Mr. Hartman. Something horribly traumatic. Something she's not ready to talk about."

I thought for a moment.

"All of that about thinking I was going to molest her. Could that be it? Was she . . . sexually abused?"

The very thought made my stomach churn.

Ms. Chaves gave her pen a little chew.

"Possibly. That's not an illogical conclusion."

"How do we get her to talk about it?"

"We can't."

"What's missing?"

"In a word . . . trust."

Moonguyen was the best game I'd ever played.

Better than Smart Vietnamese Soccer even.

Nobody else could play Moonguyen better than me and I was just a Limper Girl.

Not even Randy. And Randy was a big strong man.

Every day, we'd play Moonguyen. And I kept winning. I couldn't count high enough yet to tell you all the Moonguyens I won by.

I liked the rules.

Maybe if I hadn't gotten to make up new rules every day, I wouldn't have liked Moonguyen as much.

I made lots of new rules one day. Randy had to stand in this big metal bucket where they put all of the garbage. It smelled like potty. But that's where Randy had to stand if he wanted to make a Moonguyen!

And he tried. And he tried. And he tried.

I guess it was a good rule because Randy didn't make ANY Moonguyens from the big garbage bucket.

So, I won.

Again.

"Have you spoken with Shelley? About when she plans to come home?"

"She needs some time, I think. I'll let her call me."

"Shelley may need time but your daughter needs a mother."

I was very quiet.

"Mr. Hartman? Randy? You need to call your wife. You need to try to resolve your problems."

I looked up at Ms. Chaves.

What I said next came as a complete surprise. To me, anyway.

"You're right. Cam needs a mother. I'm just not sure anymore that it should be Shelley."

I finally got Cam to understand that I wanted her to hold still. I counted with my fingers.

One, two, three, four, five.

I pointed to the top of her very still head.

"Keep it for a five count and I'll give you a Moonguyen. You don't even have to make a basket."

Cam probably didn't understand a word of that, but I was getting a little tired of being excluded from the Moonguyen rule-making committee.

She got the gist of it, though.

I put the ball on her head.

One . . .

The ball fell off.

"MOONGUYEN!"

"NO MOONGUYEN!"

Randy still didn't have a girlfriend, which meant he didn't have a wife, which meant that somebody else had to cook and keep house.

Even though I had my hands full taking care of Hoa, I decided that I needed to be Randy's wife, all except for the lovey-dovey stuff, until he got a new one.

After I beat Randy (again) at Moonguyen, he went upstairs.

I decided to surprise him and cook dinner.

"Have you told this Trish how you feel?"

"No."

"Do you plan to?"

"Whoever . . . plans . . . things like that?"

"Good point."

Randy ran downstairs, yelling some American gibberish.

He didn't need to do that. I had everything under control. It was just a little fire.

For once, Ms. Chaves backed off and just let me sit and think. And so I sat and I thought.

"I guess I need to try to fix this, don't I?"

"I guess you do."

We could have scraped the burned part off of the water buffalo things and they would have been fine. I'd have eaten them.

But Randy put Hoa and me in the car and we went to a place where they made the water buffalo things for us.

Even after burning the water buffalo things, I still thought I could be the wife, except for the lovey-dovey part.

Maybe Randy could have two wives. I could do the cooking and cleaning and the other wife could do the lovey-dovey.

Yes. That would work, if we could find Randy a wife who wouldn't mind me doing the cooking and cleaning so she could just lovey-dovey all day.

Choices

Tonight on Prep Focus: troubling new data on concussions may prompt expensive new football helmet rules; a look at some possible late bloomers who could turn into senior-year stars; plus a report on rumors that Randy Hartman's coaching career may not be the only thing in his life on the rocks.

posted by HARTMAN_HATER:
So that's Hartmoron's problem? He's not getting any [REMAINDER OF POST DEEMED INAPPROPRIATE FOR PUBLICATION].

posted by MOONGUY:
Whoever was responsible for leaking Coach Hartman's possible marital issues to the press should be drawn and quartered! A coach's personal life is off-limits! Always! NO EXCEPTIONS!

"MOONGUYEN!"

Cam pointed to the face of an astonished Kelvin Jones. The junior point guard had just surrendered a basket shot from the top of the key by a ten year-old girl who could barely walk.

"Three!" Cam bubbled. "Three! Three! Three!"

Kelvin shot me a "seriously?" look.

I shrugged. If I could get used to it, what's his problem?

"That wasn't a three, girl!" Kelvin argued (sort of good-naturedly). "The line's back there!"

"You're not going to win that one!" I barked out to Kelvin.

Third day of summer basketball camp at Bishop Mathis.

I couldn't impose on Trish to babysit Cam, no matter how enthusiastically she might insist that it was no imposition at all.

Ms. Chaves had helped me come to grips with the reality that Trish was the thin ice at the middle of my emotional pond and I was a pretty sorry skater.

"What is it about this Trish that attracts you?"

I had to think real hard. Surprisingly enough, I was having trouble coming up with an answer.

"She's cute."

So, I came up with what seemed like a brilliant idea.

Why not just bring Cam along to camp every day? She seemed to like basketball. She could sit with me on the bench, watch and learn.

"MOONGUYEN!"

But . . . that wasn't how it was working out.

"Cute? That's *it*? You have an overwhelmingly strong urge to risk your marriage over 'cute'?"

"No! You didn't let me finish."

"I waited three full minutes for you to say something after 'cute.'"

Cam had quickly made herself the center of attention. I could see now that shyness was not ever going to be a major issue in this girl's life.

"All right, guys! Playtime's over! Let's get to work! Cam! Come over here and sit down!"

"She's . . . she's . . . I don't know."

"She was a gymnast, you say?"

"Still is, I guess . . ."

"Most gymnasts are . . . diminutive, are they not?"

"Yes."

"So, Trish is small for an adult woman?"

"I guess you could put it that way."

"Cam! I'm serious! The boys have work to do!"

"MOONGUYEN!"

"Cam! I know that you understand what I'm saying! Get over here! Now!"

"Childlike?"

"What?"

"Female gymnasts often look much younger than their chronological age. They are childlike."

"Yeah. So?"

"When you first met Shelley back in college . . . was she . . . childlike?"

"I said I'd be happy to watch her."

The sound of Trish's voice startled me.

As she sat down next to me on one of the folding chairs that make up a "bench," it flashed through my mind that Trish Manders was both the person I most wanted to see and the person I absolutely did not under any circumstances want to see.

"I've got this under control. CAM! NOW!"

"MOONGUYEN!"

"I guess 'under control' is a relative concept?"

"CAM! DO NOT MAKE ME WALK OUT THERE AND DRAG YOU BACK!"

"Hey Cam! Aren't you going to say hi to me?"

Cam turned toward the bench and got a face-breaking smile.

"TRISH!" Cam squealed as she fast-limped toward us.

"The problem is . . . I don't know *how* to fix it."

"Just take the first step."

"And what would that be?"

Stupid America was getting less stupid all the time. Maybe someday I might actually not mind it so much.

Randy took me back to the place where I'd met my friend Trish.

I thought that I was going to get to see Trish but then we went into this great big giant room. A lot of boys were there.

I was sad at first that Trish wasn't there, but then I figured out that Randy had brought me along so that I could teach the boys Moonguyen. Some of them were pretty good at it.

Randy kept making me sit down and watch while he tried to teach the boys Moonguyen. But he wasn't doing it right. We'd been there two days already and Randy hadn't made anybody throw the ball from a garbage can yet or hold the ball on their heads.

That morning, Randy was yelling at me to stop teaching. I pretended like I couldn't understand what he was saying. The boys needed somebody who knew what she was doing to teach them Moonguyen.

But then I heard Trish's voice!

Time to take a break!

Other than competing with my daughter for coaching time, camp was going well.

Sort of . . .

"Does anybody here have the slightest idea what I mean when I say 'set a pick'? I know you don't see it a lot on Sports Center, but it is an important part of the game of basketball."

Nobody was arguing. Nobody was loafing. Nobody was yawning in my face.

But something was missing.

The guys seemed to be listening.

But my instruction didn't seem to be leading to much in the way of on-court performance.

"All right . . . take a break. It's hot in here. Let's stay hydrated."

I headed back to the bench, where Cam was excitedly explaining something to Trish with a combination of Vietnamese, quasi-English and some very emphatic hand motions.

Cam looked up at me and grinned.

"Trish your girlfriend."

No helping the fire-engine red my face was turning.

"No, Cam! Trish is my friend! She is NOT my girlfriend!"

I maybe said that a little too loudly. There was a noticeable lull in conversation throughout the gym for a few seconds.

Cam apparently took my return to the sidelines as an invitation to start haranguing guys into playing Moonguyen with her. I was just as happy to get her out of the picture.

I sat down and endured a brief mutually embarrassed silence.

"Your daughter seems to have some very definite ideas about how your life should be run."

I snorted. "She does at that."

More silence. More uneasiness.

"That guy on Prep Focus had no business talking about your marriage."

"Yeah, well, it was going to come out someday."

Trish took in a deep breath.

"I guess this is the part where I say how sorry I am and offer you a shoulder to cry on?"

"Actually, I think this is the part where I have a sudden and violent nervous breakdown, am carried from the gym in restraints by a pair of bald-headed nurses with tree trunks for biceps and spend the rest of my life having earnest conversations with invisible talking animals."

"At least you haven't lost your sense of humor."

"You think I'm kidding."

"No, I think you're hurting."

"MOONGUYEN!"

I looked over at Cam, who was once again astounding poor Kelvin with her uncanny shooting ability. She was a welcome distraction.

And, at that very second, I suddenly became aware that Trish and I were very much the center of attention. Guys were guzzling from water bottles, messing with their shoes or checking their text messages . . . but nearly all of them had one surreptitious eye on Coaches Hartman and Manders.

"Actually, Trish . . . this is the part where I say that I'm getting really uncomfortable, don't quite know what to say and need some time to think a few things through."

"Fair enough."

Trish rose to her feet.

"I've got some stuff that needs doing in my office."

"All right . . . listen up . . . scrimmage time."

I'm Still A Goalie

Randy? Ruth Henderson . . . I mean Colton! Sorry. Force of habit. Bad habit. Listen, I got your message about Shane missing basketball camp. I'm really sorry. He meant to be there, but with everything that's going on, he's still in a bad place. I'll try to get him there tomorrow, Friday at the latest. And I'm sorry your marriage breaking up made the headlines. Call me if you need anything . . .

I had counted four days. Yes, I could count that high.

One, two, three, four.

Four days that Randy had been taking me to try to teach Moonguyen to the boys. It had been hard work, but I liked it. I still wished Randy would let me use trash cans, though.

I had only gotten to see Trish once that whole time.

I tried to tell her that she could come and be Randy's lovey-dovey wife and I'd be the cooking and cleaning wife and we'd all be happy together, but I didn't know enough American words (yes, they were words, I guessed, not just stupid sounds) to make her understand.

So, Randy still didn't have a wife. And the boys still didn't know how to play Moonguyen right.

I hoped we'd have a rest day, but Randy got me up again on the fifth day and we went straight to the Moonguyen school.

I went out and made some Moonguyens with the boys. They all seemed to like me. And I liked them.

Not that I liked boys.

I was never going to like boys.

No lovey-dovey for me!

But if I could just get Trish to say that she'd be Randy's lovey-dovey, then I could just go be the cooking and cleaning wife and I wouldn't ever have to think about boys again! Wouldn't that be nice?

The boys who were trying to learn Moonguyen were really big and tall. They were even bigger and taller than Randy and Randy had been the biggest and tallest man I'd ever seen!

Well . . . I thought that the boys had been big and tall . . .

I had put Hoa down for a nap on a chair and she'd been sleeping for a long nap time when a new boy walked in.

And that boy was the biggest and tallest boy I had ever seen.

Ever, ever, ever.

The other boys stopped playing when the Really Tall Boy walked in and started whispering to each other.

A girl walked in with the Really Tall Boy.

Well, she wasn't really a girl. She was more like a wife-lady. And she was very tall for a wife-lady. Very tall.

I giggled when I saw the Really Tall Wife-Lady. I thought she'd forgotten to put her skirt on! But then I saw that she had a little black napkin thing on that was kind of like a skirt, but no skirt I'd ever wear out where people could see me! Especially boys . . .

I wondered if the Really Tall Wife-Lady was the Really Tall Boy's lovey-dovey, but decided that the Really Tall Wife-Lady was too old to be his lovey-dovey.

Randy got up and shook the Really Tall Boy's hand. Or he tried to shake it, but the Really Tall Boy didn't seem to notice.

The Really Tall Wife-Lady, though, seemed really happy to shake Randy's hand. She smiled and she laughed. It was a stupid laugh. A stupid laugh like somebody's who pretending to be laughing but not doing a very good job of pretending.

The Really Tall Boy went off through a door that I knew I wasn't allowed to go into. That was where the boys changed clothes, so I was happy I wasn't allowed to go through that door. Who wants to watch boys change clothes?

The Really Tall Wife-Lady followed Randy over to the chairs where he liked to sit.

The Really Tall Wife-Lady sat down right next to him!

She sat down real close to him!

No!

No, no, no!

The Really Tall Wife-Lady wanted to be Randy's lovey-dovey wife!

No! NO! NO!!!!!!!!!!!!

I limped over.

I could see that Randy didn't have a happy face on about the Really Tall Wife-Lady wanting to be his lovey-dovey wife. I was glad to see that, but I wanted to make sure.

"She NO your girlfriend!"

The Really Tall Wife-Lady laughed, but gave me a little look that said: "Maybe not yet, but I am going to be his girlfriend and you can't stop it from happening!"

I looked at Randy. I wanted to make sure he had heard me.

"SHE NO YOUR GIRLFRIEND!"

Every time I'd tried to talk to Randy about girlfriends before, he'd make a shush-shush motion. But Randy didn't make a shush-shush motion when I told him that the Really Tall Wife-Lady was not his girlfriend.

For once, I think he was listening.

Just then, the Really Tall Boy came out wearing his Moonguyen clothes. He walked by and looked down at me. He smiled at me, but it didn't feel like a nice smile. It felt like a mean smile. Like the kind of mean smile that Bullygirl Tham had on her face right before she tried to knock me down.

I didn't like the Really Tall Boy at all. I didn't like the Really Tall Wife-Lady with the teeny-tiny oh-look-at-me skirt.

I decided that I was not going to try to teach the Really Tall Boy how to play Moonguyen. Only nice people should get to play Moonguyen! So, I sat down next to the Really Tall Wife-Lady. I was going to keep my eye on her!

The other boys tried to shake the Really Tall Boy's hand. He didn't even seem to notice.

Summer basketball camp is not varsity basketball practice.

It's just that. A camp. A camp open to any boy who can pass a physical and pay a fee.

And there's always one poor guy who shows up, works his tail off and all he does is prove that he has no business on the court.

Clayton Bosch had tried out as a freshman. And I mean, he had really tried. He'd hustled hard. He'd taken criticism well. He'd shown up on time and done everything I'd asked of him.

A model player.

Except . . . Clayton was not a basketball player. Period.

It wasn't so much that he was short. I'd seen some 5'7" guys work into being pretty effective as guards. But that was because they had brought something else to the party. Athleticism. Ball-handling skills. An instinct for being where the ball happens to be.

Poor Clayton had none of that to offer. Slow, awkward and utterly incapable of competently executing two consecutive dribbles, Clayton Bosch was pretty much a catastrophe on the basketball court.

But . . . he passed the physical. His parents had paid the fee for camp. And there he was.

Wrong place. Wrong time.

Wrong everything.

There was this one boy at the Moonguyen school who wasn't tall. At all.

He'd throw the ball at the orange thingee and miss it completely. I knew it would be a long time before I'd be able to teach him to throw it from a trash can.

I called him Oh No. Which was because whenever he tried to throw the ball into the orange circle thingee I'd think "Oh no!"

And now I'm sorry I called him that silly name.

Maybe Oh No couldn't play Moonguyen, but that didn't mean he wasn't nice.

I'd fall down a lot when I was trying to teach Moonguyen. It's like I would forget I was a Limper Girl and try to run but then my leg would say: "Excuse me! Limper Girl Leg here!"

And I'd fall down. Sometimes on my bottom. Sometimes on my face.

And Oh No was the only boy who ever came over to try to help me up.

So, maybe I didn't think much of Oh No as a Moonguyen player, but I liked him as a person.

Not as a boy! I just liked that he was nice, okay? Geez! You say you like a boy and everybody starts thinking you want to lovey-dovey him! Stop thinking that!

Oh No kept coming to Moonguyen school. Every single day. So, he was there the day that the Really Tall Boy and the Really Tall Wife-Lady who didn't care what people could see when she sat down showed up.

Which was kind of too bad, don't you think?

Randy had been talking to the boys and then lined them up like they were Smart Vietnamese Soccer teams.

I didn't think that the boys knew enough yet to play a real game of Moonguyen, especially the Really Tall Boy because he hadn't come to any of the other classes, but Randy wouldn't listen to me (maybe because I didn't know all of the right American words yet).

The boys started trying to play Moonguyen. I decided that maybe Randy was right about not putting trash cans out. There was no way they were ready to do that!

I saw a problem right away. The Really Tall Boy was so tall that he was able to get the ball all the time.

And he never once shared! He just kept throwing the ball into the orange circle thingee!

I am sorry, Really Tall Boy, but that is NOT Moonguyen!

You share in Moonguyen! You let other people have chances in Moonguyen! And you do not knock other people on their bottoms in Moonguyen!

The Really Tall Boy was knocking a lot of other boys on their bottoms!

The Really Tall Boy was a bully, just like Tham!

A bully!

I hated bullies!

Why was Randy letting a bully into our Moonguyen school?

What if Randy really did want the Really Tall Wife-Lady for his lovey-dovey and that's why he was letting the Really Tall Bully knock everybody on their bottoms?

Just when I was about to give up hope, Randy stood up and started yelling. The boys stopped playing and Randy walked out to the Really Tall Bully.

"Dial it back a little, Shane! This is a high school basketball camp, not the NBA Finals!"

Shane loudly chomped on a piece of gum.

"Okay."

The word suggested agreement, but the tone implied otherwise.

"This is about technique. You're not showing me any technique. Just brute strength."

More chomping followed by another tepid "Okay."

I tromped back to the bench. Ruth was frowning.

"I thought that there might be somebody at this level who could challenge him."

Suddenly, I was finding nothing in the world that could grate on my nerves as badly as Ruth Henderson-Oops-I-Mean-Colton's voice.

"After all he's been through . . ."

Okay, so the Really Tall Bully maybe hadn't understood that Moonguyen was not a game about knocking boys on their bottoms. So, he had an excuse . . . to start with.

But after Randy talked to him, he didn't have any excuse.

After that, he wasn't stupid. He was just mean.

Oh No hadn't gotten to play and I was happy about that. Oh No was nice and I didn't want to see him get knocked on his bottom.

Randy pointed to some boys who'd been sitting down. Oh No was one of them. They got up and walked out onto the Moonguyen field. Some other boys left.

They started playing again.

The Really Tall Bully, just like always, got the ball. He started bouncing the ball and running toward the orange circle thingee.

And there stood poor Oh No.

The Really Tall Bully threw the ball up at the orange circle thingee, but he didn't stop running.

He ran right into Oh No.

Oh No didn't just fall on his bottom. That would have been bad enough.

Oh No went backwards real fast after the Really Tall Bully ran into him. He tumbled head-over-heels. Three times. He hit his face hard against the wall.

Oh No lay kind of still for a couple of seconds.

Randy got up and ran to him. I tried to limp as fast as I could.

Oh No started to sit up. There was more blood on his face than there was face.

And he was crying.

Randy knelt down and looked really hard at Oh No's poor face.

Everybody was really quiet.

Except the Really Tall Bully . . .

The Really Tall Bully was laughing.

Can you believe that? He was laughing at poor Oh No, just like Tham had laughed at me. Laughing because he had hurt Oh No. Laughing because Oh No was crying like anybody else would be crying!

Nobody had picked up the Moonguyen ball. It rolled right to my feet.

Oh No was trying to stand up, but I think Randy was trying to tell him to stay down.

The Really Tall Bully just kept laughing and laughing and laughing.

There's only one thing to do with a bully, I don't care if it's a girl or a boy!

I picked up the Moonguyen ball.

I lifted the ball up, pulled my arm back . . .

"I THINK SHANE'S NOSE IS BROKEN! THAT LITTLE BRAT OF YOURS BROKE MY BOY'S NOSE!"

From the little crunching sound we'd all heard when the ball hit Shane's face, I guessed that Ruth was probably right.

"AFTER ALL SHANE'S BEEN THROUGH! YOU'RE THE COACH! YOU'RE SUPPOSED TO PROTECT YOUR PLAYERS, NOT LET SOME LITTLE MONSTER OF YOURS INJURE THEM! HE'S GOING TO HAVE TO GO TO THE EMERGENCY ROOM!"

"Maybe he and Clayton can go together. Maybe the emergency room has a two-broken-noses-for-the-price-of-one deal . . ."

"MY BABY IS HURT AND YOU'RE MAKING JOKES?"

"No, Ruth. I'm not making jokes. They're more like wry ironical observations."

"YOUR GIRL DELIBERATELY TRIED TO HURT SHANE! AND SHE SUCCEEDED! WHAT ARE YOU GOING TO DO ABOUT IT, RANDY HARTMAN? WHAT ARE YOU GOING TO DO?"

Once again, just as it had been after I'd emphatically denied to Cam that Trish was my "girlfriend," the gym was quiet. Very quiet. All eyes and ears were focused on me.

"I think . . . I'm going to buy her a pony."

We All Have To Grow Up Sometime

posted by HARTMAN_HATER:

I am speechless! We had Shane Henderson! We had him! He was ours! And Hartmoron's kid pops him in the face with a ball? And Hartmoron laughs about it? And now Henderson's off to St. Vincent? Why is this clown still coaching? Why doesn't Hartmoron just take his stupid crippled kid and [REMAINDER OF POST DEEMED INAPPROPRIATE FOR PUBLICATION].

posted by CLAY313:

U r the moron, not Coach Heartman! Coach Heartman got rid of Shane Henderbutt because he was a big dumb stupid bully! Coach Heartman got rid of Shane because he didn't have any commitment! I like Coach Heartman! He is a good man! I don't want him to go!

posted by LANCERS_HOOPS_BOOSTERS:

If you're in town this weekend, be sure to come out to Overin Park for our Annual Independence Day Hoops Bar-B-Que! The fun starts at 11:00! There will be a bounce house and face painting for the kids! Plus a silent auction for all of you adult fans, featuring basketballs signed by Coach Ty Roberson. Plus there will be a raffle for a copy of Coach Roberson's new book, "The Keys To Success Are Already On Your Chain!" with a personal message inscribed from Coach R himself! All proceeds will go to career counseling and placement for Almost Former Coach Randy Hartman.

posted by MOONGUY:

I'm hearing this great wailing and gnashing of teeth over Coach Hartman dismissing Shane Henderson. Yes, I agree that Bishop Mathis has just lost out on one of the great raw talents in the history of the sport, but I think that it has also gained something in integrity. Coach Hartman has just made very clear that his program has standards and that those standards will be enforced regardless of talent. For the first time since taking over the reins, Coach Hartman has finally done something worthy of the title "Coach." Having said that, I will acknowledge that Shane Henderson's broken nose was a regrettable unforeseen consequence . . .

It was going to take some getting used to, I guessed.

Nobody was staring. But everyone was glancing over their shoulders, whispering remarks to one another.

Cam, thankfully, was oblivious. She'd set the newest baby doll ("Wah" or something) up in a high chair and was spooning little bits of oatmeal up to the baby's mouth.

I guess maybe it should have been a bit of a comfort. Would it be completely unreasonable to assume the possibility of foul play to see a white adult male transporting an obviously Asian girl?

But the covert attention we were receiving at the little diner inside the truck stop was making me a little nervous.

Cam chattered on, apparently admonishing Wah to eat more or not dribble her food or something.

Cam was holding up pretty well, considering that we'd been on the road close to seven hours. I'm not sure that the trip would have been possible before she had mastered the word "potty" in English.

"Wah! No!"

I had no idea what Wah had just done, but Cam seemed to think it was pretty flagrant.

Our jovial and unattractively over-buxomed waitress, Jojo, was a walking cliché. Call Central Casting, tell them you need a truck stop waitress. They send Jojo. Every time.

"Can I get you anything else, Hon?"

"Hon" seemed to be Jojo's nickname for anything male.

"No, thank you. We really need to get back on the road."

Jojo ripped our bill off the pad and slapped it down on the table.

"Whatcha doin', Sweetheart?"

"Sweetheart" seemed to be Jojo's nickname for anything female.

"You feedin' your baby doll? Isn't that precious? What's your name, Sweetheart? You look just like Pocahontas. Is that your name, Pocahontas? Is she Indian?"

I really didn't want to be discussing Cam, or anything else really, with a stranger, even a stranger as energetically friendly as Jojo.

"No. She's Vietnamese."

"Vi-et-nam-ese! Really! Well how about that? My brother, Cole? He was in the Army. Went to Vietnam. He didn't like it much. Cole didn't get into the fighting part, really. He was in Saigon, mostly. You know them helicopters they used? Cole ran this big warehouse where they kept all these spare parts. On account of the Viet Cong kept shooting at the choppers . . ."

"Very interesting. Do I just pay this to you or should I take it up front?"

"Cole says he didn't like Vi-et-nam-ese people much. Kind of lazy, I guess, was his beef with them. Said why should we be fighting to protect their country when they couldn't be bothered fighting for themselves?"

"Cam! We need to go!"

"But I know it's not like all the Vi-et-nam-ese are lazy. I can see Pocahontas here is just workin' up a little storm with her baby doll, aren't you, Sweetheart?"

After the Really Tall Lady-Wife with the tiny little skirt swung her purse at Randy, she yelled something at the Really Tall Bully and they left together.

I wanted to feel bad about hurting the Really Tall Bully, but I didn't.

All of the boys in the Moonguyen school must have felt good about it, too, because they came up to me and were laughing. Some of them patted me on the back. Which was kind of nice but kind of weird, too.

I was worried that the Really Tall Wife-Lady's purse might have hurt Randy's eye or something, but he seemed to be all right. After the boys had gotten done patting my back and saying nice things to me, Randy told them to all sit down.

Randy talked to them for a long time. I didn't know most of the word-sounds he was making, but the Moonguyen boys seemed happy. They clapped their hands a bunch of times.

When Randy was done talking, the boys all got up. Some of them patted me on the back again. It still felt kind of good and kind of weird.

That night, Randy put some of his clothes and some of my clothes in one of the big bag things. He dragged the big bag thing out to the car and then pointed for me to get in.

I said: "No!" I didn't say it because I didn't want to go with him but because I didn't have Hoa. I limped back to the house, picked up Hoa and was ready to go.

We kept passing motels at every off-ramp and each claimed to have vacancies.

It was tempting. I was tired. I'd had a long day.

But, time was short.

I didn't know for sure if I still had a job. But, until I was formally booted off the campus, I needed to act like I did. And that meant being back bright and early Monday morning for week two of basketball camp.

There wasn't much room in the schedule for anything other than driving.

I also wasn't sure how well it would go over for me to try to check in to a cheap motel with Cam.

I looked over at Cam, who was chastising Wah about something Wah had either done or failed to do.

The language barrier had developed some major cracks, but it was still there.

Even so, there were things I needed to get across and I needed to do it before we got to Oregon.

"Cam! We're going to see . . ."

I realized that I wasn't entirely sure what to call Shelley.

"Mom. We're going to see Mom. Do you understand?"

Cam gave me a blank look that seemed a pretty definitive "no."

"Mom . . . umh . . . We're going to see your Mom. She misses you and she wants to see you."

Good thing I was a real boy or my nose might have punched right through the windshield.

"Mom needed some time away. But I think she's going to want to come home now. I think . . ."

Cam's facial muscles hadn't so much as twitched.

"Mom . . . you know . . . Shelley . . ."

A grimace. That was at least a reaction.

"Shelley is your Mom. Now, you shouldn't call her 'Shelley.' Call her . . ."

"Peep-Peep!"

"No! No Peep-Peep! Mom!"

"Peep-Peep!"

"Mom!"

"PEEP-PEEP!"

"MOM!!"

"PEEP-PEEP! PEEP-PEEP! PEEP-PEEP!"

The situation was calling for another approach.

I pointed to myself.

"Dad!"

"Randy!"

"Dad!"

"Randy!"

"You are Cam! I am Dad! We are going to see Mom!"

"Randy! Peep-Peep!"

"No Randy! No Peep-Peep! Mom and Dad!"

Cam abruptly shifted her combat strategy to ignoring the enemy and started fussing with Wah again. They were apparently having quite a conversation.

The wheels in my brain slowly ground their way through my options.

"Wah!"

Cam kept on ignoring me.

"Cam is Wah's Mom."

More ignoring.

"You are Cam. Wah is your baby. You are Wah's Mom."

"No Mom! Nanny!"

Humh . . .

"What about Ling?"

"NO LING!"

"I thought you were Ling's nanny, too!"

"NO LING! NO LING! NO LING!"

"Okay. No Ling. I guess I fixed her for nothing?"

"NO LING!!!!!!!!!!!!!!!!!!!!!"

"No Ling? But Wah? Why? Why Wah and no Ling?"

Cam suddenly turned very quiet.

For a minute, anyway.

And then she started crying.

And crying. And crying. And crying.

It was a good thing that I wasn't a Crybaby Girl.

Nannies shouldn't cry in front of their babies, so I didn't. But Randy was making me sad talking about Hoa. I didn't want to talk about Hoa. I didn't want to talk about Hoa or Ling or Peep-Peep or anything.

I didn't want to talk. Period.

And I didn't cry. I just told Randy to be quiet and not talk to me about Stupid Baby Doll Ling anymore.

But then Hoa started talking.

"Randy made Ling all better. Maybe he could fix me, too."

"Ling was just a stupid baby doll. You are real, Hoa. It's easy to fix a stupid baby doll. It's not easy to fix a real baby."

"Don't you love me, Cam?"

"Of course I love you! I'm your nanny!"

"Then why won't you let Randy try to fix me?"

"Because . . ."

"I am dead, Cam. Do you want me to stay dead?"

"No! That's not what I'm . . ."

So then I cried. I was a Crybaby Girl.

Ms. Chaves apparently had known what she was talking about.

Cam sobbed for a good two hours. Or a bad two hours, depending on your point of view, I guess.

She clutched Wah like the doll was the last friend she had on Earth.

I drove on in silence. Just didn't seem like a good time for me to be sticking my nose in.

We were well past Shasta when Cam finally exhausted herself and nodded off to sleep.

I checked my watch and calculated an ETA.

So . . . what exactly do you say to your almost-estranged wife when you show up at 3:00 a.m. Unexpectedly. With a daughter in tow who has almost single-handedly driven her to a nervous breakdown?

We were about to find out . . .

Lovey-Dovey

"Hi, Shelley."

If this were a movie, Shelley would have come to the door in a silk nightgown, demure yet enticing. Her face would have lit up. Her lips would have parted. She would have blushed, hesitated and thrown her arms around my neck.

"Oh my God!" she would have sobbed. "I thought I'd lost you forever! Oh, Randy, I've been such a fool! Can you ever forgive me?"

The little bow at the center of the nightgown's neckline would have caught my attention. I would have fingered it, drawing out Shelley's suspense.

"No, darling. We've both been fools. Come, let us dance in the pale moonlight."

It was a terry-cloth robe, not a silk nightgown.

Oh . . . and . . . it wasn't Shelley who came to the door. Not at first.

It was Doreen. I won't tell you what she was wearing, just in case you're eating right now.

"You must be really threatened by me."

"Good to see you too, Doreen. I need to talk to Shelley."

"To come all this way. Are you afraid that I'm going to cast some spell on Shelley and make her love another man?"

"You're not a witch, Doreen."

"So quick to condemn what you cannot understand . . ."

"Any more than you were a Druid, a medium, a reincarnation of Marie Antoinette or any of the other identities you've tried on while I've known you. What do you run on these? A six-month cycle?"

"I am too a witch!"

"No, you're not, Doreen. Although I have to admit that the term does kind of fit in some ways."

"I wouldn't expect you to understand . . ."

"And I wouldn't expect you to have the slightest idea what you're ever talking about, Doreen."

It was then that Shelley appeared in the doorway behind Doreen. Yes, in that terry-cloth robe. I wish I could say something romantic here, like I'd have thought she was beautiful if she were wearing burlap. Notice that I'm not saying that or anything like it.

Shelley's face did not light up. Shelley's face didn't do much of anything, really.

"Cam's asleep in the car. May I come in?"

"He's threatened by my mystical feminine power, Shelley. Why won't he bring her in? Afraid I'll put a spell on her too?"

Shelley gently tapped Doreen on the shoulder and then pointed toward a hallway.

"What? You're ashamed of your sister now? After I've put you up and . . ."

"Shut up, Doreen, and go to bed." The very flatness of Shelley's tone conveyed something uncharacteristically powerful.

Doreen slunk off to bed, muttering about her family's nineteenth century attitudes.

Shelley's eyes met mine. There were blank, emotionless.

I guess I could have lived with screaming and yelling, a slap on the face and a brutally slammed door. That would have been something. A reaction. Anything . . .

"I'm probably unemployed come Monday. I may even be getting sued. Cam . . . umh . . . assaulted one of our prospects with a basketball. The guy was being a real jerk and Cam picked up a ball and she just . . . just . . ."

I couldn't help myself. I started to giggle.

"I mean, the guy's a monster, right? Huge . . . and there's Cam . . . barely comes up to his kneecaps and . . ."

My giggle turned to outright laughter.

"Everybody else is like scared of him . . . but not Cam . . . so, she doesn't even aim, really . . . and . . . POW! . . . flattened his nose . . ."

I was laughing so hard, I was starting to cough.

"CRACK! They could hear it break like out in the parking lot! And . . . umh . . . hold on a second . . . his mother, you know, she's been like all flirty with me and everything . . . and she like hits me in the face . . ."

Yes, I know. It really wasn't THAT funny, but . . .

I doubled over and did my best to compose myself.

"Hits me in the face with her purse . . . and so she and the kid are like leaving in this big huff . . . and she's got on this tight little skirt . . . wouldn't have made a good washcloth . . . and so Cam picks up the ball again . . . and . . . WHAM! . . . nails her right on her wiggly little fanny . . . and . . ."

Shelley's expression still hadn't changed. It was sobering me back up real fast.

"So, I'm probably going to get fired. My wife has left me and I've got no clue whether it's permanent. I'm in this place of questioning like everything I've ever done. It's pretty much your standard sense of everything spiraling out of control."

I looked back at the car.

"This is going to sound funny . . . but you want to know the one thing about my life that's working right now? Cam. She maybe just got me fired, but . . . She really is something special, Shelley. She's smart. She's funny. She's stubborn as a damn mule. And she needs . . . us . . . both of us.

"Ms. Chaves, who I know isn't high on your favorite people list right now, says that Cam is hiding some trauma. And I believe it. She cried for like two hours straight on the drive up. The doll she got from Ms. Chaves . . .

"I did a lot of thinking, after Cam finally fell asleep. And, I guess all I can say is it's time for me to grow up. Maybe it's time for me to give up coaching. That English class we met in? You know, I liked it more than I could admit at the time . . . I don't know . . . You're a writer . . . Do you think I could be? Babbling, aren't I?

"Maybe I need to talk to Ms. Chaves about this, but I do seem to babble whenever I'm really scared or nervous or something and I'm scared and nervous because I want to get our family back together and I really don't know how to do that and you're just standing here not saying a word to me . . ."

I woke up in a strange room. In a strange bed. With my clothes still on. Hoa was on the pillow next to me.

That's a kind of scary thing. To wake up someplace and not know where you are or how you got there or if you're alone.

I kind of crawled off the bed and leaned against it.

"Hoa, where are we?"

Hoa didn't say anything. And then I remembered that Hoa had died because I was a bad nanny.

I was alone, so there wasn't anybody to see if I was a Crybaby Girl, so I picked Hoa up, hugged her and started crying again.

"Cam?"

Limper Girls can't jump. Well, we can't jump very far. So, I didn't jump. I just kind of bobbed up and down a little bit.

Randy sat up. He'd been asleep, I guess, on the floor on the other side of the bed.

I was idly pushing some scrambled eggs around my plate. It was the coffee that I really needed and I'd already put away four cups.

Cam sat across from me. The size of the booth made her seem even smaller than she was. She would not let go of the Wah doll. Her hamburger was untouched.

"Sorry about this. Dumb stupid wild goose chase. Just looking to get control over something, you know."

If Cam understood a word, she wasn't letting on.

"So, here's the deal. I'm your Dad. And I like that. I know it sure didn't seem like it at first, but I want to be your Dad. Which would be great and terrific and all of that except I don't have the slightest idea where we're going to be living.

"We came all the way up here to see if I could get your Mom back at least."

Cam was softly stroking Wah's hair.

"Let me get this part right . . . let me be your Dad . . . that's the important part . . . and then maybe we'll see about the rest."

"SLAM DUNK!!!!!!!!!!!!!!!!!!!!!"

I was hoping against hope that it would be Shelley calling. Part of me was disappointed . . . but then . . .

"Whoa, Dude! SHE is like calling EWE!"

Seventeen Year Old Randy was leering at me from somewhere inside the mists of my libido.

"Shut up," I said sullenly to Seventeen Year Old Randy.

"Trish . . . what's up?"

Trish's tone was frantic.

"Randy! Where are you?"

"Umh . . . well I was making a heroic effort to save my marriage . . . kind of trying the knight in shining armor deal. But maybe the dragon ate me. I wish I could give you something more definitive on my marital status. Don't want to leave you hanging . . ."

"What do you mean . . . leave me 'hanging'?"

"Well . . . umh . . . you know . . . you and me . . . the Thing. You know . . . the THING! Except . . . we never really had a Thing, did we? I mean . . . there was just the flirting . . . was there flirting? I've had about two hours sleep in the last forty-eight and I've figured out that I've got this babble problem, so maybe best that you just ignore anything I say."

"Randy . . ."

The quivering voice on the other end of the line seemed to be weighing its options.

"You're just not a guy who has . . . Things."

"I'm an overgrown frat boy."

The sound Trish made was an odd cross between a rueful laugh and a choking-to-death cough.

"You're either more out of touch with yourself than any person I've ever met or you're a pathological liar."

"I'm . . ."

For a brief instant, I kind of knew what Shane must have felt like when he realized that he'd been hit in the face with a basketball and the damage wasn't going to be minor.

"Forget that. You have to get down here to the school!"

"Why?"

I kind of knew what she was going to say and I was already wondering why I didn't seem to care.

"The whole thing with Shane has really hit the fan. Principal Frank called this big meeting. Shane's here. His mother . . ."

"What's she wearing?"

"What?"

"Shane's mother. What is she wearing?"

"What difference does THAT make?"

"Never mind . . ."

"You have to get down here and defend yourself! I think they're going to . . . oh jeez . . . is that Ty Roberson?"

Well, that part made sense. I hadn't gotten the impression that Ty had really been enjoying retirement all that much. What better way for Bishop Mathis to damage-control this catastrophe than to bring back Coach Waterwalker?

And not a single call to me from anybody at the school except Trish . . .

"You have to get down here, Randy! They're going to crucify you!"

"Trish . . ."

Cam suddenly perked up. "Trish?"

" . . . I've been doing a lot of thinking . . . like I tried to tell Shelley . . . I got off-track somewhere along the way . . . what is it they say about an alcoholic . . . he has to bottom out before he can start back up . . ."

"You are talking nonsense!"

"No. I've been living nonsense. Little boy in big body. Coach Hartman isn't real."

Trish's response was short, rude and unprintable. The phone clicked. I tossed it back down on the table.

"Trish?"

"No Trish. Just you and me. Just Cam. And Dad. And Wah. And Ling."

"No Ling!"

"Okay . . . no Ling . . ."

"Wah . . . Wah . . ."

Cam wasn't crying. I think she was beyond crying.

"I can't help you. God, I wish I could speak Vietnamese."

I looked down at the phone. Maybe I couldn't speak the language, but we knew somebody who did.

I hadn't talked much on a phone. I don't think I'd talked at all. So, I guess I pushed some button I shouldn't have pushed because there wasn't anybody there.

Randy said something that didn't sound very nice as he pushed the buttons on his phone and then handed it to me again.

"Hello? Cam? This is Katherine. Remember me?"

Did I remember Katherine? Yes! She knew Vietnamese. Somebody I could talk to!

I was almost forgetting that I was sad about Hoa, but then Katherine said . . .

"Your dad said you've been crying a lot. Is that right?"

"I guess so . . ."

"Have you been crying about your baby doll?"

"She's not a doll! She's real!"

"Okay . . . sure . . . and her name is Hoa?"

I didn't want to talk about Hoa. How could I tell Katherine that when she was being so nice to me?

"I don't want to talk about Hoa, Katherine. And that's final. Don't bring her up again! And thank you for being so nice to me."

"Cam, I want you to be happy. Your dad wants you to be happy. He's worried that you are crying so much about Hoa."

"I'm not crying about Hoa. I'm crying because I'm tired and because Randy needs a lovey-dovey wife."

"Excuse me?"

"Peep-Peep wasn't a very good wife. I don't think she lovey-doveyed or cleaned up or cooked or anything! I can be the cleaning and cooking wife, but I can't be the lovey-dovey wife. So, I'm trying to find a lovey-dovey wife for Randy, but he doesn't seem to like any of the girlfriends I pick out for him!"

Katherine didn't say anything.

"I think Trish should be Randy's lovey-dovey wife. She's nice and she's pretty."

"Cam . . . your dad and your mom are still married."

"No, they're not! Peep-Peep left! She's gone!"

"That's not how it works . . ."

"It's not fair! Randy is nice and needs a lovey-dovey!"

"That's something your dad and mom need to work out."

"THAT STUPID AMERICAN WOMAN IS NOT MY MOTHER!"

"Well, she is still your dad's wife and . . ."

"SHE IS NOT HIS WIFE! SHE LEFT HIM!"

"That's not how it works . . ."

"SHE LEFT ME!"

"I think she just needs some time to think . . ."

"I WOULD NEVER LEAVE A CHILD! EVER! I WOULD NEVER LEAVE HOA! I DIDN'T LEAVE HOA! SHE WAS SICK AND I TRIED TO HELP HER BUT SHE DIED AND IT WAS MY FAULT AND . . ."

I had used up all of my talking voice and had to stop.

Stupid Babytears were coming out, but I wasn't crying! Don't say I was crying because I wasn't!

Katherine was quiet for a few seconds.

"Can I talk to your dad, please?"

Life As I Knew It . . .

Monday morning. Caffeine had finally met its match.

I was exhausted.

But, I wasn't exhausted because I had driven all night.

I wasn't exhausted because my marriage was crumbling.

I wasn't exhausted because my career was imploding.

I was exhausted because I could not get an image out of my mind, an image poor Katherine had been forced to paint for me over the phone.

A little girl holding a baby. A very sick little baby. The little girl pouring all of her love into that very sick little baby. The little girl waking up to find the baby dead.

The little girl struggling to live with the tragically mistaken notion that she had killed the baby.

My conversation with Katherine had pushed all of my other very substantial worries out of my head.

I kept looking over at Cam, asleep in the front seat and cradling the baby doll she called Wah.

Cam made me feel helpless.

Almost as helpless as Cam must have felt feel when she woke up with a dead baby in her arms.

I crawled into bed. I crawled into bed in a bedroom in a house that probably wouldn't be mine too much longer.

Too tired to care. Too tired, too discouraged, too burned-out on living. At that moment, I had one purpose and one purpose only: sleep.

I had some fear that I was about to suffer nightmares about dying infants and crying girls.

But, I couldn't fight off sleep any longer. I closed my eyes.

"SLAM DUNK!!!!!!!!!!!!!!"

Don't tell me I didn't turn the damn phone off . . .

"Hartman? Ty Roberson . . ."

Perfect.

"Where are you?"

"None of your business, Ty."

I clicked the phone hang-up icon and started fumbling around for the power button.

"SLAM DUNK!!!!!!!!!!!!!!!!!!!!!"

I sighed.

"Hartman! Where are you?"

"Not any of your . . ."

"I'll see you in your office in fifteen minutes!"

If I'd have had any of my wits about me, I might have said something clever and snappy like: "You're not the boss of me!" But all that came out was a garbled half-protest.

I hung up the phone and rubbed my eyes.

"SLAM DUNK!!!!!!!!!!!!!!!!!"

"Hartman? Bring your daughter!"

Cam wasn't exceptionally happy about being pulled back out of bed but the promise that she might see Trish seemed to motivate her.

On the way over to school, I began wondering about severance. Surely the school would have to pay me something, even if I was responsible for costing the basketball program a future NBA Hall of Famer.

And then it hit me that I really should be getting good and mad about Roberson ordering me to bring Cam. Sure, I'd have had no choice, but the idea that he wanted her to witness my humiliation personally grated on me.

I pulled into my COACH HARTMAN parking space for what was probably the last time.

It was quite a crowd gathered beneath The Wall Of Real Champions. Coach R, Principal Frank, a couple of guys I recognized from the Board of Trustees and then one weasely little man I did not know.

"Randall Hartman?" Weasely asked as I walked in.

" . . . umh . . . yes . . .?"

"I have some papers for you."

With that, he shoved into my hand a sheaf of documents written in the tiniest little font, all except for SUMMONS AND COMPLAINT. Prepared by Thomas MacBride, Esq.

"You have been served. Have a nice day."

Weasely walked out, leaving Cam and me alone to face the den of hostile Bishop Mathis lions.

"Don't bother reading it, Coach Hartman," Principal Frank ordered. "You, the school and just about everybody else in the neighborhood have been named in a lawsuit by Shane Henderson's mother. Pain, suffering, emotional trauma. They're asking for about 20 million dollars."

"Is that all?" I drawled in a tone that I hope sounded calm and unconcerned. It probably didn't.

"So," Roberson pointed to Cam, "this is the girl that cost us Shane Henderson?"

"Leave her out of this, Ty."

Did I just call him "Ty"? Really?

"It's a little late to leave her out of any of this, Coach Hartman," Principal Frank snorted. "Do you have any idea how serious the situation is?"

"I've got an idea, yeah."

"The Board of Trustees voted yesterday to terminate your contract," Ty noted. "I got here . . ."

"Just in time to take your old job back," I growled.

Roberson threw back his head and laughed.

"Just in time to save yours, actually."

I wanted to sleep.

I did not want to get up and go to Moonguyen school with Randy.

I did not want to get up and go anywhere.

I had slept some in the car but it was a Stupid Nothing Sleep that didn't do any good. When Randy shook me to get up again right after I'd just gone to sleep, I said some things to him in Vietnamese that really weren't very nice. Remember when I told you not to tell Ai? I'm telling you again!

I almost fell asleep again as Randy drove us to the Moonguyen school. I thought that at least I would get to see Trish, but Randy didn't take me to Trish. We went into a room where there were lots of adults but no Trish.

A little man with a face like a mouse gave Randy some papers and then left.

An old wife-lady with a face like a duck said some things to Randy that I don't think he liked very much.

And then an older grandpa-man with a face like a . . . like, I don't know . . . It wasn't a face to make fun of, so I'll just say it was the kind of grandpa face where you know you'd better do what he says or else . . . Anyway, he looked at me and said something.

It didn't sound like the older grandpa-man was happy to see me. You'd have thought I'd made potty in his hat or something.

Randy sounded like he was sassing back to the older grandpa-man, but then the older grandpa-man said something that made Randy get real quiet.

Randy was quiet. The older grandpa-man was quiet. The old wife-lady with the face like a duck was quiet. There were some other older grandpa-men who were quiet, but then they hadn't said anything yet anyway.

Just then, when everybody was still being quiet, Trish walked in.

Was I happy to see Trish!

"Trish!"

Trish smiled, but made a kind of unhappy face.

I knew why Trish was unhappy. It was time to do something! I had to get Randy and Trish together!

"Trish your girlfriend!"

"Moonguyen?"

I'd told everybody to leave my office. Everybody but Cam. She was sitting under the Neil Armstrong poster.

"I don't know."

She hugged the Wah doll tightly.

"Moonguyen?"

I absently sipped from the steaming cup of motor oil that passed for coffee in the Bishop Mathis Athletic Department.

"Moonguyen. Let's talk about that. I guess it's as much your decision as it is mine now."

Cam stared intently at me. She clearly understood that something important was being considered.

"I came here today thinking I was getting fired. But then it turns out that the very guy whose great big giant shadow has been cast over my work is also the guy who just talked the powers that be out of canning me."

I took another sip. Awful coffee . . .

"So . . . what should we do, Cam? Should I stay in this pressure cooker just for the sake of having a job? If I'm going to be your dad, that's going to be a lot of work too. I don't know if I can do both."

"Moonguyen?"

"On the other hand, if I quit, then what? Still have to pay the bills. What would I do? Go coach someplace else? Open a sporting goods store? I don't know . . . what should we do, Cam? Just you and me now. What should we do?"

"Moonguyen?"

She looked so small underneath that moon landing poster.

"And how can I help you with this dead baby thing? How can I help you understand . . . you didn't kill that baby. Okay? That was not your fault . . ."

"Moonguyen?"

"I want to help but . . ."

Somewhere deep in my sleep-deprived brain a couple of puzzle pieces were fitting together.

"But . . ."

"Moonguyen?"

I stared at Neil Armstrong and his one small step.

Ty Roberson had told me that those posters had something to teach me, if I'd just pay attention.

Maybe it wasn't Ty had in mind, but Neil Armstrong had just helped me make sense of something.

A question had just been answered.

Not that I liked the answer . . .

I was confused. Again.

Why were we sitting in that room?

I hadn't wanted to get up and go to Moonguyen school, but, as long as we were there, why weren't we teaching the boys how to play it right?

Randy talked and said a bunch of things I could not understand. I couldn't understand what he was saying, but I was liking the way he was saying it. Soft, gentle . . .

And then, all of a sudden, Randy jumped up. He made a motion with his hand that I think meant I was supposed to stay and not follow him.

I followed him anyway.

Randy was walking real fast, almost running. It was hard for me, the Limper Girl, to keep up. He disappeared around a corner.

I heard his voice. It wasn't the soft, gentle Randy voice he'd been using in the office.

It sounded like he was trying to say "Moonguyen," but he wasn't saying it right. Just "Moonguy."

I limped around the corner. Randy was talking to (shouting at, really) the old grandpa-guy with the okay face. Randy was putting his finger in the old grandpa-guy's face.

He was saying "Moonguy" a lot.

How could he teach anybody a game if he didn't even know what to call it?

"All along . . . it was YOU?"

Ty just kept smiling a "gotcha" smile. Which just made me all the madder . . .

"And now you say you really want me to succeed? But you've been undermining me the whole time?"

"You ready to talk about this like an adult, Coach Hartman?"

"No! . . . Yes! . . . I . . ."

"What did you think of me when you were first hired?"

"I . . . well . . . I respected you . . ."

"But were you going to listen to me?"

"What? You never came to me and said . . ."

"Of course you weren't. Walk with me."

Ty started down the hallway.

"Moonguyen?"

Cam was standing next to me.

"I told you to stay in the office!"

"Let her come! No harm in it!"

Ty stopped in front of the massive Bishop Mathis athletic trophy case at the entrance to the gym. He pointed to a grainy photo.

"Clem Miller. They called him 'Pap.' Coached basketball here since back before we had fifty states. Beloved by all."

Of course, I knew who Pap Miller had been. Why were we talking about him?

"But weren't his teams . . . umh . . . mediocre?"

"Course they were. Pap Miller didn't know a free throw from a French kiss, but he had a way with his players. Father figure. Dispensed wisdom. Made them feel good about themselves. Different era. Winning really wasn't everything.

"When I was hired, everybody thought they wanted another Pap Miller. What they got was me. Pap wanted to be loved. I wanted to win. I was kind of a shock to the system.

"My first year was rough . . ."

"I thought . . ."

"Yeah, I know what you thought. You thought I'd been this big iconic figure guy from the get-go. People got short memories sometimes. Some folks were ready to give me the heave-ho before we played our first game. Discipline was kind of a new idea, I guess.

"And Pap kept sticking his nose in the middle of it. Calling me up, telling me to go easier on the players and all of that. Showing up at practice, telling me off in front of the team. When

I finally told him to stay away, I had my own lynch mob to deal with."

Ty grimaced.

"Came close to wrecking my career here before it really got started. Now, I knew you wouldn't listen to me. Nor should you, I guess. But . . . I was hoping that a little intelligent well-taken criticism in amongst all of the worthless crap that gets put up on the Internet . . . well maybe you'd listen to that . . ."

He grinned a little through the grimace.

"Or maybe not . . . But I had to try . . . I had quite an investment in you, reputation-wise."

"What do you mean?"

"Went out on a limb picking you as my successor. The less imaginative in the administration . . . and there are quite a few matching that description . . . couldn't see hiring somebody who didn't already have a resume three miles long. It took some persuading . . . Not outright threats, I guess . . . but . . ."

"Why me?"

"I'm not going to answer that question. I think I'd rather let you figure it out for yourself. Read what Moonguy has had to say. That might give you an idea or two."

"Why am I not fired? What did you say?"

"Humh . . . well a lot of it you don't want to hear . . . and I mean that . . . your life will be happier that way . . . but, basically, I said that it didn't make any sense to let the boy go just when he's starting to figure out he's got a backbone."

He gave Cam a wry little smile.

"And, besides, if he forgets, he's got somebody alongside to remind him, doesn't he?"

Cam smiled back. Like she actually understood.

"But if you don't get your rear end out to the gym floor, they might change their minds again. Can't have a coach who doesn't show up for camp on time, now can we?"

The old grandpa-guy smiled at me like I'd done something good. And then he pointed at Randy like the old grandpa-guy and I knew some kind of secret about him.

I didn't think the old grandpa-guy liked me, so I was happy that he smiled. I didn't know what the Randy secret was, but I didn't want him to think I was a Stupid Girl who couldn't figure it out.

Besides, how was I going to ask him?

Randy took me by the hand.

Which was kind of nice and kind of weird. He hadn't done that before. I wanted to pull my hand back away, but Randy was holding it tight. Not tight like it hurt. Tight like he really wanted to hold my hand.

So, I was nice about it and let him hold onto my hand.

We walked into the Moonguyen school. All the boys were wearing their Moonguyen clothes. They clapped and whistled and shouted when we walked in.

I think Randy thought they were clapping for him. But since I was the one who was trying to teach Moonguyen the right way, I knew it was for me. Don't tell Randy I said that.

I figured I was going to have to get used to Vietnamese food someday. So, that night, I took Cam out to some place called "Saigon Pho Express."

I'd hoped there'd be somebody there who spoke Vietnamese, but no such luck. From the look on Cam's face, I gathered that the food wasn't much more authentic than the service.

It was the thought that counted, right?

I'd considered asking Trish to come, but . . .

Well, that would have just complicated things.

And the last thing Cam needed was another complication.

Me either, I guess.

Cam got a big kick out of the fumbling around I was doing with the chopsticks.

She pretended to feed some of her whatever it was to the Wah doll and then fussed and scolded like Wah had dribbled food all down her front.

After cleaning Wah's little baby doll nightgown, Cam got a mischievous grin on her face and held the doll out to me.

"Grandpa!"

I don't know where she'd picked up "Grandpa," but she seemed quite proud of herself.

"Grandpa!" she said insistently as she pushed Wah my direction.

I glanced around the restaurant and made sure no one who might question my masculinity was watching and took Wah.

Cam motioned that I should hold Wah like she was a baby. I didn't have much (any) practice holding an actual baby, so I did the best I could.

Cam motioned that I should feed Wah, accompanied by several very insistent "Grandpas!"

Fighting the flush that was creeping over my face, I picked up two chopsticks full of whatever pork thing I'd ordered and held it to Wah's mouth.

"Grandpa!" Cam giggled.

"Grandpa," I admitted reluctantly.

Cam giggled.

I think Wah was happy, too.

Cam went to bed promptly and was snoring before I got out of her bedroom.

I wanted desperately to go and collapse, but I knew I had one more item on the to-do list before I could permit myself the luxury of sleep.

I screwed up my courage, picked up the phone and dialed.

"Hi. It's me. Of course you knew that. Caller I.D. Just thought I'd call and see if, umh, you've decided our future yet. Because it turns out I'm not fired and our daughter loves me and I was hoping that you were ready to . . . I'm babbling . . . again!"

One Year Later . . .

Tonight on Prep Focus we preview the upcoming Division One State Semi-Finals. How will Montoya Beach's backcourt match up against St. Francis' potent guard tandem of Percy Morgan and Chantral Carmichael? Can the Bishop Mathis Lancers sustain their amazing comeback momentum or will their storybook season have an unhappy ending when they square off against undefeated Cielo del Oro?

posted by MOONGUY:
Randy Hartman's failure to use his final time out in the last minute against Cielo del Oro was a rare tactical error on his part and an unfortunate black mark against him in what was otherwise a stellar sophomore coaching season. The Lancers came within fifteen seconds of a trip to the state championship game. Not bad for a guy who was almost fired a year ago.

posted by LANCERS_HOOPS_BOOSTERS:
If you don't have your reservation yet for Wednesday night's Lancers Hoops Awards Banquet at McGee Center, you're out of luck! It's a sellout! If you do have your reservation, get ready for an evening of great food and plenty of accolades for our Centennial League and Southern Section champions!

posted by CLAY 313:
So, where r u, Heartman Hater? U have been so quiet lately. I thought u said Coach H was an idiot, but I guess u r the idiot!

Tonight on Prep Focus we investigate the unfolding scandal at St. Vincent involving freshman center Shane Henderson's academic eligibility. Did school officials deliberately alter Henderson's fall quarter grades? Also tonight, a heartwarming story about a Hartman, as we look at the special relationship that developed this past season between the Bishop Mathis Lancers and their unofficial mascot Cam, the adopted Vietnamese daughter of head coach Randy Hartman.

Mercy House seemed strange. Nothing had changed. But everything had changed.

It was good to see my friends again and very good to see Ai and all of the other nannies.

But it wasn't what I had expected. I guess I had become much more American than I realized. I had forgotten so much of my Vietnamese.

I acted happy and part of me was happy. But part of me was very sad. The nannies were very loving and did the best they could, but what was going to happen to these kids when they got too old to stay anymore?

I laughed and hugged all of them, but I wanted to cry. Who was going to adopt a blind child or a child with a scrunched-up face? Where would they go? What would they do? I wished that we could take all of them back to America with us.

I had to keep telling myself that the important thing was we were going to get to take Ling home with us.

I had been proud to be Ling's nanny. But I was going to be even prouder to be her sister.

The paperwork said that Ling was two years old. She looked more like an infant. A tiny, sickly infant.

"Failure to thrive" was all that Mercy Worldwide could tell us about her condition. That and the sad fact that she was completely blind in one eye.

Trinh had taken us to Mercy House first thing in the morning, but it was July and this was Vietnam. The sweltering heat was augmented by a bottom-of-the-ocean level humidity.

Ai greeted us at the front door with a little bundle of Ling and a very brave smile.

Ai had clearly done her best to make Ling look healthy for us. She was wearing a new little pink nightgown and Ai had found a patch of just enough hair for a little pink ribbon.

Ling had the tiniest little beads of sweat on her forehead and each breath seemed to drain another ounce of her little energy.

This was a very sick little girl.

But, I seemed to be the only one in the family who noticed.

Cam was jumping out of her skin and it was all she could do to keep from grabbing Ling right out of Ai's hands. I had told Cam, in no uncertain terms, that Shelley was going to get to be the first to hold Ling.

Shelley's face lit up when Ai handed Ling to her. For all practical purposes, Ling was the infant that Shelley had wanted in the first place.

Give Cam credit. She waited patiently while Shelley oohed, aahed and cooed at Ling.

Ling's face was more red than brown and her breathing seemed very labored.

I finally nudged Shelley and nodded toward Cam. Grudgingly, Shelley handed Ling over.

"Ling! It's me! Cam!"

Cam's smile started to fade as she realized that Ling did not remember her. Ling squirmed a little and then let out a cry.

"Ling's hungry!"

Ai produced a small bottle, which Shelley grabbed.

Cam gave Shelley a look that suggested a very ugly standoff over who was going to feed Ling. Only one way to avert that looming disaster . . .

"May I hold my newest daughter?"

Cam gave me one of her I-know-what-you're-up-to looks, but surrendered Ling to my care.

"Hi, Ling. I'm your dad. You look hungry."

I got it. Okay?

Shelley's the mom and so she should get to do all of the mom stuff.

But, I was the big sister! And I had big sister stuff to do!

I knew Dad had taken Ling just so that Shelley and I wouldn't fight over her. I was a little mad at him, but I understood.

The best thing for me to do was to go play with the kids and wait for my turn to be the big sister.

But none of the kids knew who I was. Did I look that different? Maybe they were expecting a Limper Girl, but the special shoe thingee I'd gotten from Trish's doctor friend made me walk like a Normal Un-Limper Girl.

The kids were staring at me the way kids stare when there is a stranger. But I wasn't a stranger. I was Cam, the Nanny-Goalie.

"Who wants to play?"

I think that's what I said. It was frustrating to have forgotten so many Vietnamese words.

No. They didn't know me. That made me sad. I walked out of the play room and into the nursery. Maybe playing with babies would make me happy.

There were lots of new babies. They were new babies at Mercy House. That meant they had the same missing arms, scrunched-up faces and blind eyes that all of the other kids had.

So, I found the babies but I wasn't any happier.

I stopped right next to Hoa's crib. Well, it was some other baby's crib by then, but it was the same crib where I'd tried to take care of Hoa.

"Hoa . . . I am so sorry . . ."

"This was her crib?"

I knew it was Dad behind me. Shelley wasn't with him, so I didn't try to stop crying.

"Yes," I kind of mumbled.

"It wasn't your fault."

It had been six months since Cam had finally told me herself about the baby that had died in her arms. I'd heard the story already from Katherine the night we drove back from Oregon, but it sounded all the more heart-wrenching coming directly from Cam.

I had told Cam it wasn't her fault on an average of five times a day. I don't think she believed me . . . yet . . .

"Hoa was very sick. She was going to die. There was nothing you could have done."

Cam whimpered something unintelligible.

"You did something beautiful for Hoa. You let her know somebody loved her and cared about her. She died feeling loved."

Cam wiped her eyes and blew her nose on her sleeve.

"I know you don't believe that, but it's true."

I was ecstatic that Cam had come to think of me as Dad. But, she still set a few boundaries. Like, I still couldn't hug her. Ms. Chaves said that was normal and I shouldn't take it as a rejection.

So, I didn't try to rub Cam's shoulder or anything. I just let her play out the crying cycle.

"I still feel sad."

"I don't blame you. You loved Hoa."

Cam was very quiet for several seconds.

"You said that your school was close? I'd like to see it."

"There isn't much to see."

"I don't care. It was your school. I want to see it."

Cam was doing her level best not to smile.

It was a lot easier to get from Mercy House to the school than when I'd been a Limper Girl.

I knew that Dad was just trying to help me not think so much about Hoa, but I was happy he had asked to see my school anyway.

It was summer. Nobody would be at the school. Maybe that was best. I was kind of hurt that none of the kids at Mercy House knew me, so maybe I shouldn't try to see any of my old friends from school.

"You walked this every day? With your limp?"

I nodded. "It was hard, but I made it."

"Did you like going to school?"

"Yes . . . I guess . . . except I missed Ling. But that was where I learned to be a Goalie."

"I still can't believe you were able to do that, play soccer I mean. I don't know how you did it."

"I just wanted to play. So I played."

We were almost to the school. I could see a boy and a girl sitting on the steps.

"Gross! Dad! They're smack-smacking lips!"

The girl looked up.

"Cam?"

It took me a minute.

"Mai?"

Mai had changed . . . a lot. Mai looked more like a wife-lady now. When she stood up, she looked even more different. She had grown wife-lady things.

Mai ran down the steps and hugged me. I don't think the boy was very happy about that. He wanted to do more lovey-dovey.

"[Vietnamese words]!"

"I'm sorry. I forgot my Vietnamese, Mai. Dad, this is my friend Mai. She said that you were going to try to touch my bottom."

"[Vietnamese words]!"

"I missed you, too. This is my Dad. He didn't try to touch my bottom."

"[Vietnamese words]!"

"I wish I could talk to you . . ."

Mai turned to the boy and said something to him. He still didn't look happy. He got up and walked around to the back of the school.

"[Vietnamese words]!"

"I have a sister now, Mai. Do you remember Ling? We're adopting Ling. Shelley will be the mom. But I will be the big sister. Which is more important than being the mom . . ."

The boy came back holding a Smart Vietnamese Soccer Ball.

"I think Mai wants to play soccer with you."

"It's been a long time. I don't know if I remember how."

"I'd like to see you play . . . even if you don't remember."

So, I went out onto the field. Mai walked beside me, saying a lot of things in Vietnamese. I think they were all nice things.

I walked to the goal.

"Dad? Are you watching?"

It was absolutely amazing.

Mai kicked ball after ball after ball at Cam. She stopped every one of them with a shout of "Goalie!"

And she threw the ball back to Mai every time with that weird spot-on aim of hers.

Mai's boyfriend stood next to me, a sullen look on his face.

"Do you speak English?" I asked innocently.

All I got back was a glare. I decided not to pursue the conversation any further.

"Goalie!" Cam shouted.

"Hey, Cam! How about we show Mai a real game?"

Cam grinned. Instead of throwing the ball to Mai, she threw it to me.

"Stand on one foot!"

I complied.

"Jump up and down on it!"

I jumped up and down.

Mai and the boyfriend looked understandably confused.

"Now . . . bounce the ball off your head into the goal."

"Cam . . . I'm like fifty feet away . . ."

I bounced the ball off my head. It fell at my feet.

Cam ran over, giggling.

"Okay . . . now . . . YOU balance the ball on your head for five seconds!"

"Come on! You know I can't do that . . ."

"If you want to score, you'd better learn fast."

Cam stood as perfectly still as she could and put the ball on her head. It rolled off.

"My turn . . ."

"NO! Let me try it again!"

Cam put the ball back on her head. It lingered there for about a second and a half before rolling off again.

"Okay, NOW it's my turn!"

"NO! Let me try again!"

Cam put the ball on her head a third time.

"One one thousand . . ."

The ball teetered perilously to the left, but Cam shifted her feet and the ball stayed on . . .

"Two one thousand . . ."

"I didn't say you could move . . ."

"SHH! Three one thousand . . ."

"It's about to roll off!"

"Four one thousand . . ."

"Oh no! It's going to fall right off . . ."

"Five one thousand!"

Cam grabbed the ball from the top of her head and smiled that triumphant little smile of hers.

"MOONGUYEN!!"

The Hartman Adoption Saga Continues in 2015 With . . .

The Magical Adventures of Princess Ling

Enjoy This 2 Page Excerpt and Preview

PRINCESS LING AND THE RED HORSE NAMED SAMMY
By Shelley Foster Hartman

Beautiful Princess Ling lived with her father, King Randy, and her mother, Queen Shelley, in a great big castle in the Kingdom of California.

Princess Ling's favorite thing to do was to wake up early in the morning and ride her big red horse named Sammy.

Princess Ling and Sammy would ride through the forest, across the babbling brook, through the meadow, and over the hills. Princess Ling loved Sammy and Sammy loved her.

Now, Princess Ling was special for lots of reasons, but one of the things that made Princess Ling very special was that she could talk to the animals . . . and the animals could talk to her!

One day, just after they had crossed over the babbling brook, Sammy stopped and flicked his big horsey ears.

"What's the matter, Sammy?" Princess Ling asked.

"Princess Ling . . . do you hear someone crying?"

Princess Ling was very still as she listened.

"Yes, Sammy! I think you're right! Someone is crying!"

"And it's coming from over behind that

"Cam! I am working! Do NOT grab things from out of my typewriter! Give that back!"

Cam gave me one of her patented looks of defiance and held up the page she had ripped from the typewriter carriage.

"This is wrong!"

"It's a children's book! There is no 'right' or 'wrong' to it. Give that back to me this instant!"

"Where's Princess Cam?"

"There is no Princess Cam in this story!"

"Well, there's Princess Ling . . . and King Randy . . . and Queen Shelley . . . There should be a Princess Cam!"

"Cam . . . it's a story! Just a story! It's not about us!"

"Yes, it is!"

"No, it isn't!"

"And Sammy's a cat, not a horse!"

"It's not about us!"

"And he's not red! He's yellow!"

I took in a very deep breath. I tried to remember everything Ms. Chaves had worked with me on. Patience. Maturity. I'm the parent. She's the child. I'm in charge. I am an adult. I am . . .

"And he can't talk!"

"It's not about Sammy the yellow cat. It's about Sammy the red horse! Now, please give me . . ."

"YOU HATE ME! YOU HATE ME! YOU WON'T EVEN PUT ME IN YOUR STUPID BABY BOOK STORIES!"

I'm the parent. She's the child. I am the adult. She's the child . . .

"I HATE YOU AND YOUR STUPID STORIES! AND LING HATES YOUR STUPID STORIES!"

With that, Cam ripped the sheet in two.

And I forgot some things. I forgot that I was the parent. I forgot that she was the child. I opened my mouth . . . and . . .

16182510R00144

Made in the USA
San Bernardino, CA
21 October 2014